IDLE H

Harrison Phillips is an English author of extreme horror and splatterpunk fiction. His literary influences range from Clive Barker and Stephen King, to Jack Ketchum and Edward Lee. He was born and raised in Birmingham, England, where he still resides with his long-suffering wife, their two daughters, and a schnauzer named Minnie.

www.twitter.com/harrisonhorror

www.facebook.com/harrisonphillipshorror

vestigialpress@hotmail.com

Idle Hands: Extended Edition
Copyright © 2023 Vestigial Press

Cover artwork by
InsaneCamel
(insanecamelcorp@gmail.com)

Harrison Phillips has asserted his right to be identified as the author of this work.

First published in 2021
© 2021 Vestigial Press

All rights reserved. This book, or any portion thereof, may not be reproduced or used in any manner, without the express written permission of the publisher.

This book is a work of fiction. All names and characters are the product of the authors imagination. Any resemblance to actual persons, living or dead, is entirely coincidental.

IDLE
HANDS

CONTENTS

KNOCK DOOR RUN	1
A PRIVATE SHOW	27
FILTER	57
WHAT HAPPENED IN THE QUARRY?	83
THE BINMAN	111
THE SCARECROW	123
THE HOLE	145
MUM	171
DON'T LISTEN	191
THIS STORY SUCKS!	209
THE MEETING	215
ARTIST	231
THE BALLARD OF JOHN SMITH	247
PORNOGRAPHER	253
COME OUT	279
THE CONFESSION	309

KNOCK DOOR RUN

"If you little shits knock my fucking door one more goddamn time," said the one-eyed man. "I swear to fucking God himself I'll skin you alive!"

He was stood beneath the canopy of his small porch, protected from the drizzling rain that was falling from the grey November sky, the front door to his small, end-of-terrace house wide open behind him. He looked crazy, like a man possessed by the devil Himself. The moonlight - what little of it could penetrate through the thick blanket of cloud - reflected from his single, solitary eye, as he peered up and down the street, hoping to catch a glimpse of whoever had dared to knock his door seven times already tonight.

Tommy was scared. No - more than that. He was terrified. But there was something exhilarating about it all too. The adrenaline coursing through his veins caused his heart to beat out of his chest. He could feel it hammering away at the inside of his ribcage, trying to break free. For a moment, he even thought he could hear it over the pitter-patter of the rain chipping away at his hood, although that was probably just his imagination. The old man may have been in his sixties, but there was still something horrifying about him. It was that eye. The moonlight caused it to glow blue as it scanned the darkness. And it was looking for *him*. After all, it was *he* who had knocked the door on this occasion.

"You hear me, you little fuckers?" the one-eyed man said, his deep voice a menacing growl - the voice of a man who smoked too many cigars. "If I catch you, you're fucking dead!" And then he re-entered his home and slammed the door shut behind him.

"Holy crap balls," David said, sniggering. "He's pissed now, huh?"

Of course he is! Tommy thought, although he decided against saying it aloud. That was the seventh time this evening - in the last of fifteen minutes, actually - that he'd been forced to come to his door, only to find nobody there to greet him. It wouldn't be the last time either - he could probably expect it to continue for another half hour or so, before David got bored and agreed to cause trouble elsewhere.

"Yeah," said Mikey, chuckling too. "Proper pissed off he is."

Mikey was David's little brother. He was only ten, but he was small even for a ten-year-old. His laugh sounded more than a little nervous, but Tommy couldn't tell if the nerves were due to the possibility of getting caught, or if it was due to the fact that he'd just used the word 'pissed', and that was - so Mommy had always taught him - a naughty word. But he wasn't with Mommy now; he was with his big brother David, and the use of such words was actively encouraged.

Idle Hands

The three boys were currently crouched down behind the bushes that lined the side of Whitechurch Street, directly opposite the one-eyed man's house. The rain had been falling all day. It had eased up a little since they'd left school this afternoon, but still, Tommy hadn't been so keen on going out tonight. But it hadn't been his choice. David had knocked on his door and asked if he was coming out to play. That meant that Tommy *had* to go - you always *had* to do whatever David said. If you didn't, you'd never hear the end of it, and you'd likely make yourself an enemy for life. Even when his mother had shown concern about two twelve-year-olds and a ten-year-old playing out on the streets at night - and in the rain, no less - Tommy had reassured her that they'd be fine.

Playing 'Knock Door Run' was one of David's favourite pastimes, along with throwing eggs in front of oncoming buses and spray-painting crude graffiti in underpasses (more often than not, he'd draw a cock and balls, with three lines of spunk shooting from the end - *hilarious!*). And the one-eyed man had soon become his favourite victim, mainly because he would always fall for it. Plus, it seemed to really get to him, making the whole thing all the more satisfying for David.

The one-eyed man was somewhat of a legend amongst the local kids. They all knew him, and they all feared him to some extent. It was that eye. No, that wasn't true. It was the missing eye that caused so many of the kids to suffer sleepless nights. A large, jagged scar lined the right side of his face. It seemed to start right on his cheek bone, with numerous legs – like those of a spider - that radiated out from the centre. One of those legs crossed the eyelids of his right eye, which now hung loose, with nothing behind them to prop them up, to stop them from collapsing into the empty socket. His whole face seemed to have dropped on that side. The skin hung loose from the bone beneath and the eye - or what remained of it - was placed low; probably a good inch lower than it had any right to be. And there were stories about him too. Most seemed to agree that he'd lost his eye during the war (although nobody was ever specific about which war - he was too old for Afghanistan and too young for WW2). When he came back from the war - his eye now missing, his face drooping as if it were melting from his skull - his wife upped and left him, taking their young daughter with her. There were rumours amongst the kids that he'd killed his wife and daughter. They said that he'd butchered them, chopped them up into tiny pieces and flushed them down the toilet. Of course, the story said that the police couldn't prove anything, as everything would've been washed away in the sewers. Then there were the rumours that he was a cannibal. They alleged that, during the war (whichever war that was), he'd been taken hostage and had to resort to cannibalism in order to survive. They said he'd eaten his wife and daughter, as he no longer knew any better. People also said that he was a vampire, as nobody ever saw him leave the house during the day.

It was those stories that gave kids nightmares.

Even Tommy wasn't immune. Although he'd never admit it, he'd had nightmares about the one-eyed man too. In his dream, he'd been playing 'Knock Door Run', much like he was at this precise moment. In his dream, he approached the door confidently, not at all like he would do in real life. In his dream, he banged the door loudly, pounding it with his fist. And then, in his dream, he did something wholly bizarre - he just stood there. He didn't turn, he didn't run. He wanted to, for sure. But something wouldn't let him. It was as if his legs had seized, as if his entire body were encased in concrete. In the dream, his heart would be thumping and thudding as the door slowly opened, the hinges creaking. Beyond the door, inside the house, was nothing. *Literally nothing.* It was an abyss - a black hole - where nothing, not even light, could escape the darkness. And then he'd emerge - the one-eyed man, taller now than he was in reality, his single good eye glowing red. His hands, his fingernails long and pointed like the talons of a bird, clawed at the door frame, and dragged him out of the house. As he stood before this subconscious version of Tommy, at least eight feet tall now, his body was all out of proportion, tall and thin and gangly, as if he had been stretched. It was at that point that Tommy could run. In the dream, he turned and fled. But the one-eyed man gave chase. He was fast, sprinting like a cheetah, his long stick insect legs taking five-meter strides. But Tommy was quick. Quick enough to maintain his distance. But the one-eyed man was right there behind him, swiping at his heels with six-inch claws. As Tommy ran, looking over his shoulder, he watched as the one-eyed man grew taller and thinner by the second. Even his head was growing elongated. And then the eye opened. Not the red eye, fixed upon Tommy like a predator latches onto its prey, but the missing eye. And inside was nothing, just as there had been nothing behind that door. Nothing but a darkness - an empty, black void. And, in the dream, Tommy continued to run. But the one-eyed man caught him easily. He picked Tommy up with one hand, his fingers wrapped tightly around his entire body. He was a giant now, the one-eyed man, the cyclops, perhaps thirty feet tall. And the gaping eye, now bigger than Tommy himself, had grown row upon row of sharp, shark-like teeth, and it was chomping at him, desperate to feed upon his tasty, youthful flesh. The one-eyed man then fed Tommy into the eye, into the darkness, where the teeth tore into his flesh and mulched his bones.

That was when Tommy had woken up. He'd wet the bed. His mother had scolded him, had threatened to make him wear nappies again if he didn't learn to control his bladder. Of course, he told nobody about his nightmare. Especially not David.

Fortunately, he'd only had the dream once. But once was more than enough.

But now, here he was. Crouched down behind the bush, David to his left and Mikey beside him, waiting for the right moment to strike once again.

The one-eyed man's gonna eat you! his brain urged. *He's gonna gobble you up! Feed you to his missing eye!*

Tommy ignored it. *Stupid brain!* Several people had told him before that he thought too much. He thought they were probably right.

"Okay," David said, peering over the top of the bush. "Coast is clear."

"Who gotta go next?" Mikey asked.

"You do," David told his little brother.

Tommy saw a sudden look of terror cascade over Mikey. His snickering grin, as nervous as is it already was, dropped. The corners of his mouth turned downwards. His eyes were, all of a sudden, much wider than they had been. He looked as though he might cry. You see, Mikey *never* had to knock the door - he was too little. But it seemed as though David had decided that now was the perfect time for his little brothers first go at doing the knocking and the running, rather than just sitting back, and watching while others took the risk.

"N-n-no way," stuttered Mikey, seemingly unable to force the words out first time. He'd never been a stutterer, at least, not as far as Tommy had been aware. This was a sudden tick he'd developed, as the fear took a hold of his heart. "Whuh-why m-me?"

"Don't be such a pussy!" David said, his voice hushed, but the emphasis still apparent. "I've done it, like, five times already tonight. So has Tommy. You haven't even done it once! *Not once. Not ever.*"

Tommy thought for a second that he saw a tear run down the side of Mikey's cheek. But then he realised it was nothing more than a rogue raindrop that had somehow infiltrated its way under the peak of Mikey's hood. Still, he felt sorry for him. He felt as though he ought to volunteer to go again. But then, there was no way David would accept that. He'd decided it was Mikey's turn, so Mikey had to do it.

"Come on, bro," David urged Mikey. "Time to be a man. Time you grew a pair of balls!"

The look of dismay on Mikey's face began to straighten out. Now it was a look of anger. *How dare David suggest he didn't have no balls!* Tommy knew right then that Mikey was going to do it. He was a man, after all.

Mikey stood. Slowly, he stepped out from behind the bush and began his approach. As he reached the kerb, he looked back over his shoulder, to where Tommy and David were peering out of the bush. "D-d-don't leave me, you g-guys," he pleaded, his nerves still getting the better of him.

"Go on!" David said, waving his arms, ushering him on.

Mikey turned and continued on.

It was at that point that something occurred to Tommy - Mikey's coat was bright red. Tommy's coat was dark blue in colour, while David's was black. Poor little Mikey - his coat was bright red, and it screamed out in the darkness like a beacon. If anybody was going to be seen, it was him. And then, if the one-eyed man gave chase, Mikey's coat would be like the red flag of a matador, daring the bull to strike. It was as simple as that. *Mikey was dead meat.*

But he continued on, clearly unaware of the mortal danger his own coat presented. He crossed the road - it was a quiet residential estate, so there were few cars to present any risk. And then he was there, standing before the porch of the one-eyed man's end-of-terrace house. He looked back one more time, to find David smiling and nodding like a lunatic. Tommy thought for a second about calling Mikey back. Perhaps it was unfair to send a ten-year-old out there all alone. But then again, what was the worst that could happen? It was a harmless prank, that was all. It's not like the one-eyed man was really a cannibalistic monster, was it? He wouldn't really skin Mikey alive if he caught him, would he?

Would he?

Mikey stepped forward. He reached out for the door knocker, which resided on the right-hand side of the door, at what would've been greater than head height to little Mikey. The knocker itself was shaped like a lion's paw and it pivoted from the top.

Idle Hands

Once you lifted it, you could simply drop it and run, allowing it to fall and knock against the brass plate below. Mikey was moving slowly, cautiously. Tommy felt nervous for him. He needed to just get on and do it. *Knock the door and run!* Just standing there like that, he was more likely to get himself caught.

And then, as Mikey's fingers brushed against the brass, the door swung open.

Within nanoseconds, the one-eyed man had leaned out and grabbed a hold of Mikey's coat. He'd been waiting there, like a coiled spring, ready to pounce. "Come here, you little shit!" he said, as he dragged Mikey into the house. Mikey screamed, but those screams were soon cut off by the slamming of the door.

David jumped to his feet, the sudden realisation of what had just happen slamming into him like a fist. "Holy shit!" he said.

Tommy had sprung to his feet just as quickly as David had. He wasn't entirely sure what he'd just witnessed. The one-eyed man had snatched up poor little Mikey and dragged him inside. But was that all it was? Was it the one-eyed man? Or was it the one-eyed monster of his nightmares, the razor-toothed eye socket opening up, ready to feed on the flesh of a ripe, young child? No. *Don't be so stupid!* It was the one-eyed *man*. That's all he was – a man. But that didn't make things any better. Somehow, it made things worse. This wasn't a dream, wasn't a nightmare - this was real life, and Mikey had just been dragged into the lair of the beast.

David was panicking, his voice pitched higher than Tommy had ever heard it. "What the *fuck* do we do now? What the *fuck*..." he was repeating.

Tommy didn't know. It seemed to him that the best course of action would be to run. If they ran quickly, as fast as their legs would carry them, they would be at David's house in ten minutes flat. They could tell his parents and let them deal with it. They would almost certainly call the police. That was *definitely* the best thing to do. This was a matter for grown-ups to deal with, not a pair of twelve-year-old boys. But then, if they did that, if they turned and ran, by the time anybody came to help, it might already be too late. The one-eyed cannibal may have stripped the meat from Mikey's carcass by then. The police would find him, the one-eyed man, sitting at his dining room table, tucking into a feast of raw, bloody offal. Or perhaps the one-eyed maniac may have chopped Mikey up, and flushed the little pieces down the toilet.

"We've gotta help him!" David was crying, his eyes pleading with Tommy for assistance. "We gotta get Mikey out of there!" He looked terrified; almost certainly he *was* terrified. He didn't look like the big, brave leader anymore. Not at all. Now he looked like a small, frightened twelve-year-old boy.

And that's exactly what he was.

Tommy's mind raced from one possible outcome to the next. Then it settled on one; the one that, in all probability, seemed to be the most likely scenario - the one-eyed man had simply sat a sobbing Mikey down on his sofa, and was now lecturing him on how (and why) playing pranks on the elderly was wrong, informing him that many old folks live alone and that they get scared when kids play pranks on them. Perhaps he might even have provided a refreshing glass of lemonade for Mikey to drink while the lesson was doled out.

Idle Hands

Tommy told David as such.

"So, what do you suggest we do then, Tommy?" David had asked. "Nothing? Huh? Huh?"

Tommy thought for a moment. He watched as the raindrops dripped from the front of his hood, right before his very eyes. He listened as it plink-plonked into the puddles it had itself formed. He sniffed at the air - it smelled stale. And then he motioned for David to follow him. "Come on," he said.

For reasons unknown even to himself, Tommy was feeling brave. But then, he'd already convinced himself that nothing bad was going to happen. When David had asked him where they were going, Tommy had told him that they were simply going to take a look. "We'll just look through the window," Tommy said. "Let's see if we can see anything, alright?"

David nodded affirmative.

They approached the end-of-terrace house cautiously. A short path, made up of three paving slabs, lead to the front door. To the left of the front door was a large bay window, which would've looked in on the living room, had the curtains not been drawn. Before the bay window laid a small, dying lawn. A few patches of grass seemed to be indulging in the futile task of clinging onto their meaningless lives. But mostly the grass had died and withered away, leaving behind bare patches of dirt. Tommy and David crossed this lawn in deep, hunched-over strides. They kept themselves as low as possible, hoping to remain out of sight of any eyes - or any eye, *singular* - that may be watching them.

Crouched down, they both clung onto the sill of the large bay window, as if they were clinging on to the edge of a cliff with only their fingertips. Tommy looked over the edge of the sill. The closed curtains hung a little above the bottom of the window - perhaps a millimetre or two. The gap was too small to see anything more that shadows, obscuring the light as they moved across the room.

"I can't see shit," whispered David, so quietly that Tommy could hardly hear him over the rain.

"I know. I can't either," said Tommy.

Further to the left, at the corner of the building, a wooden gate blocked entry into the alleyway that would lead to the rear of the houses. Tommy knew they shouldn't go down there - that would be trespassing. But they *needed* to. If they wanted to see into the house, they had to go around to the back and try the windows there.

Tommy made a move for the gate. He pushed it, half expecting to find it locked. But the metal latch slipped up easily and the gate swung open. It was dark beyond the gate (*was this the abyss?*), with little light able to penetrate the narrow void between the two houses. A feeling of dread pumped its way through Tommy's body, as his heart raced. It wasn't as if he was scared of the dark - at least, he never had been before. But the darkness was where the monsters lurked, be they human or be they… something else.

Nevertheless, both he and David slowly made their way along the alleyway. It was too dark to see anything. Tommy had visions of his foot catching on something, sending him crashing to the ground, the noise of which would alert the one-eyed man to their presence here now. The alleyway was narrow enough so that he could touch the walls on both sides. So he did just that, allowing his fingers to drag gently along the rough surface of the brick.

From the front, the one-eyed man's end-of-terrace abode looked small. Tiny, even. But, in all actuality, what it lacked in width, it made up for in the depth. The house must've been at least three times deeper than it was wide. It was something Tommy had never considered before. If he thought about it at all, he'd have expected the interior of the house to contain, perhaps, a kitchen and lounge downstairs, and a single bedroom and bathroom upstairs. But as he traversed the alleyway, David following nervously behind, it was becoming more apparent that this house was much bigger than he'd expected.

The alley continued on past the one-eyed man's garden, turned the corner and then continued along the back of the houses, where another gate opened up to the rear of each houses in the terrace. The fence that surrounded the gardens was high - way too high for Tommy to see over - and they were constructed from overlapping timbers, preventing any chance of seeing through.

At least, now that they'd passed the houses, there was more light to afford them slightly improved vision.

The gate to the one-eyed man's back garden was unlocked too. Tommy pushed it open slowly and peered in. It was dark, but he could still make out the overgrown bushes and unkempt lawn that lined either side of the narrow stone path that lead to the back door. There were no lights on in the house. He turned back to David and nodded. "We going in?" he said, hoping that David would say no, hoping that he might suggest they go back, run home, and tell their parents everything. But he didn't. He simply nodded.

Tommy pushed the gate a little further now. It was stuck. It had dragged along the floor, where weeds had grown and matted into a thick blanket of undesirable vegetation, and clogged up beneath the gate. But he didn't need it open much further - just enough for him to slip through. So he pushed the gate harder, with both hands, forcing it to inch the tiniest bit further. That was enough. He squeezed through, into the garden. David followed behind. Quickly, they scooted across the garden, once again keeping themselves as low to the ground as was humanly possible.

There was only one window at the back of the house. Tommy assumed that it looked upon the kitchen. However, behind the window, the horizontal slats of the wooden blind were closed. There was no chance of seeing into the house here either.

Tommy squatted down and pressed his back against the wall below the window. He felt exhausted. He surely would've sat on the ground, had it not been for the fact that it was soaking wet. David followed suit.

"What now?" David whispered. There was an urgency in his voice, as if he knew what they needed to do, but didn't quite want to say it himself, as if he didn't want to be held accountable for getting them both killed.

Tommy thought for a moment. How should he know what to do next? It wasn't as if he'd been in this situation - or even any remotely similar situation - before. He wanted to go. Just leave. Let somebody else deal with it. Mikey would be fine. Perhaps they should've just knocked the one-eyed man's door and apologised. If they promised not to do it again, maybe he'd let Mikey go. For sure he would. He wasn't a monster - he was a man. He would've been a kid once. Surely he would've done stupid things too. He'd understand. He'd get it. They could apologise, leave, and never go back.

But what if he was a monster? What if he was a cannibal? Or a vampire? He'd almost certainly drag them into his lair and consume them too, just as he had done to Mikey.

Poor little Mikey. It was Tommy's fault he was in there. He should've done something. He should've offered to go instead. Mikey was too little to stand up to his big brother. But Tommy wasn't. He should've said something.

Too late now. Mikey was inside and they had to get him back. "We've gotta get in there somehow," Tommy said.

David nodded his agreement.

Together, they moved for the back door. Surely it would be locked. It had to be. Nobody left their doors unlocked around here anymore - at least that's what Tommy's mother had once told him. But, much to his surprise (and to his concern, if he had to be totally honest), this door was unlocked. It seemed too good to be true, as if it were a set-up. The one-eyed man had left the door unlocked on purpose, an invitation for them to enter. Once inside, the one-eyed man would be ready to strike, the blade of his butcher knife sharpened to perfection.

But enter they did. Moving cautiously, Tommy pulled on the door handle. It clicked and the door popped inwards. He looked back to David, who only nodded. Tommy nodded in return and pushed the door open.

Inside, Tommy and David found themselves in a small, narrow cloakroom, which must have run alongside the kitchen. As the light from outside entered through the open door, Tommy could see a number of coats and jackets hanging from hooks on the wall. On the floor were various shoes and Wellington boots, all piled up on top of one another. And there was a horrible stench. It smelled like rotting food mixed with animal urine, topped off with stale cigar smoke. It smelled dirty, unclean. Truth be told, Tommy kind of thought it smelled like death might.

When Tommy looked back over his shoulder. Despite the fact that David's face was shrouded in shadow, Tommy could see that he was grimacing. "What the fuck is that smell?" David said, pressing the back of his hand against his nose, an effort to block out the stench.

"I don't know," replied Tommy, deciding not to mention the idea that perhaps the smell was coming from Mikey's rotting corpse.

They continued on through the cloakroom, which itself opened out into the hallway. There, at the other end of the hall, they could see the front door. Directly to their left was an open door, which lead into the kitchen. Thankfully, the kitchen was empty. The small amount of light that filtered in through the slats of the blind revealed stack upon stack of dirty plates, most of which were still encrusted with the remnants of long finished dinners. *That's the source of that disgusting smell* thought Tommy, his mind wandering to the potential here for a rat infestation. *How could anybody live like this?*

Idle Hands

Then there was a noise from somewhere further along the hallway. It sounded like the muffled groan of someone pleading for help.

Mikey!

There were two doors on the left-hand side of the hallway. Both were closed. The sound had come from behind one of those doors. Slowly, Tommy and David made their way along the hall. There was no carpet here, only bare floorboards which threatened to squeak with every step they took. The walls were bare too, stripped back to the cracked, crumbling plaster. In some places, roughly torn slivers of floral wallpaper hung from the walls, as if somebody had given up on the redecoration halfway through the job. Tommy made a mental note of the stairs on the right of the hall, which ran up to the second floor, the paint flaking away from the banister.

They reached the first door. Instead of opening It, Tommy pressed his ear against it and listened.

"What are you doing?" David whispered, his hushed voice sounding more urgent now.

Tommy his forefinger against his own lips. "Shhh!"

A thought ran through Tommy's head - if this were a horror movie, like the ones Uncle Chris had brought for him to watch when he came to babysit a few weeks ago, this door would be suddenly wrenched open and the one-eyed man would be standing there, axe in hand, ready to chop him into tiny pieces.

And then there was that noise again. It came from behind the second door.

David's eyes widened and his eyebrows raised to the top of his forehead. It was hard to tell with such little light to go by, but Tommy thought he look pale. He looked more terrified now than he ever had before. Tommy imagined that he probably looked the same.

They moved to the second door. The grunts continued to emanate from inside. Tommy and David listened. Tommy felt certain that Mikey was behind this door. It sounded as though he had been gagged. He looked back to David and nodded silently. David nodded in return.

Slowly, Tommy wrapped his fingers around the spherical doorknob and turned. He pushed the door gently and peered in through the gap that opened before him.

David looked over Tommy's shoulder. "Holy fuck!" he said, failing to maintain the quietened volume of his voice. The one-eyed man was nowhere to be seen. But in the middle of the room - a room that was practically bare, save for a two-seater sofa, a small coffee table and a bookcase - was Mikey. He had been tied to a chair and he was gagged, just as Tommy had thought. Tears were streaming down his cheeks, building up on the ledge formed by the nylon rope, which had been tied around his head to secure the rag stuffed in his mouth. He no longer looked like a ten-year-old boy - now he looked like a fifty-year-old man, death creeping up on him day by day.

David pushed past Tommy and into the room. He darted across to Mikey. "Oh my God, Mikey," he said, all sense of needing to remain silent seemingly gone from his thoughts. "Don't worry. We'll get you out of here!"

Tommy followed David into the room. "Quiet!" he tried to urge David. "He's gonna hear us!"

Idle Hands

It was suddenly dawning on Tommy that they might actually be in far more danger than he had imagined they would. He hadn't expected this. If the one-eyed man was capable of kidnapping a young child, what else was he capable of?

David was tugging at the knots which bound Mikey to the chair. They gave easy enough, and soon Mikey was able to stand. Immediately, he pulled the gag over his head and spat out the rag.

"Alright," Tommy said. "Let's go!"

They didn't need to be told twice. They sprinted from the lounge, back into the hall and made for the back door.

But the one-eyed man was stood there, blocking their path. He was no more than a shadow - a black shape, silhouetted against the tiny amount of light that entered from the back of the house. "What the fuck are you doing in my house?" the one-eyed man growled.

"Shit!" Tommy yelled. He didn't normally swear - he wasn't allowed. But this situation certainly seemed to call for it. "Come on! This way!"

Tommy grabbed a hold of David and Mikey and pulled, dragging them towards the front door. Tommy slammed into the door and groped at the handle. It didn't budge. *Great! He leaves all his doors unlocked, except for this one!* "Shit!" Tommy said again.

Immediately, without thinking, Mikey turned and scrambled up the stairs. David followed. Tommy knew that was a stupid thing to do - they'd be trapped. Either that, or they'd have to jump from an upstairs window. But there was no other option now. The one-eyed man was walking slowly along the hallway. "Who the fuck gave you permission to come in here?" he said.

Tommy bolted up the stairs.

The landing was narrow, with four doors leading off into different rooms. Tommy followed as David and Mikey ran into the room at the end of the landing. He turned and slammed the door shut behind him.

It was pitch black inside the room. Not a single sliver of light entered through the window. The stench in here was worse than it had been downstairs. In here it was almost unbearable. Had he not been more concerned about the psychopath he could hear slowly creeping up the creaking stairs, Tommy surely would have vomited. He ran his fingers across the wall until they landed upon the light switch. He flicked it. The bare bulb that hung from the ceiling blinked on, flooding the room with bright white light.

And then the room was flooded with Mikey's screams.

Tommy spun around. He could hardly believe his eyes. In the corner of the room, a woman was laid on a filthy mattress, stained with faeces and urine and blood. She was naked. Her skin was dirty. Her greasy hair had been roughly sheared, almost back to the scalp. Her mouth had been sewn shut, the thick grey threads looping from top lip to bottom lip, then back again. Lengths of chain bound her cuffed wrists to the pipework of the nearby radiator. And she was trying to scream. Her lips, sealed tightly shut, prevented her from doing so. She struggled onto her knees. Her outstretched hands begged for them to help her.

"Jesus Christ!" Tommy said. He darted across the room and dropped to his knees next to the woman. He'd never seen a naked woman before, not in real life anyway. But there was nothing remotely exciting - or arousing - about this encounter. She was trying, yet failing, to speak. There was a sense of urgency about her though, as if she'd been here for years and Tommy's was the first friendly face she'd seen in all that time. "It's okay," Tommy said. "I'll help you." He traced the chains back to where they were hooked onto the pipes. He pulled at them. They were fixed solid.

David and Mikey were watching. Neither of them noticed that the one-eyed man was now inside the room and that he was standing right behind them. It wasn't until Tommy looked back to ask for assistance that anyone noticed his presence.

"Look out!" screamed Tommy, at the top of his lungs.

It was too late.

The one-eyed man grabbed David by the throat and lifted him up, slamming him back against the wall and holding him there, choking him, his legs flailing a full two feet from the ground. "You think you can come in *my* house?" said the one-eyed man, through gritted teeth. "You think you can fuck with me?" He then plunged the blade of the knife he was carrying into David's tummy. Immediately, blood began to pour from the wound and drip to the floor.

Tommy was panicking now. He didn't know what to do. It didn't seem there was much he *could* do. His senses were being assaulted from all angles. Mikey was screaming again. David was grunting as he writhed on the wall. The chains that bound the woman rattled as she tugged at them. Without thinking, as if on autopilot, Tommy grabbed the chains and pulled. The pipe that the chains were wrapped around splintered and gave way. Both Tommy and the woman tumbled back as the chains fell loose.

Tommy watched as the woman sat up. She reached up to her mouth and felt the threads that sealed her lips. She seemed to think for only a second, before pushing her fingers between the tightly wound threads. Blood began to ooze over her lips as she forced her fingers inside. And then she pulled, tearing her mouth open. The blood flowed freely now, as she gasped deeply.

And then she was on her feet, screaming, charging towards the one-eyed man.

The one-eyed man didn't notice her coming - he must've been too engrossed in the pain he was inflicting upon David. He didn't notice her until the chain was wrapped around his neck and she was clinging onto his back.

The one-eyed man dropped David. He fell to the floor and landed in a seated position, the knife still stuck in his belly. His breaths were shallow and laboured, but at least he was still alive.

The one-eyed man, wearing the dirty, naked woman like a rucksack, stumbled backwards. She pulled the chain tight. His bony fingers clawed at it, trying to pull it away, trying desperately to allow the air into his lungs.

Tommy scrambled across the floor on his hands and knees. He placed his hand on David shoulder and looked into his eyes. "You okay?" he asked, already knowing that that was a stupid question.

David coughed. "Of course I'm not okay!" he said, barely able to form the words.

"I'm sorry," Tommy said, apologising in advance. "But I need this." Without warning, he pulled the knife from David's belly. David yelped in agony.

The one-eyed man was spinning now, trying the shake the naked woman loose. But she was on too tight. She wanted him dead and there was no way he was going to stop her.

Mikey ducked out of the way as the one-eyed man careened towards him. But he wasn't quick enough. They collided, sending Mikey flying. But the one-eyed man dropped too, landing on top of the woman. Her grip loosened only momentarily, but it was enough for the one-eyed man to break free. He flipped over, immediately striking her with the back of his hand. He then climbed on top of her, pinning her arms beneath his legs. "You're just like your fucking mother, you know that?" he said, before proceeding to hit her again. And then he spat on her. "You're a fucking cunt, just like she was." He hit her again. "The pair of you can rot in hell together!" He raised his fist to hit her again.

It was then that Tommy stuck the knife in the one-eyed man's back. He didn't know much about human anatomy, but he was fairly sure the heart was on the left side of the chest. So that was where he'd aimed.

The one-eyed man peered back over his shoulder. His good eye looked at Tommy, taking in every inch of his face. There was a look of dismay in that one eye, which almost seemed to beg Tommy for help. *Why?* it seemed to want to cry out. *Why did you kill me?* Blood spilled over the cracked, chapped lips of the one-eyed man and then he dropped down dead.

The woman - her lips torn, her eyes blackened and swollen, every inch of her face plastered in a thick mask of blood - started to laugh.

Tommy dropped to the floor. He looked to David, who had now propped himself up against the wall and was clutching his stomach, his hands soaked with blood. He looked to Mikey, who was balled up on the floor, his hands over his ears, a shivering wreck. He looked to the woman, the corpse of the one-eyed man laid upon her, her face and body a broken and battered mess of blood. And she was still laughing.

Laughing hysterically.

***

The police came to see Tommy a few days later, just to give him (*and* his parents, more importantly) an update on what they'd found.

It seemed that the rumours were - at least in part - true. Upon investigation, the police had found the dismembered remains of the one-eyed man's wife wrapped up in bin liners and hidden away in the loft. As best they could tell, during the time that he was away fighting in the Falklands conflict, she had been having an affair with their next-door neighbour. When he had returned, she had asked him for a divorce. It was this, compounded by the fact that he was suffering from a severe case of PTSD, that had led him to kill her and take their daughter hostage, keeping her locked up in the house for the last thirty-five years. She had only been five at the time.

Apparently, he had sewn her mouth shut after she refused to stop screaming. That was, at a guess, about twenty-five years ago. Since then, her diet had consisted solely of liquidised meals.

David was going to be just fine. The knife had missed all of his vital organs. Wounds like that tended to bleed a lot, or so the police officer had said. He had lost a lot of blood, but he was in hospital and he was going to be okay.

Mikey was a little shook up, but the police officers who had checked him over had found him to be in good health, both physically and mentally. They had no concerns about him. Given time, the memories of what had happened in that house would fade and he too would be just fine.

When the police had first come to the house on Whitechurch Street - they had been alerted by one of the neighbours, who had witnessed the boys scattering from the building, covered in blood - they had taken all three of them to the station for questioning. Tommy had told the truth - he told them about the game of 'Knock Door Run', about Mikey being snatched, about entering the house, and finding the bloody, broken woman. He hesitated at first, but soon enough he told them that it was he who had killed the one-eyed man. They were understanding. They told him he'd acted in self-defence. They told him it was fine.

It didn't feel fine to Tommy.

But perhaps it would, in time. It might take five years. It might take ten years. It may even take twenty. But eventually the memories would fade, and everything would be just fine.

Sure.
Everything would be just fine.

THE END

A PRIVATE SHOW

Claire took a sip of her rose wine and returned the glass to its place on the shelf that ran beneath the bathroom mirror. She then proceeded to shave the remaining hair from her cooch. She had to be perfectly clean shaven - even the slightest amount of stubble could be a turn-off for the most discerning of viewers. Once finished, she looked herself over - gave herself the final inspection - and decided she was perfect. She was nineteen. Her C-cup boobs were perky and full of bounce. Her tummy was flat - a slight hint of abdominal muscle showed though the thin layer of subdermal puppy fat that had yet to melt away. And her tight teenage pussy - now devoid of even a single hair - was every man's fantasy.

She had curled her hair. The tightly wound, dirty blonde locks hung just above her shoulders. She always wore minimal make-up - nowadays, men seemed to prefer the natural look. A small amount of eye liner - just enough to accentuate the blue of her eyes - was all she wore tonight.

She pulled her thong on and clasped her bra behind her back. Both were black, trimmed with white lace - a matching pair that Steve had bought for her on

Wednesday, especially for this occasion. She looked cute and she knew it. She had a good a feeling about tonight.

She picked up her wine and gulped down the small amount that remained. As she did so, the door opened and Steve entered the bathroom. He was wearing only his boxer shorts, his toned and muscular physique proudly on display. "Wow," he said, as he looked her over.

Claire smiled at him via her reflection in the mirror. "You think he's gonna like me tonight?"

"*Like you*? He's gonna love you! If he doesn't, then there's clearly somethin' wrong with the guy."

Perhaps there is *something wrong with this guy,* Claire thought to herself. It wasn't as if either of them had met him before.

Claire ignored the thought. She laughed and returned her empty glass to the shelf, before turning to face Steve, beckoning him in for a kiss.

Steve obliged. He squeezed her tightly, digging his fingertips into the flesh of her back as he caressed and kneaded her skin. His tongued wrapped around hers as they pressed their lips together so hard it almost hurt. Claire loved him - she felt sure of it. Of course, she didn't *really* know what love felt like (she always considered herself to be too young to know), but she felt sure this was it. There was a fire that burned inside her whenever Steve held her. It made her feel a kind-of delirious happiness, unlike anything she'd ever known. If this *wasn't* love, she didn't care - love could wait.

"Okay, mister," Claire said as she pushed Steve away. "Let's save it for the show, yeah?"

Idle Hands

Steve laughed and kissed her one last time. "Alright. Well, hurry up then. Two minutes 'til show time." And with that, he took one of the fluffy white bath robes from the hook beside the shower, slung it over his shoulder and left the room.

Claire watched him as he went, admiring the way his boxers hung loosely over his firm buttocks. Then she turned to look at herself in the mirror once again. She squeezed her breasts together and pushed them up, giving herself even more of a cleavage than the bra alone provided. It crossed her mind that, perhaps, she ought to get herself a boob job. Not yet though - they were perfect as they were right now. But in a few years' time, once her body began to give way and they started to sag, she would definitely get them enhanced. Nothing too big though, just something to firm them up.

She left the bathroom a few moments later, the other robe now wrapped around her. It was 4:00 a.m. and outside the sun had already begun to raise its head above the horizon. Claire crossed the room and closed the curtains. The hotel room was nice. It was clean and comfortable. They always used the same hotel and all of the rooms here seemed to be almost identical. The artwork that hung above the bed appeared to be different in each room, but that was about the only discernible difference.

Steve was sat in the middle of the bed, his legs folded, the laptop balanced on top of his knees. His fingers tapped away at the keyboard. He was no doubt messaging *MattyMoo149* to let him know that they were ready to begin.

MattyMoo149 was one of their regular customers. He always tipped well.

"Is he there?" asked Claire, peering over Steve's shoulder at the computer screen.

"Not yet. I've told him that we're about to start streaming, so I expect he'll be along any second."

"Well, he best not keep us waiting too long."

"I'm sure he won't. But, hey, if he doesn't show, it makes no difference to us - he's already paid, remember?"

"I know," Claire said with a sigh. "But the extra tips he promised sure would come in handy." Cam girls didn't tend to make a lot of money. Even the most popular ones (and Claire was certainly popular - she always got hundreds of viewers per show) struggled to make anything worth shouting about. Most of the girls doing it had to work a day job as well - Claire worked part-time as a waitress in an Italian restaurant. But then, it wasn't as if camming was a difficult job. Not at all. Most people, Claire and Steve included, did it purely for the excitement of being watched by strangers. It was a dirty hobby and the extra income that those voyeurs provided was always more than welcome. But the truth was that, even if your number of viewers peaked in the thousands, the vast majority of them would only hang around for just as long as it took them to jerk themselves off and shoot their load into a handful of crinkled tissue. And then they were gone, with no sign of a tip.

It was the regular customers – those who tuned in to each and every show – that paid the majority of tips. Even then, they'd be lucky to walk away with anything more than a few hundred pound.

That was why, when *MattyMoo149* had offered them £5,000 for a one-hour private show, Claire had

Idle Hands

agreed in an instant. Had he have been there with her in person, she'd have practically bitten his hand off.

She'd half expected nothing to come of his offer. But sure enough, once they'd arranged a time and date, then the £5,000 appeared in their account.

And that time and date was now.

Steve stood from the bed and carried the laptop over to the dressing table. There, a camera was already set up on a miniature tripod, aimed at the bed. He plugged the cord from the camera into the port on the side of the laptop. "You ready?"

Claire nodded. She sat on the edge of the bed and plastered a smile onto her face, one that showed off her perfectly white, perfectly straight teeth. Steve clicked a few on-screen icons and their broadcast began.

The majority of the laptop's screen was taken up by the image from the camera. Claire could see herself sat on the bed. She adjusted her robe, opening it just a little, to show off the top of her cleavage. Down the right-hand side of the screen was the chatbox, where, during any normal show, the viewers could leave their messages. It was here that they could make their requests for what they wanted to see Claire and Steve do to one another. It was fulfilling those requests that earned them the most tips.

At the top of the chatbox was a number. It showed the amount of people watching. It currently stood at zero.

"You sure he's gonna show?" Claire said to Steve, as he sat on the bed beside her.

"I'm sure," said Steve, smiling reassuringly. He was a handsome guy. Claire had met him three years ago, on their first day of college together. They were in the same class, both studying economics. They'd hit it off immediately. He was funny and charming and intelligent. Of course, it didn't hurt that he was incredibly good-looking too. He'd asked her out a few weeks later and of course she'd said yes. They were pretty much an 'official' couple after that. After a few months of casual dating (and incredible sex), they'd began filming themselves and uploading the footage to porn video sharing websites. It had been Steve's idea, but Claire had gone along with it gladly. She found the idea of people masturbating to videos of her getting fucked to be quite the turn-on. When Steve had suggested they broadcast themselves live, explaining how they could make money from the tips, Claire had thought it was a great idea. They'd been camming for nearly 2 years now, and Claire had built up quite a following.

The computer bleeped. The number at the top of the screen had increased to one.

'Hi MattyMoo!" Claire waved enthusiastically at the camera. "You there?"

A reply quickly appeared in the chatbox.

MattyMoo149 - Good evening.
MattyMoo149 - I'm here.
MattyMoo149 - I must say, you look as beautiful as ever tonight.

"Thank you," giggled Claire, shying away from the camera.

MattyMoo149 seemed like a nice man (or woman - he had said he was male, but Claire had no way of knowing for sure). They'd first noticed him watching about six months ago. He was polite, although he didn't really say much. His messages were well composed, unlike those of most of the other perverts who watched. More often than not, their chatbox would be filled with such delightful messages as *'SHOW US UR CUNT!'* and *'STICK IT IN HER ASS!'*. They were the sort of crude message you soon got used to, soon learned to ignore. When Claire had first started as a cam girl, the kind of things people would say had been quite shocking. Back then, as a seventeen-year-old, the fact that somebody could message her, telling her that they would rape her if they ever saw her on the street had been quite scary. But Steve had assured her that none of these people could ever hurt her. He'd convinced her that they were nothing more than a bunch of perverts who believed they could say whatever they wanted as they hid behind the anonymity their username provided. Soon, Claire had learned to play up to it. Someone once threatened to drug her and fuck her arsehole while she was unconscious. She pretended she'd like it. She pretended to orgasm at the thought of it. That guy had left a pretty generous tip.

Steve scooted around and climbed on to the bed. He positioned himself behind Claire. He began to massage her shoulders through the fluffy material of her robe. Claire closed her eyes, tipped her head back and moaned gently. "Oooh. That feels *so* good..." Steve lowered his head and kissed her on the neck. He allowed his hand to work its way down Claire's front and inside her robe. He slid his fingers inside her bra and ran them over her stiffening nipples. Again, Claire moaned passionately. She smiled at the camera. "So MattyMoo," she said. "What do you wanna see us do?

MattyMoo149 - Take off your robe.

"You got it," Claire winked at the camera. She bit her lower lip, as if contemplating whether or not she should remove her robe. She would, of course - *MattyMoo149* had paid for a show after all.

Slowly, Claire untied the belt from around her waist. Steve continued to kiss her neck as he slid the robe downwards, off of her shoulders. He then returned his hands to Claire's breasts, once again reaching inside the bra, squeezing, and pinching her nipples.

"You like what you see?" said Claire into the camera, her voice sultry, seductive.

MattyMoo149 - Sure do.
MattyMoo149 - Let me see your breasts.

Claire raised her eyebrows flirtatiously. She stood from the bed and fully removed the robe, dropping it into a heap on the floor. Steve sat back and watched as she turned and crawled onto the bed, on her hands and knees. Claire knew that, for only a second, her buttocks would be spread, giving *MattyMoo149* a quick glimpse of the thin strip of material that comprised her thong, the only thing that hid her tight, wet pussy from sight. And then she straightened up, hiding her thong from view. She reached around and unclasped her bra. Slowly, she lowered it, watching over her shoulder as she did so. She could picture *MattyMoo149* (for some reason she imagined him to be forty-something, a well-paid professional, who always wore a smart suit) at home, stroking his hard dick as she looked into his eyes. She held the bra up and dropped it onto the bed. Then, once again biting her bottom lip, she turned to face the camera, her forearm covering her breasts. She allowed a long, drawn-out moment to pass, before finally moving her arm. She laughed and said "Well? You like?"

*MattyMoo149 - *Of course.*
*MattyMoo149 - *They're the best breasts I've ever laid eyes on.*

"Why, thank you." Claire giggled and sat down on the edge of the bed once again. "So, do wanna see me play with my friend?"

*MattyMoo149 - *Yes.*
*MattyMoo149 - *Please.*

"Any special requests?"

*MattyMoo149 - *No.*
*MattyMoo149 - *Do whatever pleases you.*

"Sounds good to me." Claire stood from the edge of the bed and beckoned Steve to join her. He climbed off the bed and circled around to where she was stood. Immediately, they began to kiss passionately, as Steve began to knead and squeeze her breasts. Claire untied Steve's belt and opened up his robe. His penis was already erect inside his boxer shorts. Claire knew that Steve found all of this a massive turn-on, just as she did. He'd even do it for free, of that she was sure. She pulled down the front of his boxers and released his member. She then took a tight grip of it and began to stroke back and forth. As she did so, Steve bent and took her nipples in his mouth, biting them, flicking them with his tongue.

Claire peered over his shoulder and looked into the camera.

Steve ran his hands down Claire's back and took a hold of her buttocks. He squeezed them tightly, just as she liked.

The computer bleeped as a new message came through.

MattyMoo149 - Eat her pussy.

Claire smiled. She pushed away from Steve. "This one's for you, I guess," She said.

Steve read the message on the screen.

"Oh," said Steve. "Well, I don't need to be told twice."

Claire kissed Steve again as she took a hold of his robe and pulled him down onto the bed. She shuffled back, propped up on her elbows. Steve followed her move, manoeuvring between her legs and pushing her thighs apart. There, sat back on his own heels, he took a hold of the waistband of Claire's thong and pulled it down along the long length of her smooth legs. He dropped it to the floor and then lay flat on his stomach. Claire watched as he began to lick and nuzzle at her vagina. His tongue slid between her labia and probed inside her. She moaned softly, her mouth wide open. She dropped back, onto the bed and began to squeeze her own breasts, moaning loader now as Steve's tongue encircled her clitoris.

She lifted her hips from the bed and began to thrust against Steve's tongue. She reached down and

Idle Hands

grabbed his hair, pulling his head into her crotch. Soon, she climaxed. There were times when she faked it for the benefit of the audience - they wanted to see her cum multiple times during any one show. That wasn't always possible. But sometimes she could cum two of three times, depending on how horny she was. Tonight, she was pretty horny. The warm, tingling rush that flooded her body caused her to gasp for air.

Steve sat up. Claire ran her fingers through her hair and laughed. "Oh God. That was so good!" She swung her leg over Steve's head and shuffled to the edge of the bed. "Do you think I should reward him?" she asked the camera.

MattyMoo149 - Indeed I do.

"How should I reward him?"

MattyMoo149 - I think it's only fair if you give him oral in return.

Steve laughed aloud. "I couldn't agree more, Matty!"

"You know what," Claire said. "I think that's a great idea." She took Steve by the hand and ushered him off the bed. She then knelt before him and slid his boxers down. His erection - all seven inches of it - sprang to attention as the elastic popped free. Claire giggled once again. "Wow," she said, speaking to Steve, but really it was for the benefit of *MattyMoo149*. "I don't think I've ever seen a dick as big as this before." With that, she took a hold of the shaft and wrapped her lips around the end. She had decent technique (or so *she* thought). Sure, she couldn't deep throat (even the thought was enough to make her gag), but she knew how to suck a dick, no problem. One hand stroked up and down the length, while the other cupped his balls. Steve liked it when she would pinch and tug at his scrotum, so she did this occasionally. Her tongue licked around the tip of his penis as her head bobbed back and forth. She removed his penis from her mouth and began to lick back and forth along the length. She then reinserted his penis into her mouth and continued to suck and lick at it.

After a few minutes of this she stopped to address the camera. "I'm so horny, Matty. Can he fuck me now?"

MattyMoo149 - Of course.

"Thank you."

Steve crossed the room and picked up a condom from the bedside table. He tore open the wrapper and removed the condom from inside. He then sat on the edge of the bed and rolled the condom down the length of his erection.

Claire shuffled back on the bed and lay back. Steve crawled between her legs and laid on top of her. She loved to feel his weight on top of her. He was broad and heavy. But he was also strong, and the feeling of him pressing down on top of her reminded Claire that he would always protect her.

She could feel the tip of his penis sliding along her labia. It felt nice. But she wanted to feel his girth inside her. She wrapped her legs around him and dug her heels into his buttocks, pulling him into her. The length of his penis slid into her. She moaned as he hit full depth, as a wave of intense pleasure - combined with a slight twinge of pain - pulsed from her genitals. And then he began to thrust in and out, slowly at first then picking up speed. He pushed himself up on his hands and sat up, onto his knees. He continued to fuck her, reaching down, and squeezing her breasts. Claire stretched out, reaching her hands up to grasp the headboard. Steve grabbed a hold of her ankles and flipped them onto his shoulders. He wrapped his arms around her thighs and began to pound harder. Claire moaned with ecstasy every time Steve thrust into her.

Claire heard the computer bleep. She read the message on the screen.

MattyMoo149 - Take the rubber off.

"Sorry Matty. No can do," Claire said, in between her deep gasps of pleasure. "I'm not looking to get pregnant tonight." She smiled and winked at the camera.

MattyMoo149 - You can take the morning after pill tomorrow.

There was something about this that made Claire feel somewhat uncomfortable. Why was it so important to him that they went unprotected? What difference did it make to him? It didn't make sense at all. Him suggesting that she should risk her health just so he could get off wasn't exactly pleasant.

MattyMoo149 - I'll make it worth your while.
MattyMoo149 - Just take the rubber off.

Steve's rhythm had slowed. He too was reading the message on the screen. Claire could see by his face that he wasn't sure how to react.

MattyMoo149 - Check your account.

Steve climbed off of Claire. He grabbed his iPad from the bedside table and loaded up the online bank account they shared. A payment of £100 had been made into the account.

Steve showed Claire the screen. "Oh my God," she said, understanding that *MattyMoo149* had made that payment, in order to get them to follow his instructions. They could refuse, of course. But if they did, the show would be over - no more tips from *MattyMoo149*.

And he was right, of course - she *could* take the morning after pill tomorrow.

"What do you think?" Steve asked, without even looking at her.

"Fuck it," she said, shaking her head. She reached down and pulled the condom from Steve's penis. She held it up, displayed to the camera. "Happy now?"

MattyMoo149 - That's much better. Far more intimate.
MattyMoo149 - He'll be able to feel you now.

Claire pushed Steve back on the bed. He willingly obliged. She then swung her leg over his chest and straddled him, facing the camera, reverse cowgirl style. From there, she lowered herself down onto Steve's erection. It felt so much nicer as it slid inside her once again. There wasn't that rough feeling as the latex pulled and nipped at her skin. It felt natural. There was a feeling that - all of a sudden - they were closer than they had ever been before.

Slowly, Claire began to ride him. She lifted herself up and then dropped back down. The length of his thick, hard penis pushed deep inside her. She could feel it pressing against her cervix. It felt good. She moaned with pleasure - a sound she wouldn't have been able to suppress, even if she wanted too.

*MattyMoo149 - Good girl. You're enjoying it. I can tell.

*MattyMoo149 - So much better without the condom, yes?

"Oh, yes," Claire said, her voice little more than a whisper. She reached up and squeezed her breasts hard. The pain was nice - a fine companion for the pleasure currently coasting through her body.

And then she came. A warm wave of orgasm emanated from her pubis, causing every inch of her body to tingle. Without even noticing, she was moaning louder now, riding Steve's dick harder than she had been before. And then, as her orgasm tapered off, she stopped.

There was a new message on the screen.

*MattyMoo149 - Do you like being choked?

"What the fuck," Claire muttered to herself, before asking the camera - "What do you mean?"

She had now climbed off of Steve and was once again sat on the edge of the bed. She wanted to get closer, to ensure she'd read the message correctly.

She had.

Steve read the message too. "What the fuck is this?"

MattyMoo149 - Simple question.
MattyMoo149 - Do you like being choked?

"No," said Claire, sternly. "I don't. At all."

MattyMoo149 - I'd like to see you being choked.
MattyMoo149 - I think you'd enjoy it.

"No, I wouldn't. It's not going to happen."

MattyMoo149 - Please check your account again.

Claire's heart was beating hard. She could feel it throbbing inside her chest. She felt nervous - a sensation she hadn't felt in a long time. But she knew what Steve was going to find in their account. She hadn't been prepared for how much would be there though.

"He's paid us five-hundred pounds," Steve said.

"What?" Claire said, unable to hide her disbelief. She shuffled along the bed and looked at Steve's iPad.

Sure enough, there was another new payment. It was for £500.

MattyMoo149 - Let him fuck your mouth.

Idle Hands

*MattyMoo149 - I want you to gag on it.
*MattyMoo149 - I want to see you choke.

Claire looked to Steve. He was still sweating, and his cheeks were flushed, but she could see that he looked nervous. Neither of them spoke as Claire considered the money in her account and all she had to do to earn more.

She nodded to Steve, then turned to face the camera. "Ok," she said. "I'll do it."

*MattyMoo149 - Great!
*MattyMoo149 - Lie on the bed with your head hanging over the side.
*MattyMoo149 - That way I'll be able to see.

Claire did as instructed. She shuffled on to the bed and laid back, so that her head hung over the edge. Now upside-down, Steve stood before her. He squatted a little, so that he could place the tip of his penis against her lips.

Claire opened wide. Steve guided his penis into her waiting mouth. Immediately her gag reflex took a hold and tightened up her throat. She could feel the tip of his erection pressing onto her tonsils and already she wanted to gag. The fact of the matter was that, no matter how hard she tried (and, believe me, she *had* tried), she could only take half of his length in her mouth before it hit the back and her oesophagus closed up tight. Steve pulled out and then slid back in, each time pressing a little harder.

*MattyMoo149 - Tell her to relax.

"He says you need to relax," Steve said, as he continued to push his dick further into Claire's mouth.

Claire tried to relax. She took a deep breath through her nose.

*MattyMoo149 - Choke the bitch.
*MattyMoo149 - I want to see her gag.

With every thrust of Steve's hips, Claire's stomach wanted desperately to expel the contents of her stomach. But just before the urge grew too strong, Steve would pull out. But then he began to pick up speed, fucking her mouth harder and harder. As his dick slammed into the back of her mouth, pressing against her tonsils, her gag reflex began to work overtime.

*MattyMoo149 - Push your dick in as far as it will go.
*MattyMoo149 - Choke her.
*MattyMoo149 - Make her turn blue.

Steve continued to fuck Claire's mouth, reaching forward, and squeezing her breasts aggressively. She was gagging. Thick balls of spit leaked out of her mouth with each of Steve's thrusts, and trickled down her face. She felt disgusting.

She felt scared.

She couldn't breathe. She knew that Steve would never hurt her, but right now she had surrendered all control to him. It was that which frightened her the most.

And then Steve slowed. But instead of removing his dick, he slowly pushed it in deeper. She could feel it working its way past her tonsils, past the sphincter that prevented her from vomiting, and into her oesophagus. She was choking. She tried to push Steve away, thinking that as soon as he knew she wanted him to stop, he would. But he didn't. He pushed in deeper. Her stomach began to tighten. It was painful. She reached around and dug her fingernails into Steve's buttocks, attempting to tear his flesh away.

Steve pulled out. Immediately, Claire flipped over and puked on the floor. The taste of bile made her wretch further.

She could feel the tears streaming down her cheeks. Once the vomiting had stopped, she looked up at Steve through foggy, bloodshot eyes. "Are you okay?" he asked her.

"Do I look okay to you?" she replied.

The computer bleeped.

MattyMoo149 - Don't clean yourself up.
MattyMoo149 - I want to see you looking like the dirty whore you are.

Claire scoffed back a laugh, as she coughed up and spat out a mouthful of phlegm. "You wanna see me covered in puke? What kind of a sick pervert are you?"

MattyMoo149 - The kind that expects you to do as you're told.
MattyMoo149 - Move closer to the camera.

Claire shook her head in disbelief, yet she did as instructed. She moved in front of the camera and crouched, so that her tits and her stomach - both of which were sticky with bile and saliva - were perfectly framed. "You like what you see, you dirty old man?"

*MattyMoo149 - Indeed I do.

"So, are we finished here?" Claire had had enough now. She was regretting having ever agreed to do the private show.

*MattyMoo149 - Not yet.
*MattyMoo149 - I haven't cum yet.

"Well perhaps you ought to try a little harder."

*MattyMoo149 - Maybe I will.
*MattyMoo149 - Show me your asshole.

Claire rolled her eyes. Steve was now sat on the end of the bed. Claire stood, turned her back to the camera and bent over. She grasped her buttocks and pulled them apart with her fingers.
There was a horrid smell filtering in through her nostrils. She looked down at the floor where the puddle of her sick still festered. She closed her eyes, for fear that she may vomit once again.

*MattyMoo149 - Check your account.

Steve picked up the iPad. "Holy shit," he said.
Claire opened her eyes and looked at the screen. £1,000 had been paid into their account.
"What's this for?" said Claire, wiping a trail of drool from her bottom lip with her hand.

MattyMoo149 - I've never seen you do anal.
MattyMoo149 - Do you do anal?

"No. I don't."

MattyMoo149 - Never?

"No."

MattyMoo149 - I'd like to see you lose your anal virginity.

"No way. Not happening."

MattyMoo149 - Name your price.

Claire was beginning to feel as if this whole situation was crazy. It was almost unbelievable. She thought about it for a moment. Anal sex wasn't something with which she just wasn't comfortable. She couldn't imagine how painful it would be. It wasn't something she ever hoped to experience. But then, *MattyMoo149* was essentially offering her a blank check. She could say any amount and chances were he'd pay it. "Ten grand," she told the camera.

Silence befell the room. It seemed to last for hours, despite being only seconds.

"Claire..." Steve began to say, before being cut off by the bleep of the computer.

MattyMoo149 - Done.

Claire and Steve looked at their account. The £10,000 was there. Claire shook her head and laughed. It was insane. The thought crossed her mind that they could just end the show now; call it a day, more than fifteen-thousand pounds richer. But that would surely be the end of their camming career. Bad word of mouth spread like wildfire in the online community.

Claire looked to Steve. He was simply staring back. She nodded, assuring him that she was happy to do this. Steve stood from the bed. There was a bottle of lube on the dresser, one that they rarely had to use. He grabbed it and squeezed a generous amount onto his fingertips. Claire climbed onto the bed, once again on all fours. Steve massaged the lube around Claire's anus.

Slowly, he worked a finger in. It felt strange. It felt surprisingly good. Still, it was just a finger. She felt sure something bigger - an erect penis, for example - would feel a whole lot different.

"Be gentle," Claire said, looking back to where Steve stood behind her. He nodded in return.

Steve squeezed a dose of lube onto the shaft of his cock and stroked it along the length. He then placed the tip of his penis against Claire's anus and began to push.

Claire closed her eyes and bit her lip as she felt the pressure against her rectum. She soon felt her sphincter open up and allow entry to Steve's hard cock. She gasped as a wave of pain flooded her body.

"Ughh…" Claire moaned. "Stop. Stop, stop."

*MattyMoo149 - Don't stop.

Idle Hands

Steve didn't stop. He continued to push, sliding his dick in deeper. The pain continued. Claire's natural reflexes caused her to squeeze her buttocks together. But that only caused more pain. "Arghhh" she practically screamed, biting her lip even harder. "Stop. Stop now."

*MattyMoo149 - Keep going.

Steve ignored her. He began to thrust in and out of her anus.
Claire was crying. She grabbed a pillow a bit into it, smothering her own screams.

*MattyMoo149 - Hit her.
*MattyMoo149 - Spank her.

Steve slapped Claire's right buttock. She could barely feel the stinging sensation over the intense pain she felt in her colon.

*MattyMoo149 - Hit her harder.

Steve spanked Claire harder. This time she felt it. She lifted her head and yelped, before burying it back into the pillow.

*MattyMoo149 - Do it again.
*MattyMoo149 - Harder.
*MattyMoo149 - Make the bitch scream.

Steve raised his open palm and swung it full force into Claire's buttocks. She did scream this time. Once again, she begged him to stop. But he didn't.

She tried to pull away, but Steve kept a tight grip on her hips. "Stop! Please!"

MattyMoo149 - Keep going.
MattyMoo149 - Fuck her harder.
MattyMoo149 - Hit her again.
MattyMoo149 - Again.
MattyMoo149 - Harder.

Steve fucked Claire's ass as hard as he could, pulling out and slamming back in, ignoring her screams, all the while spanking her as hard as he could, turning her buttocks a violent shade of red. He reached forward and grabbed a hold of her hair, pulling her back. Claire gasped, her face free of the pillow. "Please stop!" she begged once again.

Steve grunted. His pace slowed. Claire could feel his penis pulsing inside her as warm semen filled her colon.

Panting like a dog, Steve pulled out and flopped back on the bed. Claire slumped forward. She hugged the pillow against her chest and started to weep.

MattyMoo149 - Did he cum inside you? Show me.

Claire didn't see the message. Steve did though. He grabbed Claire by the arm. "Come here," he said, as he dragged her off the bed. He spun her around and pushed her back down over the edge of the bed, her behind facing the camera. He grabbed a hold of her cheeks and spread them. Claire could feel the semen trickling out of her anus and running down the inside of her leg.

MattyMoo149 - Very nice.
MattyMoo149 - Very sexy.

Claire continued to sob. She felt so ashamed. She felt abused. No amount of money would ever have been worth the ordeal that Steve had just put her through.

Steve gritted his teeth. "I think we're done here," he said. He sounded angry. Claire thought that *he* must've felt ashamed too; angry at what he'd allowed himself to do to her.

MattyMoo149 - Eat it.

"What?" Steve said, the tone of his voice an angry, bemused embarrassment.

Claire didn't see the message of course - she was lying face down on the bed, muffling her own sobs in the quilt. She felt disgusting, violated.

MattyMoo149 - I'll give you another £10k if you suck the jizz out of her arsehole.

A silence befell the room. Claire didn't know what had been asked of Steve, but she could tell he was contemplating it, whatever it was.

And then she felt Steve's face between her buttocks. She could feel his tongue working its way inside her rectum. She lifted her head and moaned; not a moan of pleasure, but one of despair.

Then Steve tore himself away and spat a mouthful of thick, slimy semen onto the floor. "That's it!" he said, the anger still present in his voice. "That's it! We're done!"

*MattyMoo149 - Okay.
*MattyMoo149 - I have one more request, then we're done.

Claire sniffed back her tears as she slid from the bed and sat on the floor, unaware that she was sitting in the puddle of vomit. Either she didn't know, or she didn't care. She read the message on the screen. "No," she said. "No more requests."

*MattyMoo149 - This one isn't for you.
*MattyMoo149 - It's for him.

Steve sat in the edge of the bed and read the messages on screen.

*MattyMoo149 - I have £1 million here, with your name on it.

Claire read the message too. She looked back to Steve, whose eyes had widened.

*MattyMoo149 - I have a simple request for you.
*MattyMoo149 - Do it and the money is yours.
*MattyMoo149 - Kill her.

Claire felt her heart racing. Steve was sat in silence. His eyes were flicked back and forth across the screen, taking in each and every single word.
She could tell that he was contemplating it.

Idle Hands

*MattyMoo149 - Kill her, then fuck her corpse.
*MattyMoo149 - That's the only thing that will make me cum.

"What the fuck?" Claire said between deep, rasping sobs. "Steve, we have to end this."

*MattyMoo149 - £1 million.
*MattyMoo149 - You'll be rich.

Claire stood. She reached for the laptop. Before she could lay her fingers on it, she was pulled backwards. Steve had taken a handful of her hair and yanked. "Wait a minute," he said, pushing her down onto the bed. "I need to think about this."

*MattyMoo149 - Don't think.
*MattyMoo149 - Do it.
*MattyMoo149 - Kill her.
*MattyMoo149 - £1 million.

"How would you want me to do it?" Steve asked the camera.

Claire rolled from the bed. She looked back to where Steve was looking at the screen. His face was blank, as if he no longer resided in his own body. She looked to the door. She could make a run for it. But it was locked, of that she was sure. If she fumbled and failed to get it open, she would surely be done for.

*MattyMoo149 - Cut her throat.
*MattyMoo149 - I want to see her bleed.

"Alright," Steve said. Claire could hear him breathing heavy. His voice seemed to falter as he spoke. He stood from the bed and began to rifle through the holdall on the floor. Claire's belongings were in that bag, including her cosmetics. In her make-up bag was a small pair of scissors. She guessed that was what Steve was going for.

Slowly - painfully - Claire scrambled onto her knees. She crawled towards the dressing table. She reached up and took a hold of the dresser. Before she could heave herself up, Steve was on top of her, dragging her up to her feet. He spun her around and pushed her back. Just as she had thought, he had found her scissors.

"I'm sorry," Steve whispered.

"So am I," said Claire.

She swung for Steve. The empty wine bottle she had grabbed shattered as it collided with his skull. Shards of glass splintered, slicing the skin of her forearm.

Dazed, Steve stumbled back. Blood was pouring down his face, from somewhere above his hairline. As his vision cleared, he stared at Claire. There was a look of distain on his face. He squeezed the scissors tightly and stormed towards her.

Claire screamed. She still held what remained of the wine bottle by the neck. She lifted it and plunged it into Steve's throat.

He dropped the scissors. As he pulled away, the broken glass tore free. The gaping wound in his neck split wide. Blood gushed from the exposed arteries. As he choked on his own blood, he tried to speak. No words came. He slumped back onto the bed, where he fell limp.

Idle Hands

Claire took a long, deep breath. A sense a relief swarmed her. She stepped towards the bed. Steve was dead, no doubt. His eyes were wide and glassy, his tongue hung from his mouth.

The computer bleeped. Claire turned to face the screen.

*MattyMoo149 - Thank you.
*MattyMoo149 - I just came.

Claire could only stare. She had no response.

*MattyMoo149 - I've transferred you your money.

Claire picked up the iPad. Sure enough, the amount in the account was now more than seven figures.

She sat on the edge of the bed. She could feel the warm blood that now saturated the bed sheets squelching between her thighs. She stared at the screen.

*MattyMoo149 - And here's a little bonus for you too.

Claire watched as another payment appeared in the account. It was another million.

*MattyMoo149 - Thank you again.
*MattyMoo149 - Goodnight.

The counter at the top of the chatbox flicked down to zero.

Claire looked into the camera. She wondered if he was still there. She wondered if he was still watching her somehow.

She smiled at the camera.

"Goodnight."

THE END

FILTER

I was beautiful.

At least that's what *they* used to tell me. I can't really say that I was ever in agreement. And don't get me wrong, it's not as if I ever considered myself to be ugly. But the truth of the matter is that I think I look much better like this.

I used to have blonde hair, which hung shoulder length in tight, thick waves. So many people told me how much they loved my hair, how they wished they had hair like mine. Really? I hated it. No. I didn't hate it; that's too strong of a word. But I did often wish that it was straighter and more easily managed.

My skin was relatively clear, save for the freckles that littered my nose and the few spots that seemed to be permanently engraved to my forehead. Most girls of my age tended to suffer with spots much worse than I did, so I guess that's one thing I should've been grateful for.

My eyes were green, although anybody who took the time to look a little closer would see that they were actually flecked with grey. I liked my eyes. Should anybody ask which part of my body was my favourite,

I'd always say my eyes. Time and time again I'd been complimented on them, as if I somehow had a hand in creating their colour. If only. No, that was the work of my mother and father (although, I suppose they didn't have to put much effort into it either).

My friends often told me how much they envied my body. I wasn't sure why. Oftentimes, I wished I had *their* bodies. I was tall (only an inch or two shorter than Jake, my boyfriend - we'll get to him shortly). I was slim, although I had put on a few extra pounds recently, and I did feel like I was getting a little bit chubby. My boobs were firm and pert - being only 17, I suppose they really *ought* to be. My legs were long and slender; it was them that seemed to get the most compliments, especially whenever I wore a skirt or a dress.

I'd never really like my body. I'd always found looking at myself naked to be awkward, and somewhat embarrassing. The feeling only got worse once I hit puberty, when my breasts began to fill out, and my menstrual cycle kicked in like a fucking bitch. But still, for the most part I was always able to suppress those feelings. I was always quite happy being naked around other people, just so long as I didn't have to look at myself in a mirror.

But as I look at myself now, I think I look good. All of my imperfections are gone. I look pure. There's nothing for anybody to pass comment on now. No way for anybody to make fun of me for the way I look. Not that anybody ever did. Again, *they* always said I was beautiful. But now, that wasn't even possible. Right now, I *am* beautiful. And I'll be even more beautiful once I've washed away all the blood.

Idle Hands

Jake had been shocked to see me like this. No - shocked isn't the correct word. He was *horrified*. I really don't understand why. I'm not sure he loves me anymore. Actually, I am sure; he *doesn't* love me anymore. He *can't* love me anymore. The dead aren't capable of feeling emotions, are they?

Anyway…

This all began just a few days ago. Let me take you back to the start.

Growing up, I'd never considered myself to be pretty (see above). But so many people told me I was good looking that, I guess, I just accepted it for what it was. It didn't make any difference to me and my life, so I didn't think too much of it. And thinking back now, they may not have really meant it anyway. I, myself, often complimented my friends on the way they looked, even if I didn't really believe what I was saying. It's just the kind thing to do, right?

Truth is, I'm no different to any other teenage girl. I have my insecurities, but I also enjoy the compliments I receive.

Social media was pretty much my life. I loved it. I loved posting selfies to Instagram and Twitter. It was on there that I mostly socialised with my friends. Our days at college were so busy, that any time spent socialising in person was, more often than not, very short. Of course, we'd see each other on the weekends. But still, we spent more time chatting online, posting photos, and commenting on each other's selfies.

Even Jake took the time to like and comment on my pictures. Of course, we spent a lot more time together in person, than I did with my friends. But whenever we weren't together, if I posted a selfie, he'd always comment, telling me how beautiful I was.

I loved Jake. I mean, I *still* love him. He doesn't love me anymore though. He said he wanted to help me. He said I needed to see *someone*. And now he's gone. He left me here, all alone. That's fine. I'm happy. When he first saw me looking like this, the look of disgust on his face wasn't hard to miss. I told him that I thought I looked beautiful. He said I needed help. That had broken my heart. I'd screamed at him. I'd threatened to cut his fucking throat with the knife I was holding at the time. I hadn't meant to actually do it.

We first met around eight months ago, in the college cafeteria. I had been alone at lunch that day. So had Jake. He had been standing in the queue, waiting to pay. I'd joined the queue behind him, at which point he'd turned to me and cracked some joke about how painfully slow the service was. I can't remember exactly what he'd said, but he was funny. I could feel the warmth emanating from him. I liked him. He'd invited me to sit with him and I had agreed.

After that, we sat together during most of our lunch breaks. About a week later we exchanged numbers. Jake would text me every night. Sometimes we would speak right through until the early hours of the morning.

I could tell Jake liked me. I liked him too. A few more weeks passed before he built up the courage to ask me out on a date. I felt nervous for him; as soon as he started to ask - and I could already tell just *what* he was about to ask me - my heart started pounding. Several times he stuttered, choking on his words. Finally, he managed to get his words out.

Idle Hands

I said yes, of course. Why wouldn't I? He was handsome and funny, and he really seemed to care about me.

He took me to the cinema. He let me choose the film (I forget what we watched now, but I seem to remember it being a comedy). Once the film was finished, we went to the Italian restaurant around the corner and shared a pizza. Once we were finished eating, we caught the bus home, and Jake walked me to my front door. He had wished me goodnight; I had said the same in return. Then I leaned in and kissed him.

I was nervous then. Not that I thought, even for one second, that he might pull away from me, that he might turn me down. I *knew* he wouldn't. But still, I couldn't suppress the feeling of apprehension growing inside me.

Jake kissed me back. We were girlfriend and boyfriend going forward.

Three days ago, my parents went on holiday. They had invited me of course, back when they'd booked it six months ago, but I'd said I didn't want to go. They were fine with it - I'm seventeen, and quite capable of looking after myself for a week. Back then, as soon as I'd known that they were leaving me with the house all to myself, I'd told Jake. We'd agreed for him to come and stay with me. Neither of us could wait. Neither of our parents were keen on us spending the night together. Don't get me wrong, we were allowed into each other's bedrooms (and it wasn't like our parents forced us to keep the doors open either). But they knew - or, at least, I assumed they knew - that we were fucking. And it wasn't as if Jake was my first sexual partner either.

He was the best though. He really knew how to please me, gently nibbling at my nipples as he slid deep inside me. And the way he probed me with his tongue... I could barely describe how intense the pleasure was.

No, we couldn't wait. Unfortunately, my parent's flight was in the middle of the night, so we'd have to wait until the following day before he could come around to stay. Thankfully, that day would be a Saturday; we'd have the whole day at home together.

The night before - the Friday that my parents were due to fly out - I was in my bedroom, doing what I *always* did; browsing social media and taking selfies, hoping for one good enough to upload. Earlier that day, I'd received an email from a company, looking for 'influencers' to test their new camera app. I wasn't any kind of an influencer; I only had around two thousand followers on Twitter. But, *whatever*, I decided to give it a go. If it was any good, I might even give them some feedback.

I had installed the app and opened it up. It was called 'BeuatifyU'. The email in which I'd received it had described it as *"the easiest way to improve your selfies"*. However, when I first opened it up, what I found (after agreeing to the end-user agreement) was a plain and simple camera app, no different to my phone's standard camera app. In fact, this one was even *simpler*. There was nothing to it, no choices of filter, or anything.

Still, I struck a pose and snapped a selfie.

I had to admit, it looked good. I wasn't sure why. I think, in that first photo, I just looked fresher, less tired maybe.

Idle Hands

I posted it to Instagram. Within a few moments, the photo started to receive likes.

And then my phone rang. It was Jake. I answered immediately. "Hey," I said, my voice audibly upbeat, even to my own ears.

"Hey Millie," said Jake. "How's it goin'?"

"Good. And you?"

"Yeah, good. Have your parents left yet?"

I listened. I knew they hadn't left yet; they wouldn't go without saying goodbye. But still, I could hear them shuffling around downstairs, quietly arguing over something or other (probably something as simple as whether or not they'd packed enough towels). "No," I replied. "They're still here."

"That's too bad; I was really hoping I could come and see you tonight."

"I'd have really liked that," I said, giggling. "But I'm afraid that'll have to wait."

"Too bad. So, what you up to?"

We spoke for about thirty minutes, before my mother knocked on my door and entered. I told Jake that I loved him and that I'd see him soon. He replied likewise, before hanging up the phone.

I joined my parents downstairs, where they proceeded to inform me of all the rules they expected me to follow while they were away. Thankfully, not once did they mention Jake; to my mind, that meant they were happily agreeing to the concept of him coming to stay. At around ten-thirty, their taxi arrived to take them to the airport. I waved them goodbye, then locked the door behind them as they disappeared down the street.

After that, I watched some TV, then headed to bed at around midnight.

The next morning, I overslept. That was unusual for me; I was normally up bright and early. I guess there was nobody else in the house to disturb me. I got up and showered. As I sat on my bed, my towel wrapped around my body, I opened up that new camera app - my first feedback for the developer would probably be that the name, BeuatifyU, was stupid - and snapped a quick selfie. I loved the way I looked, with my wet hair, thick and straight, hung over one shoulder. Again, I had to admit, I did look good in the photo. I had no idea what filter this was (or why there was no option to change it; I'm sure whoever made the app could've come up with some other really great ones), but I loved how good it made me look. My skin just looked much clearer in those pictures.

Needless to say, I posted the selfie to Instagram. It got over a hundred likes in the first five minutes.

At around ten o'clock, there was a knock at the door. I opened it to find Jake stood there, a bunch of flowers in his hands. I'm not sure why, but just the sight of him made me feel elated.

Jake smiled. He really was gorgeous. "Are you wearing makeup?" he said.

That surprised me, but I took it as the joke I was sure it was. "No," I said. "Why? Are you saying I *need* to wear makeup?"

Jake laughed. "No. Not at all. Your freckles just look lighter, that's all."

At that point, I wasn't really listening to him. I just *wanted* him so badly. I *needed* him to make love to me. Biting my lip, I smiled. "Are you coming in, or what?" I said.

"I am, if you're inviting me."

Idle Hands

I grabbed him by the collar of his t-shirt, pulled him into the house and kicked the door shut behind him. As soon as he was over the threshold, I was kissing him. Immediately, I slid my hands under the material of his t-shirt and prised it up over his head. He then did the same to me, pulling off the white vest top I'd been wearing and tossing it aside. He unclasped my bra, then instantly took my left nipple in his mouth. The feeling was incredible, as his tongue circled my areola. And then his hands were inside my pants, his fingers sliding over my clitoris, then pushing their way inside me.

We fucked in the lounge. It felt so wrong, doing it there, where, less than twenty-four hours ago, my parents had been sitting, watching some crappy game show on the television. But there - with Jake sat on the sofa, and me, grinding on his lap, allowing his throbbing penis to slide in and out of me - everything just felt so right.

After I had climaxed for the third time, Jake finally came (I loved the feeling of his warm semen, oozing inside me). I kissed him, then took myself off to the bathroom, to clean myself up. Standing there naked, looking at myself in the mirror - and I never really liked to look at myself naked, remember - I felt like I was somebody else. Like the person looking at me from the other side of the mirror was a different person entirely. I felt happy and I looked incredible.

And Jake was right - my freckles had faded.

Jake left not long after, as he had arranged to play five-a-side with his mates. He promised he'd be back before nine. With little else to do, I decided to spend the rest of the day just slobbing around the house. I watched some TV. I listened to some music. I took many more selfies. I'm not sure why, but I just loved the way I looked in the photos - my skin was pale and clear, my features looked petite and perfect (I normally hated my nose, but in these pictures, it looked amazing).

It was in the early evening that I first noticed a problem.

I say problem… *You* might call it a problem. But me… I'm not so sure.

One on the selfies I took looked wrong. It took me a few minutes to figure out exactly why, but once I'd seen it, I couldn't *un*see it. I guess the app was just being too clever. The information I'd received with the email the app came in, claimed that the filter would '*remove all undesirable imperfections*'. I can only assume that some of my hair had traced along my face when I took the photo, as the app seemed to decide that my hair - a good chunk of it, at least - was not supposed to be there. The resultant picture showed me with a large bald patch running from my right ear, all the way up to the middle of my forehead. When I first saw it, I had to reach up and touch my hair, just to make sure it was still there.

It was, of course.

I brushed my hair back away from my face and took another selfie. This one showed the bald patch too. It had to be something to do with the settings - clearly, the app was remembering what changes it was making, and applying them to all subsequent photos.

The next picture I took, as well as making half my head bald, seemed to remove half of my left eyebrow. It also seemed to have erased the edges of my mouth, making my lips a third smaller than they truly were.

Idle Hands

It was ridiculous; the app was obviously broken. I closed the app and I decided to put my phone down for a while.

As promised, Jake returned just before nine o'clock. He'd brought some vodka with him. We drank the whole bottle between us - mixed with lemonade - while watching some documentary series on Netflix.

As we watched the TV, I allowed my hand to creep into Jake's lap. Of course, he did nothing to try to stop me. I slipped my fingers beneath the waistband of his boxers and began to massage his stiffening cock. He turned to me and kissed me, long and hard, deep, and passionate. I slid downtown the floor and onto my knees. I reached beneath him and pulled his trousers away from under him. I then took him in my mouth.

Before I knew it, we were upstairs, in my bed. Jake was behind me, thrusting into me, as I laid face down on the bed. I must have come three or four times before he pulled out and blew his load over my back.

We both laughed. He grabbed a tissue from my bedside table and wiped up his mess. We then lay together, naked, our bodies entwined, until Jake fell asleep.

I slipped away then, to the bathroom. As I left the room, I pulled my dressing gown over my shoulders and slipped my phone into the pocket. In the bathroom, I looked at myself in the mirror. My skin was clear and pale. For a moment, it almost looked translucent, as if I could see the white of my skull beneath. I shook the thought away. My hair seemed to be straighter than normal. I liked that.

I pulled my phone from my pocket and shrugged my gown from my shoulders. Standing their naked, a wave of embarrassment washed over me. I could feel my cheeks flushing. In the mirror, they turned only the slightest shade of pink. I opened up the BeautifyU app and took a photo of myself in the mirror.

My body looked amazing.

But my face was wrong. My hair was almost all gone; only a few wispy strands - mousey blonde and brittle looking - remained. The app had removed my eyebrows too, and my mouth was almost non-existent.

Despite this - and I can remember the feeling now, as clear as day - I felt exhilarated. As bizarre as this must sound, it felt right. It felt like this was the real me. This was how I was supposed to look.

Jake stirred as I got back into bed, but he didn't wake. I fell asleep shortly after. This was the best night's sleep I've ever had.

The following morning, I woke to Jake leaning over me, a frantic look on his face. He was holding me by the shoulders, repeatedly shouting my name. God knows how I hadn't heard him.

"Holy Jesus, Millie," he said, as I sat up in the bed. "I thought you were *gone*!"

"Gone?" I said. "Gone where?" I should've known what he had meant; the inflection in his voice told me everything I needed to know.

"I thought you were *dead*! You weren't breathing, I'm sure of it. And look…"

He pointed to the bed behind me, to where my pillow lay.

It was covered in a thick layer of hair. *My* hair, to be precise.

Idle Hands

I reached up and felt my scalp. There was still plenty of hair on my head, although I could feel that it was much thinner. My fingertips brushed across a patch of bare skin on the side of my head. Suddenly, panic filled every inch of my being. *People lost their hair when they had cancer*, I thought. I was dying, I was sure of it.

"Come on," said Jake, grabbing me by the arm. "We have to get you to the hospital."

The doctor who examined me also took a sample of my blood. They confirmed that I didn't have cancer. They told me that they believed I was suffering with a mild form of alopecia. They asked if I was under any stress. They asked if I took drugs. They asked me all kinds of questions, to try and find out what was wrong with me.

But I already knew - there was nothing wrong with me. This was the true me. Those photos I took yesterday weren't *just* photos - they were more than that. They showed the real me, and that's what I was becoming.

Of course, I never told anybody this.

The doctor said that they would refer me for further tests, and that I should go home and rest. Then we left.

Jake was great. He really looked after me. He tried to call my parents but couldn't get through - he said he'd try again later. He made me chicken soup for my lunch. After we had eaten (he'd tried my parents again; still nothing), he'd said that he needed to leave. "I promised my dad I'd help him with moving some stuff at Grandma's place," he said. "But I'll be back as soon as I can. Is that alright?"

I nodded.

"Are you sure you're okay?"

"Yes," I said. "I'm fine. I feel good now. You go. I'll see you later."

"Okay. I won't be long. I love you."

"I love you too." I really did love him.

He kissed my forehead and then he was gone. I followed him to the front door and locked it behind him. I then took myself back to the sofa, where I laid down and closed my eyes.

I must've fallen asleep quite quickly. I don't remember what I dreamed about if I dreamed at all. But when I woke, I found that I couldn't breathe. My lungs burned inside my chest, as they tried to suck in the air and failed to do so successfully. It felt as though something was covering my mouth. For a brief moment, I thought I might have been kidnapped; whoever had taken me had tied a gag around my face.

But that wasn't the case. I sat up on the sofa and groped for my face, looking to tear away whatever it was that was covering my mouth.

But there was nothing there. Nothing; quite literally. I couldn't figure it out. My fingers ran across my face, from cheek to cheek, stroking my chin as they went. There was nothing obstructing my mouth. All I felt was smooth flesh.

I took a deep breath, forcing myself to pull the air in through my nostrils. That felt good. *Remember*, I told myself. *You can still breathe through your nose.* My heart was racing, my head was pounding. I knew that something was wrong, I just didn't know what. My legs felt weak as I stood from the sofa, as if they might just give way beneath me.

Idle Hands

I crossed the living room and ascended the stairs. I made my way to the bathroom and pulled the cord to switch on the light.

My eyes immediately fell upon my reflection in the mirror. It took a few moments for me to comprehend exactly what I was looking at.

It was me, of course. But it didn't *look* like me. My mouth was gone, replaced by a solid wall of flesh. My hair was gone too, save for the few brittle strands that still hung before my face. My ears too had shrunk. They looked as though they had shrivelled, reduced to little more than wrinkled masses on the sides of my bald head.

This couldn't be real. I had to still be sleeping. It wasn't possible for this to be happening, not in real life. This was a dream. A nightmare. But then I understood; it was the app, BeautifyU. It was erasing any feature that it deemed to be an imperfection. It had started with my spots and my freckles. But once they were gone, it had begun to work on the rest of my face.

The changes it was making in the app, were somehow happening in reality.

It was trying to make me beautiful.

I touched my face. The flesh that had replaced my lips was soft, just like the flesh of my cheeks. I could feel my teeth below the flesh. The skin stretched as I opened and closed my jaw.

I began to panic then. For a moment I forgot that I needed to breathe through my nose. I began to suffocate once again. My heart continued to race. I quickly ran from the bathroom and hopped down the stairs. I entered the kitchen and tore open the draw beside the sink. Inside, I found exactly what I'd been looking for; the butcher's knife. Quickly, I took myself back up the stairs and into the bathroom.

I don't know how long I stood there, looking at myself in the mirror, thinking, trying to decide whether I was beautiful or not. I know how bizarre that must sound; I couldn't possibly think that I was beautiful, with my mouth sealed shut and my hair completely gone. But I had to ask myself; *if this isn't true beauty, then what is?*

I was being stupid (that's what I thought at the time; I'm less sure of that now). I opened my jaw as wide as possible. Thankfully, the flesh stretched willingly. I pressed the point of the blade against the skin, where I felt the corner of mouth should have been. I then held my breath and pushed. The knife penetrated the skin with ease, slicing through the flesh, into the cavity of my mouth. The pain was horrific. I wanted to scream, but the flesh that covered my mouth prevented me from doing so. Blood began to flow freely, pouring down my chin and into my mouth, where it threatened to choke me. I pulled the knife back and forth, sawing through the flesh until I reached the other side of my face, where I felt my mouth should have ended.

I tore the knife free and immediately vomited the blood into the sink.

Then I screamed.

Slowly, I raised my head, barely wanting to look at myself in the mirror. As my eyes ran across the image reflected back at me, for a moment I considered whether or not I was actually looking at myself. Then I wondered whether I was truly awake. But then I understood that I was. I understood what was happening to me. I understood that this was all I ever wanted. I wanted to be beautiful - the app was helping me do that.

With my crooked, ragged lips, I smiled.

I turned on the cold tap and splashed my face with water, rinsing away most of the blood. I then took the time to examine myself a little closer. The strands of hair that hung loosely from my head were draped across my face, sticking to my damp skin. I took a hold of them and pulled. It was painful, but their roots pulled out of my scalp with ease. A small trickle of blood ran down the side of my face.

There was a knock at the front door. The sound startled me. Who the fuck could that be?

Suddenly I remembered; Jake had come back to see me. It had to be him.

I crossed the landing and entered my parents' room. Their window looked out to the front of the house. Peering out, I saw that it was indeed Jake. He knocked on the door once again. "Millie?" he called. "You in there?"

I didn't want him to see me like this. I *couldn't let* him see me like this. I opened the window just a crack, as I kept myself hidden behind the curtain. "Go away!" I shouted. I instantly regretted it. Not because of what I'd said, but because the pain of moving my lips (if that's what you could call them now) was excruciating. I could taste blood once again; I felt the warmth of it running down my chin.

"What?" shouted Jake. I could see that he was now looking up at the window. "What's going on? Is everything okay in there?"

"Everything's fine!" I shouted, spitting blood everywhere. "Please, just go!"

"Go? Why? Let me in."

"No. Go away!"

"What's going on? Millie? Let me in."

He was persistent, but there was no way I was going to open the door to him. I needed him to leave. "No! Why won't you leave me alone? Why do you never listen? Just fuck off!"

"What's wrong with you? I'm not going anywhere. Let me in!"

I had to get rid of him. I looked around me. There was a small ceramic plant pot on the windowsill, which contained just a single, artificial orchid. I picked it up and, as quickly as I possibly could, I threw it out of the window. It smashed onto the ground, right at Jake's feet. "FUCK OFF!" I screamed, the gash in my face leaking more blood.

"Are you crazy?" shouted Jake. "I'm trying to help you."

I didn't want his help. I pressed my back against the wall and slid downwards, into a seated position on the floor. I hugged my knees and began to cry. I don't know why. Sure, I'd just had to slice my own face open as my mouth had sealed itself shut. But the truth was, that really didn't bother as much as it probably should have. I think I was just sad at the thought of not seeing Jake.

A few moments passed before Jake shouted up; "Okay. Fine. Fuck you then. I'm going."

I waited another moment before standing and peeking out from behind the curtain. Jake was already halfway down the road.

Thank God.

Suddenly, my head was spinning. I felt as though I might throw up. I guess that was because of the blood loss; I hadn't even considered that as I'd sliced my face open. I needed to lie down; if I didn't, I felt sure I would collapse. I slumped onto my parents' bed, not in the slightest bit concerned about the blood I'd leave soaked into the sheets. I felt as though I was burning up - I was suddenly pouring with sweat. I pulled my clothes off and tossed them aside.

Once I was naked, I closed my eyes and slept.

When I woke, it was dark. It had been late afternoon when I had laid down, so it must've been well into the evening by the time I climbed off the bed.

For a brief moment, I thought that I'd been dreaming all along. Perhaps even for the past few days. Perhaps I still had my hair and lips and my ears. Perhaps I still looked normal - like every other teenage girl.

But then, as I swung my legs off the bed, I realised that I couldn't see. Not properly, anyway. I could make out faint shapes and dull lights, all tinted red. And my breathing was once again restricted.

I touched my face. My mouth was sealed shut once again; the lacerated flesh now whole. And my nose was gone. There were holes in my face, where my nostrils once were - it was through them that I was breathing. I touched my eyes. They weren't there. I mean, my eyeballs were still there - it was my eyelids that were missing. They had been replaced, like my mouth, with a solid layer of skin.

I stood. Unable to see properly, I immediately became unbalanced. I put my hands out and stumbled forward, until my hands landed upon the wall. From there, I guided myself out into the hallway and across to the bathroom.

Why?

I have no idea. It wasn't like I could've looked at myself in the mirror. I was blind. It was like trying to look through your eyelids; when the light is bright enough, you can just about make out the odd movement. It was a little easier than that - the skin that now covered my eyes was thinner than my eyelids had been. Still, for all intents and purposes, I was blind.

I groped around, hoping that my hands might fall upon the knife I'd used earlier to cut open my mouth.

No such luck.

I turned and headed back out onto the landing, feeling my way as I went. Slowly, I inched my way to the top of the stairs. I had visions of myself tumbling down, so I took each step slowly, clinging tightly to the banister. Downstairs, I made my way along the hall, into the kitchen. I opened up the drawer and found another knife.

Where to start?

I needed to breathe. I needed my mouth open. As before, I pressed the blade into the skin that now covered my mouth, feeling the flesh depress between my teeth. Searing agony burned through my body as the steel pierced my skin.

The flesh gave way suddenly. I hadn't expected it. I slipped. I felt the blade dig into my tongue. I pulled the knife out and screamed. Had it not been me that had made it, the sound would've been terrifying. As my jaw opened wide, I felt the flesh split further. I spat out as much of the blood as I could, allowing it to seep from the gash that now cover half of my face, not caring where it might land. I composed myself, then continued. I pushed the blade back into the newly formed orifice and began to slice. I could tell the cut was crooked this time; the blade kept cracking against my teeth.

At least I could breathe now.

I spat out another mouthful of blood. I couldn't close my mouth anymore; if I did so, my mouth would fill with blood and I might choke. I reached up and touched my tongue. It was hard to tell by touch alone, but it felt as though I had cut halfway through it.

Holding the knife in my right hand, I used my left to feel for my eyes. I could feel my eyeballs, still rolling in their sockets, behind the wall of flesh that now covered them. I depressed the skin as much as I could between my eyeball and my skull, and placed the point of the blade into the gap.

I moaned loudly as I carefully pushed the blade through the skin. I couldn't allow myself to cut too deep; one mistake and I could take out my eyeball.

I felt the skin separate as the blade penetrated my eye socket. I gritted my teeth - my half-severed tongue lolling to one side - and began to cut. I tried my best to trace a circle around my eyeball. Once I had cut around half an inch, I pushed my fingertip into the laceration and pulled the skin away. I was in agony, but this seemed like the best solution; at least I was less likely to cut my eyeball.

Eventually, screaming as I did so, I was able to pull the skin away. It was still hanging on by a thread, hanging from my eye socket like some macabre label. I used the knife to sever the last piece of skin and then dropped them both - the knife *and* the skin - onto the kitchen worktop.

I suddenly realised I was in agony. I hunched over the kitchen side and held on for dear life, trying to prevent myself from collapsing to the tiled floor.

At least I could see now, although my vision was obscured with blood. I wished I could see myself in the mirror. I straightened up. There was a splashback fixed to the wall, just behind the cooker. It was polished stainless steel - highly reflective.

Although my reflection was distorted, as if I were looking at myself in a fun house mirror, I could see myself quite clearly. My new smile was wide and crooked, running from my right ear, down towards my chin and then across to my left cheek in a rough zigzag. Far too many of my teeth were on show. In the reflection, my eye looked to be almost perfectly round. The reason for this was obvious; what I was actually looking at was the white of my eyeball. It was hard to see, but the skin looked ragged and uneven.

I lifted the knife and placed it to my other eye.

The bang at the front door nearly made me slip and slice into my eye. From where I stood, I could look all the way down the hall, to the front door. Outside, I could see the silhouette of a person moving. It was Jake. He'd come back to see me. "Come on, Millie," he shouted. "Open up. Just let me see that you're okay."

I ignored him. I placed the knife against the side of my eye socket and began to cut. I couldn't help but scream.

Outside, Jake – having clearly heard my scream – seemed to become more panicked. "Millie! You okay? What's going on?"

And then his voice changed. "Millie?" he said, his voice louder and clearer. "What are you doing?"

Idle Hands

I looked back to the door. He was watching me through the letterbox.

"Holy fuck!" he screamed. "Stop that! Let me in!" He banged on the door again.

Once again, I ignored him. I pushed the blade of the knife into my eye socket and began to cut away the flesh.

Suddenly, Jake was in the house, stood behind me. He'd gone around to the back of the house, and in through the rear door – I'd thought it was locked; clearly not. He grabbed my wrist and pulled my hand away. "What the fuck are you doing?" he was screaming.

I pulled my hand free of his grasp, turned and backed away. I lifted the knife and pointed it at him. "Don't!" I said, my voice twisted and distorted by the blood that was gagging me, and the fact that my tongue was halfway severed. "Stay back!"

It was then that I saw his face drop. His eyes looked over me. I was standing there in the kitchen, completely naked, covered in blood. My head was bald and my face was cut to ribbons. God only knows what thoughts were running through his brain. "Oh, Jesus," he said. "What happened to you?"

I opened my mouth, allowing the blood to ooze down my chin. "This is me now," I said. "The *real* me. I'm beautiful now, don't you think?" As I said those words, I knew it wasn't true. I was a monster now. Those photos had done this to me. I'd wanted to be beautiful, but my vanity wouldn't allow it.

"You've cut off your lips."

"No," I said, shaking my head. "I created a new pair of lips."

"And your eyes… You've cut off your eye lids."

"My eyes are more open now than they've ever been. Now I can see clearly."

Jake sighed, exasperated. For a moment I thought he might burst out in laughter. But he didn't; his face remained razor straight. "We need to get you to a doctor," he said. "We need to get you some help."

He took a step towards me. I lifted the knife higher, aiming it right at his face. "No," I said. "Get back. Don't come near me!"

"You need help. Let me help you."

"I don't need *your* help."

"Please. We have to get you to the hospital." He took another step towards me.

I swiped at him with the knife. His throat offered little resistance to the steel of my blade. A deep wound opened up. Blood gushed, squirting from his arteries. He gasped, the air escaping his lungs through the gash in his neck.

He gargled the blood as he clamped his hands around his neck, trying in vain to stem the bleeding.

I didn't feel guilty. Not even in the slightest.

He stumbled back and dropped to the floor. He was dead within seconds.

And now we come full circle. This is where I stand right now, naked and bloodied in the kitchen, the corpse of Jake at my feet. Looking at myself in the polished steel, I know I don't look 'normal'. Not in the usual sense of the word. But I look perfect. I look exactly the way I'm supposed to look.

I finally look beautiful.

I place the blade of the knife to my throat and draw it sideways, opening up my neck. In the dull reflection, I see the blood seeping from the wound. And I see myself smiling, my new lips peeled back where the flesh has been roughly carved. My teeth are black, stained with blood. I don't care. I am perfect.

I am beautiful.

THE END

Harrison Phillips

WHAT HAPPENED IN THE QUARRY?

"Tell me again," said DCI Barnett, as he re-entered the interview room, having taken a much-needed cigarette break. "What - exactly - *did* happen in the quarry?"

"I already told you everything," said Samuel Fletcher, the nine-year-old boy sat on the opposite side of the desk. "You want me to tell you again?"

"I do, yes," said Barnett, as he once again took his seat. He'd brought with him a plastic cup of water for the boy, which he set down on the desk and pushed towards him. He'd brought a coffee for himself. It was too hot to drink, but he sipped it regardless, desperate for the caffeine. He'd hoped it might somewhat alleviate the throbbing pain he was feeling in the back of his skull. The caffeine - along with the four paracetamol tablets he'd consumed only moments ago - ought to take the edge off.

Barnett had been a detective for over three years now. He'd dealt with many a violent crime in his time. He'd led the investigation into more than two dozen murders. But nothing had prepared him for this. This crime was beyond belief. The level of brutality inflicted upon the victim was more than shocking. It was abhorrent.

Sam picked up the cup of water and sipped it. He looked to the court appointed solicitor sat to his left. It was obvious to Barnett that the boy was seeking guidance, but the solicitor offered none. This goddamn pencil pusher looked bored, as if he really didn't want to be there. Poor kid, he really needed somebody who actually cared what happened to him.

Not that Barnett really cared what happened to him. All he wanted was the truth. And justice for the victim, of course.

"Okay," said Sam. "Where should I start?"

"How about the beginning?"

"Like, when I got up and had breakfast? Or…"

"No," said Barnett, burning his lips on another sip of his coffee. "Let's fast-forward just a little. You told us that you met up with Patrick and Lewis just before school was due to start. Why don't we go from there?"

Sam finished off his cup of water. "Alright. Well. We always walked to school together. There's this underpass just down the road from Pat's house. That's where we met."

"Who got there first?"

"Pat and Lewis were already waiting for me when I got there."

"Right," said Barnett, as he scribbled a note in pencil, onto the pad before him. It was the same note he'd written the first time round. In all honesty, he hadn't expected to garner anything new from interviewing Sam a second time. But there were so many inconsistencies to his story - so many minute

Idle Hands

details (so small that a lesser detective might have disregarded them completely) - that he just had to make sure he wasn't missing anything. "Who's idea was it to skip school?"

Sam was playing with the empty plastic cup, squeezing it inwards, then releasing it, so that it would pop back into shape. "That was Pat's idea. He said he wasn't going to school. He said he was going to go explore the quarry, and that we should go with him."

"So you all decided to go?"

"I didn't want to. I just wanted to go to school. But they were teasing me, calling me names."

"What kind of names?"

Sam looked to the solicitor once again, as if seeking permission to say some naughty words. When he got no response (the solicitor looked as though he might fall asleep into the pile of paperwork he had stacked up on his lap), he returned his gaze to Barnett and continued - "They called me a pussy. And a faggot."

Barnett wrote both words onto the pad. "Okay. So then you walked to the quarry? That's quite a way. How long did it take you?"

"About an hour."

Barnett made a note. "And when you got there, what happened? How did you get in?"

"There's a part of the fence that's fallen down. We just walked right through it."

"Did you see anybody else around there?"

Sam paused for a moment. He tipped his head back and stared at the ceiling. He then shook his head, and said - "No. I don't think so."

"Okay," said Barnett, as he scribbled down a few more notes. His head was still pounding. He wished he could just get this over and done with, so he could get home and enjoy a cool glass of wine with his wife. But he had a funny feeling that he wasn't going to be going anywhere any time soon. "So you made your way down to the base of the quarry? Was that difficult?"

Sam shook his head. "Not really. Pat's been down there hundreds of times; he knew the easiest route to take."

Barnett assumed that the statement '*hundreds of times*' was somewhat of an exaggeration, but still he wrote himself a note. "And what did you do down there?"

"What did we *do*?"

"Yeah. What did you do? Did you play a game? Hide and seek, perhaps? Or did you have a rock fight, maybe. What did you do?"

Sam paused once again, thinking. Then he said - "Nothing. We just walked around a bit."

"Okay. So, no games? No arguments? No fighting?"

Sam shook his head.

"Okay. So, you told me earlier that Lewis hit Patrick. Is that right?"

Sam nodded.

"Why did Lewis hit Patrick?"

Sam shrugged his shoulders.

"What does that mean?" said Barnett, his frustration once again growing. "You don't know? How did it happen?"

Sam shook his head once again. "I don't know. I don't remember."

Barnett scoffed and slumped back in his chair. "Come on, Sam," he said. "You know what happened. You were there. Tell me."

"Honestly! All I remember is that Pat was in front. Lewis called Pat's name and then, when Pat turned around, Lewis punched him in the face."

Barnett sat forward. He knew now that they were getting to the nasty bit. Sam had described the scene in great detail before. Barnett didn't really want to hear it again, but he had to. He needed to listen to the story once again, if he ever wanted to know the truth. "Then what happened?"

"Lewis was just laughing. I didn't know what to do. I didn't know why he'd hit him; I barely even saw it happen. So I didn't say anything. I just stood there and watched. I don't know why I didn't say something."

"Were you scared?"

Sam nodded. "Lewis was laughing like a maniac. It was like he was possessed by the devil, or somethin'. I'd never seen him do that before."

"And that's when Lewis attacked Pat?"

Sam nodded once more.

"What did you see Lewis do?"

Sam began to cry. Tears streamed down his cheeks and dripped from his chin, onto the desk below. He folded his arms before him and nestled his face into them.

Barnett gave him a moment, before pushing him once again. "Sam," he said, sitting forward in his chair. "Look at me."

Sam lifted his head. His cheeks were flushed and his eyes were bloodshot.

"What did Lewis do?" repeated Barnett.

"There was this rock," said Sam, his voice wavering. "It was big, like a football. Lewis picked it up and held it over his head. He was still laughing."

"And then?"

"Then he slammed it down, as hard as he could, onto Pat's head. I thought Pat was dead already. There was so much blood. Where the rock had hit his head, I swear his skin had peeled off. I swear I could see his skull!"

"And what did you do?"

"Nothing. I couldn't move. I was too scared! It was like my whole body was frozen."

"So what happened next? Did Lewis say anything?"

"No, he just carried on laughing. But Pat wasn't dead. He started to move. He rolled over and tried to crawl away. So Lewis picked up the rock and hit him again. He just kept hitting him, over and over. I could hear Pat's skull cracking every time the rock landed. After about ten or eleven blows, I swear, Pat's head just popped - like a balloon - and his brains burst out of his skull. There was blood everywhere!"

"And then? What did you do next?"

"Nothing!" sobbed Sam. "I just ran away, as quickly as I could!" He dropped his head back into his folded arms and continued to sob.

Barnett sat back in his seat. He picked up his coffee and finished off the last of it. "I think we need a break," he said. "Interview terminated at fifteen-forty-two."

***

Idle Hands

"Tell me again," said Barnett, as he re-entered the interview room, having procured himself another coffee from the machine in the corridor. "What - exactly - *did* happen in the quarry?"

"I already told you everything," said Lewis Stringer, the nine-year-old boy sat on the opposite side of the desk. "You want me to tell you again?"

"I do, yes."

Barnett had brought the boy a cup of water. He placed it on the table and pushed it towards him. Lewis took the cup and thirstily drank its contents. Barnett's coffee was still too hot to drink. Despite the fact that his headache was now fading - the paracetamol finally beginning to take effect - he still wanted that sweet, sweet caffeine inside of him. Nevertheless, he'd just have to wait.

Lewis looked to the court appointed solicitor sat to his right. The solicitor - clearly more invested in this boy, than the one sat beside Samuel back in the other room - offered him a nod.

"Okay," said Lewis. "Where should I start?"

"I always find it best to start at the beginning. But maybe skip over what you had breakfast."

Lewis smiled. Barnett couldn't help but feel a little bit of sympathy towards the boy. Whatever had happened, something wasn't right.

"You told us that you met up with Patrick and Samuel just before school. Why don't we go from there?"

Lewis nodded as he finished off his water. "Okay. So… We always walked to school together, every single day. There's this underpass just down the road from Pat's house. That's where we met."

"Who got there first?"

"Pat and Sam were already waiting for me when I got there."

"Right," said Barnett, as he scribbled a note in pencil, onto the pad before him. It was the same pad he'd been writing on earlier, during his second conversation with Sam. He made sure to note down the inconsistency between Sam's version of events and Lewis' own. He had to make sure he wasn't missing anything. "So who's idea was it to skip school?"

Lewis was playing with the empty plastic cup, much in the same way as Sam had been, not so long ago. "That was Pat's idea. He said he wasn't going to school. He said he was going to go explore the quarry, and that we should go with him."

"So you all decided to go?"

"I didn't want to. I just wanted to get to school. But Sam and Pat were both so forceful. They started calling me names."

"Names? Such as…"

Lewis looked to the solicitor once again, who simply nodded and said - "It's okay. Go ahead."

Lewis returned his gaze to Barnett and continued - "They called me a faggot. And a pussy."

Barnett wrote both words onto the pad. Both words appeared there twice now. "Okay. So then you walked to the quarry? That's quite a way. How long did it take you?"

"About forty-five minutes."

Barnett made another note. "And when you got there, what happened? How did you get in?"

"Pat showed us a part of the fence that had been cut away. We just climbed right through it."

"Did you see anybody else around there?"

Idle Hands

Lewis paused for a moment. It was obvious that he was thinking, searching his brain for the correct answer. He then shook his head, and said - "No. I don't think so."

"Okay," said Barnett, as he scribbled down a few more notes. His head was still pounding. His thoughts were still on home and the glass of wine he so desperately wanted to enjoy with his wife. He knew now that was unlikely to happen. Not tonight, anyway. "So you made your way down to the base of the quarry? That must've been a difficult climb?"

Lewis shook his head. "Not really. Pat's been down there thousands of times; he knew the easiest route to take."

Barnett couldn't help but smile to himself, as he read his note from earlier and compared the two boys' respective exaggerations. "And, once you were down, what did you do?"

"What did we *do*?"

"Yeah. What did you do? Did you just hang around, talking, telling jokes? Or did you play a game? Hide and seek, maybe? What did you do?"

Lewis paused once again, thinking once again. Then he said - "Nothing. We just walked around a bit."

"Okay. So there were no arguments? No fighting?"

Lewis shook his head.

"Okay. So, you told me earlier that Sam hit Patrick. Is that right?"

Lewis nodded.

"Why did Sam hit Patrick?"

Lewis shrugged his shoulders.

"What do you mean by that?" said Barnett. "You don't know? You didn't see? How did it happen?"

Lewis shook his head once again. "I don't know. I don't remember."

Barnett sighed and slumped back in his chair. He picked up his coffee and gulped it down. "Come on, Lewis," he said. "You know what happened. You were there. Tell me."

"I don't remember! All I remember is that Pat was in front. Sam called Pat's name and then, when Pat turned around, Sam punched him in the face."

Barnett sat forward. Here came the nasty bit once again. Lewis had previously described the scene in great detail. Barnett didn't really want to hear it again, but he had to. He'd asked the question, so he needed to hear the answer. It was the only way he'd ever get to the truth. "Then what happened?"

"Sam was just laughing. I didn't know what to do. I didn't know why he'd hit him; I barely even saw it happen. So I didn't say anything. I just stood there and watched. I don't know why I didn't say something."

"Perhaps you were you scared."

Lewis nodded. "I was. Sam was laughing like a psychopath. It was like he was possessed by the devil, or somethin'. I'd never seen him act like that before."

"And that's when Sam attacked Pat?"

Lewis nodded once again.

"What did you see Sam do?"

Lewis began to cry. Tears streamed down his cheeks and dripped from the end of his nose, onto the desk below. He folded his arms before him and nestled his face into them.

Barnett gave him a moment, before pushing him once again. "Lewis," he said, sitting forward in his chair. "Look at me."

Lewis lifted his head. His eyes were bloodshot and his cheeks were flushed red.

"You *have* to tell me. What did Samuel do?" repeated Barnett.

"There was this metal bar," said Sam, his voice wavering. "I don't know where it came from. It was badly rusted. Sam picked it up and held it over his head. He was still laughing."

"And then?"

"Then he slammed it down, as hard as he could, right into Pat's face. I thought Pat was dead already. There was so much blood. I swear his nose was shattered. I swear I saw one of hie eyeballs burst!"

"And what did you do?"

"Nothing. I couldn't move. I was too scared! It was like my whole body was frozen."

"So what happened next? Did Sam say anything?"

"No, he just carried on laughing. But Pat wasn't dead. He started to move. He rolled over and tried to crawl away. So Sam lifted up the bar and hit him again. He just kept hitting him, over and over. I could hear Pat's skull cracking every time the bar landed. After about ten or eleven blows, I swear, Pat's head just, sort of, caved inwards. It was like his head had imploded. His brains were leaking out of his skull. There was blood everywhere!"

"Then what did you do?"

"Nothing!" sobbed Lewis. "I turned and I ran!" He dropped his head back into his folded arms and continued to sob.

Barnett sat back in his seat and took a deep breath. He didn't know what to believe. The two boys, the only witnesses to their friend's murder, were both giving different versions of events. They were both accusing each other. "I think we need a break," said Barnett, as he stood from the desk. "Interview terminated at sixteen-oh-nine."

As he left the room, Barnett looked back at the sobbing boy. He didn't know exactly what was going on, but he knew that both of these boys were lying.

***

The body had been found by a dog walker. It was buried in a small hole in the woods, just around a quarter mile from the quarry. The hole had been filled in and covered over with a handful of leaves. Whoever had buried it there had not been too clever; they had left two of the fingers protruding from the dirt.

The Scene Of Crime specialists had determined that the body had been buried there for at least three days.

DCI Barnett had been there as the remains had been uncovered. The body had been dismembered. Every limb had been removed, and then cut down further, into smaller pieces. The arms had been removed at the shoulder, then cut at the elbow, with the hand also removed. It was a similar story with the legs.

The head had also been removed from the torso. At least, what *remained* of the head had been removed. It was hard to tell if it was all there; it had seemingly been crushed, the whole thing mulched into little more than a mass of blood, bone and brain.

Idle Hands

It didn't take long to figure out to whom the body belonged. A young boy named Patrick Stephens had been reported missing three days earlier. There was no doubt in Barnett's mind that this corpse belonged to that boy.

The investigation into his whereabouts had already begun. They had already established that he hadn't shown up for school on the morning of his disappearance. They had also learned that he normally walked to school with two other boys; Lewis and Samuel. When they had interviewed those two boys (two days before the body was found), both had confirmed that they had been waiting for Patrick in the underpass at the bottom of his road, but that he had never shown up.

That meant that Patrick had been taken at some point between his house and the underpass, which was probably less than three-hundred yards from his front door, a distance that might only take a minute to walk.

That seemed unlikely.

A quick talk with the school informed them that none of the boys had turned up to school that day. To Barnett's mind, that meant that the three of them had gone off somewhere together. Both Lewis and Samuel had denied this, although they did admit to having bunked off school to go and play in the quarry. They had said that Patrick wasn't there.

It was only after the discovery of the mutilated body, that they decided to bring the two boys in for questioning.

It didn't take long for either of them to crack. Both of them told the same story, although they both had stated that it was the other who had killed Patrick.

It was around that time that Barnett's headache had come on with a vengeance.

***

Barnett stubbed out his cigarette on the steel tray which sat atop the bin, before posting the butt through one of the holes in the side. He then re-entered the police station.

"Well?" said DCI Smart, as he walked through the office. She was a great detective. Barnett got on with her like a house on fire. "What now?"

Barnett shook his head. "I don't know. Both of their stories are almost identical, except for the fact that they're both blaming each other."

"And their stories have been consistent, each time they've told it?"

Barnett nodded. "Pretty much."

"So, do you think they *both* took part in the killing?"

It seemed like the most logical explanation. But Barnett hadn't gotten the *sense* that either of those boys were lying. They were both lying; of that he was in no doubt. But had they have been directly involved, then he felt sure he would've been able to pick their stories apart more easily. There was, of course, another possibility.

"Maybe," said Barnett, taking a deep breath. "Either that, or they're both covering for a third party."

Smart nodded, understandingly. "Well," she said, having gathered her thoughts. "They don't know that each other is here, do they?"

"No."

"Well then, perhaps it's time you told them. Tell them that they are both blaming each other. Play them off against each other."

"Maybe you're right."

***

"Tell me one more time," said Barnett, as he took a seat at the table of the interview room, opposite Samuel. "What happened in the quarry?"

"Again?" said Sam. "I need to go through it again? Why?"

"Well," said Barnett leaning forward, his elbows on the table, propping him up. "I'll tell you why, shall I? I've got your friend Lewis in another room just along this corridor, and he's telling us a different story to the one you told me."

The solicitor - the ignorant man who had, as of yet, shown little-to-no interest in the case whatsoever - lifted his head. "You should've told me," he said. "I need to know what he said."

Sam was looking at his solicitor, with no idea what he should say or do next.

"We're about to discuss that," said Barnett. "I guess we're going to find out what *really* happened together, aren't we?"

Sam looked to Barnett. His bottom lip was quivering. "Did he tell you I did it?"

"*Did* you do it?"

Tears once again began to roll down the boy's cheeks. "Okay! I admit it! I did it. I killed Patrick."

"You mean that you and Lewis killed him together?"

"No. It was just me. I don't know where Lewis went. After I'd done killing Patrick, when I turned round, Lewis was gone."

Barnett slumped back in his chair. He couldn't quite believe it. He hadn't expected Samuel to confess. Certainly not to having done it alone. He had essentially corroborated Lewis' version of events. "Why did you kill him?" asked Barnett.

Sam shrugged his shoulders. "I guess I was just bored."

"You were bored, so you decided to kill your friend."

Sam shrugged his shoulders once again. "He wasn't really my friend anyway."

***

"Tell me one more time," said Barnett, as he took a seat at the table of the interview room, opposite Lewis. "What happened in the quarry?"

"Seriously?" said Lewis. "We need to do this all again? How come?"

"Well," said Barnett leaning forward, pushing in closer to Lewis. "I'll tell you why. I've got your friend Samuel in another room just down the corridor, and he's telling us a different story to the one you told me."

"What?" said Lewis' solicitor. "You can't do this. It's illegal."

"Is it really?" said Barnett, feigning as if he was aware of the fact. "Well, in that case, feel free to make a complaint once were done here. But right now, I'm investigating the murder of a child, so, as it stands, I'll do whatever the hell I want."

The solicitor just looked at him. There wasn't much else he could say or do.

"So," said Barnett. "Tell me the truth, Lewis."

Lewis' bottom lip was quivering. "Did he tell you I did it?"

"*Did* you do it?"

Tears once again began to roll down the boy's cheeks. "Okay! I admit it! I did it. I killed Patrick."

"So you and Sam killed him together? You took turns in hitting him?"

"No. It was just me. I did it alone. I don't know what happened to Sam. After I'd done killing Patrick, when I turned round, Sam was gone."

Barnett slumped back in his chair. What the hell was he supposed to think now? As he had returned to this room, he had felt certain that Sam had killed Patrick. He'd expected Lewis to stick to his original story. Had he done so, he may no longer have been a suspect. But what he had done was to once again say the complete opposite of what Sam had said. Barnett had no idea what he ought to do next. "Why did you kill him?" He decided to ask.

Lewis shrugged his shoulders. "I guess I was just bored."

"You were bored, so you decided to kill your friend."

Lewis shrugged his shoulders once again. "He wasn't really my friend anyway."

Barnett rubbed his forehead, using his thumb and fingers to massage his temples. He could feel his headache coming on once again. He now had two children in custody, both of whom had admitted to murdering the victim, both of whom had given an alibi for their friend.

Then something occurred to him. There was something he hadn't asked either of the boys to discuss just yet. "So," he said, rubbing the sleep from his eyes. "What did you do with the body, once you'd killed him?"

Lewis shook his head. "Nothing. I just left it there."

***

"Nothing," said Samuel, in response to Barnett's most recent question. "I just left it there."

Barnett had decided to ask Sam the same question he'd just asked of Lewis. Both had given the same answer.

"Well," sighed Barnett. "That's not where we found the body. Are seriously telling me that you didn't take it up to the woods to try and bury it."

"I didn't do that."

"So, it wasn't you that cut the body up either?"

Sam's eyes widened. It was immediately apparent that he had no idea about the dismemberment of the body. Lewis had reacted in that same way, when the same question had been posed to him.

If neither of them had attempted to dispose of the body, then who had?

Questions were running through Barnett's mind at a million miles per hour. Was either of these boys telling the truth? Were they both lying? Were they even involved at all? If not, then why would they say that they were? None of it made sense. Barnett told Sam so. "I think you're lying to me. I don't know what about, but you are. You and Lewis are both telling me the exact opposite story to one another. It's as if you'd planned this all along." Barnett felt as though his brain had been fried. He could feel the anger bubbling away inside him. He banged his palm on the table before him. "Tell me the truth! What happened in the quarry?"

"Detective!" said the solicitor, suddenly, as if awoken from a coma. "Please remember that my client is only a child. Please do not raise your voice in that manner."

Barnett gave the solicitor a scolding look, then went ahead and ignored him. "Tell me," he said to the boy.

Sam shook his head. "I… I… I just don't know. I told you what happened. That's what I remember happening."

"Why are you lying to me?"

"I'm not!" said Sam, his voice wavering, his throat dry. "I just… I can't… I…"

"You can't, *what*?" Yelled Barnett. He felt his heart burning in his chest. He was tired. His head was throbbing. All he wanted to know was what the *fuck* was going on?

Sam paused for a moment. He stared at the table, his eyes flickering side to side as he gathered his thought. *Gathering his thoughts?* considered Barnett. *That, or assembling his lies.*

"They *made* us do it," said Sam, finally.

Barnett's heart seemed to stop for what felt like an hour. "Who?" he said. "Who made you do it?"

"Them. The people in the quarry. They said one of us had to die. They said if one of us wasn't killed, then all our families would die."

"Who told you that?"

"*The people in the quarry*! They said that one of us had to be a sacrifice. They said that they needed one of us to die, so they could appease Satan."

Barnett swallowed hard. "Satan?"

Sam nodded. "They said He was watching. They said we needed to choose. We chose Patrick."

Sam burst out into tears.

Barnett had no idea what he should do now. Was this kid crazy? Had his new version of events taken place at all? It seemed so unlikely. Satanist? In *this* town? No. There couldn't be. "Tell me then; what happened in the quarry?"

***

"There were loads of them," said Lewis, choking on his own words as tears ran down his cheeks and slipped over the corners of his mouth. "At least fifty, I'd say. All kinds of people. Men and women. Black and white and Asian."

Barnett had listened to Sam's story. It all sounded - quite frankly - ridiculous. But Barnett felt like there might be some truth hidden away in there somewhere. He'd decide to tell Lewis what Sam had said, to see what story he, Lewis, would come up with now. "Did you recognise any of them?" he asked.

Lewis shook his head.

"So, what happened?"

"We went down to the quarry, just to hang out," said Lewis. "But once we got there, we realised we weren't alone. We didn't see them at first. It was like they came out of nowhere. But then they were all around us. They were all dressed in black robes, with their hoods pulled up over their heads."

Barnett doubted that. How could a large group of people dressed in robes go anywhere without being noticed? It didn't matter that the quarry was long abandoned – it had been for decades - *somebody* would've seen a large group of people entering.

Lewis continued: "They told us that Satan was alive here, in our town. They said they had to sacrifice children to him. They said that all the grown-ups knew about it."

"You can rest assured, that's not true," said Barnett. "I mean, I'm not a Satanist. I don't know of any Satanists around here." He turned his attention to the solicitor. "Do you?"

The solicitor looked up from his papers, shook his head, then looked back down.

"That doesn't matter," said Lewis. "You could be lying to me."

"I would never lie to you," said Barnett. "Please. Go on."

"They said they were only meant to serve Him. They said they needed a sacrifice. They said they could kill us all. *'Satan will be pleased,'* one of them had said. But they said they only needed one of us. They'd let us choose which one."

"And then?"

"They made, like, a big circle around us. They pushed us into the middle. They threw in a big, iron bar. Then they started singing. No - more like chanting. I couldn't understand what they were saying. They were speaking some foreign language. Then Patrick picked up the bar. He told Sam that they should kill me. He tried to hit me, but I got away."

Lewis paused for breath.

"Then what happened?" asked Barnett, leaning onto his hands.

"Sam hit Patrick with a rock!" Lewis sucked back his tears. "Patrick fell down. I picked up the bar and I hit him. And then Sam was hitting him too, with the rock. There was blood everywhere! But we kept hitting him. And then, he was dead. All the people started clapping their hands."

"So, the both of you killed him, because these people said so? Do you think that was the right thing to do?"

"They said they'd kill all of us! They said they'd kill our families! Patrick tried to kill me! I only defended myself."

Barnett sat back in his seat. He didn't know what to say next. Sam's version of the story was very similar, except, as always, his and Lewis' roles had been reversed. It was possible that somebody had influenced these boys to do what they'd done. But satanists? No. Regardless of anything else, that didn't take away from the fact that these two boys had killed their friend.

Barnett stood. "Excuse me," he said, and walked out of the interview room. He felt as though he couldn't take any more.

DCI Smart was there, waiting for him. "Well?" she said. "What now?"

"I don't know," said Barnett, rubbing his temples. "I think I've lost the plot." He walked over to the coffee machine and purchased a coffee (black, two sugars). DCI Smart followed. "Have we heard anything back from the quarry yet?" he asked her.

"I don't think anybody's been down there yet."

Idle Hands

Barnett almost choked on his coffee. "What?" he exclaimed. "We've had these boys in custody for hours now, and nobody's been down there? We *know* that was where the murder took place, not in the woods. There could be evidence down there."

"I don't think we need any more evidence," said Smart. "They've confessed. We could charge them both with murder."

"But then we wouldn't know what really happened that day in the quarry."

Smart could only stare at him.

"Didn't your grandfather once own that place? Wouldn't he want to know?"

"I suppose so," agreed Smart.

"Come on," said Barnett. "Me and you; we're going down there now."

***

The quarry was a horrendous looking place. Once one crossed the threshold, into the boundary of the quarry, it was almost as if all life there was missing. There was nothing to see but rocks all around. Only the greys and browns of the debris remained of what was once, no doubt, a beautiful place. But this enormous hole had been dug here decades ago, by greedy men who wanted the precious materials that lay buried, deep within the earth.

When DCI Barnett and DCI Smart had arrived, they had found the gates locked. Of course, Barnett knew that he could make a call and get them opened in only a few short hours. But, not wanting to waste any time, he convinced Smart to follow him around the perimeter fence, until they found the collapsed area, where both Samuel and Lewis had claimed they had entered.

Once inside, they found a route down into the base of the quarry. It struck Barnett as being somewhat perilous; on more than one occasion, he had to put his hands down to the ground to steady himself.

Smart had seemed to find the journey down somewhat easier.

At the bottom, Barnett allowed his eyes to survey the area. What was he looking for? What did he hope to find? He had no idea. But there had to be something down there, some clue to help explain what had really happened to poor, little Patrick.

There was a large open expanse in the middle of the quarry. As Barnett looked down at the ground, he could see what he thought may have been footprints. They weren't distinct; nothing more than scuffs in the dusty dirt. But if they were footprints, then they must've been made by numerous people. He called over to Smart: "Do you think these marks could've been made by people?"

Smart approached. She looked down at the ground. "Maybe," she said. "No proof that they were made by Satanists though."

"No. But look," said Barnett, as he turned on the spot, his hand stretched out before him. "They do seem to form a circle. There could've been a large group of people here."

Smart looked around. The marks in the dirt did form a sort-of misshapen circle. "But there's no other signs of a fight. You think there would be blood on the ground."

"Yeah."

Idle Hands

Barnett had spotted something. He approached it cautiously. There were more marks in the dirt, in the middle of what would've been the circle. If these were footprints, then they were headed off in all manner of directions. But these were not footprints, Barnett was sure of it. They were different widths, different sizes and shapes. They could very well have been made during a fight.

He used the edge of his palm to sweep the sand-like dirt aside. The first push revealed nothing more than a darker patch of dirt. But there was *something* there. He swept again. Some of the dirt seemed to be stained. Its colour was darker than the dirt that surrounded it. Another sweep revealed more of the stained dirt. It also revealed that the dirt had been stained a deep crimson, almost black.

Blood.

It was blood. Barnett knew it.

"Smart!" he called. "Quick! Right here! This is where it happened. I think the boys were telling the truth. At least, some of it was true."

"What?" said Smart, coolly. "*Satanists?*"

"No," said Barnett, his eyes fixed to the blood-stained dirt. "But somebody may well have been here, egging them on. Maybe they *were* forced to fight."

"By Satanists?"

"No, not by Satanists. I don't believe in that shit."

"Well, maybe you should."

Crouched down in the dirt, Barnett paused to let Smart's words sink in. What did she mean by that? He looked back over his shoulder. His heart practically stopped, right there and then. His next breath caught in his throat.

DCI Smart was no longer alone. There were people stood beside her. People in black robes, their hoods pulled over their heads.

Barnett hadn't heard them approach. They had moved silently, like ghosts. They stood on either side of Smart, who herself now looked something less than human. Her eyes seemed darker, almost black. Her skin seemed to have drained of colour. "We *are* Satanists," she said. "Lucifer is real, and our service is devoted only to Him."

"What the fuck is this?" said Barnett, standing, turning to face them. "What's going on?"

"Those boys weren't lying. We *did* make them fight to the death. Satan was ever so pleased. We told them the story that they fed to you, and they did so impeccably."

"But... I just..." stuttered Barnett, almost lost for words. Hie head was pounding harder than ever now. "I don't understand."

"The men who built this quarry were Satanists. That included my grandfather. They made a pact with the devil. That was why they were so successful. And now, we continue to worship Satan, to make our sacrifices to Him, for the good of all mankind. If we were to stop, He would rise and destroy the Earth."

"This is madness!" said Barnett. "What the fuck are you talking about? This is crazy!"

"It's really not," said Smart, a wide smile stretching her cheeks. "Eighty years ago, this town was much smaller. Every family had a stake in this quarry. Every family agreed to sell their souls to the Devil, along with the souls of all their future offspring. Making sacrifices to Him has kind-of become a tradition. We're just carrying it on."

Idle Hands

The robed people, their faces obscured in shadow, began to move towards Barnett, creeping slowly forward. Barnett himself began to back away.

"I think," said Smart, also closing in on Barnett. "You too will make a fine sacrifice. You're not a child. You're not a virgin. I *know* you're far from innocent. But you are still a good man. The Devil will be pleased to add you to his collection."

Barnett slipped. It seemed to happen in slow motion. He felt his legs go from under him. He felt himself falling through thin air. He most certainly felt the impact as his body hit the ground.

And then they were upon him. He saw them draw their blades from within their robes. The light of the setting sun flashed from the steel.

He felt his skin lacerate. He felt the blades slicing through his flesh, penetrating muscle, bone, and cartilage. He felt the warmth of his blood, leaking from his body.

He felt many things. But he did not feel pain.

No. Pain was felt in the deepest recesses of the soul. DCI Barnett no longer had a soul. Satan had already stolen it.

THE END

Harrison Phillips

THE BINMAN

Harvey was bigger than Pat in every possible way. He was taller. His shoulders were wider. He was certainly heavier. And he was also two years older, which made this whole situation seem significantly unfair.

But then again, what do bullies know about fairness?

It seemed like every single day now, Harvey was following Pat out of school – accompanied, or course, by a handful of his loyal cronies – and cornering him in the playground. There, Harvey would say horrible things to him, such as *'Hey, Pat? How does it feel knowin' you mum's a fuckin' whore?'* or *'Hey, Pat? How much does your mum charge for a blow job? My brother said she charges him a fiver, but she always does me for free!'* A rapturous round of laughter from Harvey's gang would always follow.

Then came the beating.

Harvey would normally hit him first, balling his fist up and sending it crashing into Pat's abdomen. Oftentimes, he would hit Pat so hard it felt as though he were crushing his internal organs. It was highly unpleasant. Once Pat was down, they whole gang would then take turns kicking and punching him.

They'd only ever hit his body or his limbs though – they knew better than to hit his face; teachers might start asking questions if they saw him with a black eye or a broken nose.

Once they were finished with him – it normally only took them a minute or two to inflict the punishment they felt Pat deserved for being smarter (and weaker, it would seem) than them – they would wander off to go and do whatever it was they were going to do (find somebody else to beat up?). They'd leave Pat to make his way home and explain to his mother, who never really seemed too interested, just why he was late and why his clothes were dirty and torn (he never did tell her the truth).

It was frustrating more than anything. Pat wasn't scared of them anymore. He certainly didn't enjoy the beatings they gave him, but he could take it. At least if they were beating on him, then they *weren't* beating on somebody else, not quite as mentally strong as he was.

But, seriously – he couldn't take it much more. He was going to flip. He could feel it brewing inside him.

It happened one Friday.

As per usual, Harvey and his Cronies were waiting at the school gates when Pat. As soon as they saw him coming, the snide remarks began. They often liked to comment on the way he looked; the side-parting in his hair, his wire-framed glasses, his scuffed shoes (which his mother couldn't afford to replace). As per usual, they followed him to the playground, where, once they had passed through the gates, they hustled him into the corner, where Harvey grabbed a hold as his collar and forced him up against the fence.

Idle Hands

As per usual, the steel of the fence pressed into Pat's back, inflicting the first prangs of pain he was due to feel.

But not today. Today, that would be the last pain.

"Hey, Pat? How's your mum?" said Harvey, his face pressed right up against Pat's. His breath didn't smell pleasant at all. It smelled of cigarettes. Harvey was one of the *'cool'* kids who smoked behind the bike shelter, hopefully giving himself cancer. "Has she been missing me? I haven't seen her since Tuesday, when she was suckin' on my…"

Now or never.

Pat slammed his knee into Harvey's groin as hard as he could.

"Uggghh…"

Harvey hunched over, releasing his grip on Pat.

Pat didn't know why, but he suddenly felt an urge to do something more. He leaned back and then slammed his own head into Harvey's. He heard a pop and Hervey dropped the ground, a trickle of blood already beginning to form on his forehead.

The rest of Hervey's gang just stood there, motionless and staring. It was as if they couldn't believe what they were seeing.

Quickly, Pat hopped over Harvey and ran across the playground, not daring to look back.

He did, however, hear Harvey say – "What the fuck are you doing! GET HIM!"

Pat ran as fast as he could. He exited the playground and crossed the road, only just dodging the car that nearly ran him down. As he ran along the street, he heard the familiar banging of the playground gates swinging open and clattering into themselves.

"I'm gonna get you, you CUNT! You're fuckin' DEAD!"

Pat could feel his heart racing.

He turned the corner, then almost immediately ducked into the alleyway that ran between the newsagents and the barber shop. There, he pressed his back against the wall and waited.

A moment later, a number of bodies sprinted past the entrance to the alley, nothing more than a flash of colourful jackets.

Pat closed his eyes, tipped his head back and sighed a breath of relief.

"That was close, huh?" said a voice from somewhere in the darkness.

Pat jumped. Not for a single second did he expect there to be anybody in the alley with him. He turned and peered into the darkness, hoping to catch a glimpse of whoever was hiding there. But he couldn't see a thing.

"Come a bit closer," said the voice. "I can barely see you."

Pat took a single step further into the alley. That was enough – now he could see the owner of the voice.

There was a man, sat on the ground, his back propped up against a large, grey wheelie bin. It was no wonder Pat hadn't been able to see him – he was wrapped up to his neck in a tatty, old sleeping bag, surrounded on all sides by bags of rubbish.

"No need to be shy," said the man. "Do I look like the sort of person who might hurt you?"

Idle Hands

"I guess not," said Pat, feeling absolutely no level of intimidation. He took another step closer.

"Yeah, that's it," said he man, licking him chapped lips. "Who were those kids?"

"Just the school bullies. They like to make my life hell."

"Really? How so?"

"They just pick on me. Beat me up. The usual."

"That's not very nice, is it? Why don't you let me help you?"

Pat could feel himself frowning. "Help me?" he said, a tone of puzzlement in his voice. "Help me – *how*?"

The man was smiling. His teeth were yellow, and his gums were black. There were large gaps between each tooth, making them look sharp and crooked. A few of his teeth – those at the back of his mouth – were missing. "Just bring 'em here, to me. I'll deal with them."

"Why do you want to help me?"

"Because I like you?"

"You *like* me?" said Eric, sounding almost disgusted.

The man just nodded. His smile had widened and now he looked almost maniacal. Saliva ran over his lower lip and dripped from his chin.

"Right..." said Pat, backing away. "I better be off." And with that, he turned and walked away. He looked back over his shoulder as her left the alley, to where the man was still smiling.

"Bring 'em to me," said the man. "Bring 'em to me."

Pat forgot about the man in the alley almost as soon as he arrived home. His clothes weren't torn or dirty today, but he was still late. "Where have you been?" asked his mum as he walked into the house.

"Football," he said, resorting to his stock answer. She never questioned it.

Pat disappeared to his bedroom, dreading what Harvey and his cronies might do to him if, and when, they caught up to him on Monday.

Monday came and went without incident. Harvey wasn't even waiting for Pat at the school gate.

The same thing happened on Tuesday. Nothing. How bizarre.

Was it somehow possible that Harvey and the gang of bullies who followed him around like a flock of stupid sheep had finally learned their lesson, and were now refraining from any of the activities they used to enjoy?

Of course not.

They were there Wednesday. It turned out that Harvey had merely been sick (although Pat did suspect that he may have had those couple of days off, so that he didn't have to suffer the shame of having to explain where that cut on his forehead had come from). But there he was now, stood at the gate, three of his closest minions with him. Pat recognised those other kids, but he didn't know their names.

Anyway, there was no way he would be leaving through the school gates while that lot were there. He could be certain that the next beating he received would be the worst he'd ever had to endure. His face would certainly be fair game this time around. If they caught him, Pat felt sure he'd be spending the next few days in a hospital bed.

Idle Hands

So, to that end, he decided to sneak out through the fire exit, which would lead him out to the back of the school. From there, he ran home without stopping to look behind him.

They were there again on Thursday, Harvey looking even more frustrated now, as he crunched his knuckles in the palms of his hands.

Pat left via the fire exit once again.

Pat had hoped that if he could make it through one week, then perhaps Harvey might forget all about it, and not administer the mother of all beatings to him.

That, or course, was wishful thinking.

On Friday, Harvey was waiting at the school gates once again. So, once again, Pat left via the fire exit. Except this time, as soon as he stepped out through the door, he saw one of Harvey's goons there waiting for him, propped up against the wall, cigarette in hand.

They locked eyes. "OVER HERE!" the kid with the cigarette shouted. "HE'S OVER HERE!"

Who would've thought that Harvey would be smart enough to have his mates cover all the exits, once he realised that Pat wasn't leaving in the usual way?

Pat turned and ran. The kid threw his cigarette down on the ground and gave chase.

Pat rounded the corner of the school and immediately saw Harvey and two other kids running towards him.

Pat made the sharp turn and ran across the road, Harvey and his goons right behind him. "Come here you little shit!" shouted Harvey. "I'm gonna fuckin' KILL YOU!"

Pat turned the corner onto the high street, then down the alley that led between the newsagent and the barber shop, offering only a cursory glance towards the man on the floor, who was still propped up against the bin, still wrapped up in his sleeping bag.

And then Pat hit the mesh fence that blocked the passage.

Oh – *shit!*

Harvey appeared at the entrance to the alleyway. "You stupid fuck," he said. "I know you're in here. Come out. You can't hide in there forever." Then slowly, followed by his minions, Harvey began to make his way down the alley.

As he neared Pat, he – nor any of his scumbag friends – seemed to notice the man lying at their feet. They walked straight past him, as if he wasn't even there.

"Hey Pat!" said Harvey as he drew nearer. "I'm so glad I finally got to catch up with you. I've been meaning to thank you for what you did to me the other day."

Pat's heart was racing. His mouth was dry and tasted like death.

"If you hadn't done what you did, I wouldn't have realised how keen I was to murder somebody. Thanks to you, I know that now. I think it's only right that you should be my first."

Pat turned away as Harvey loomed over him, his fists clenched into balls.

"Hey!" came a familiar voice.

Harvey turned and looked at the man on the ground, clearly shocked to see him there. "What?"

"Why you pickin' on that kid? What's he done to you?"

Idle Hands

"That's none of your fuckin' business, is it?"

"It just don't seem fair to me. You're bigger than him. And there's more of you."

"Does it look like I give a shit?"

"Perhaps you should just leave him alone."

"Perhaps you should just mind your own fuckin' business."

Pat didn't feel any more comfortable than he had just a few seconds ago. This crazy old man had said he'd help him. Fat lot of good he was doing of that right now.

"You should let him go," said the man.

"And what if I don't?" said Harvey. "What the fuck are you goin' to do about it?"

"You should let him go," said the man.

Pat could almost feel Harvey frowning, as if this dumb old man was causing him the greatest inconvenience he'd ever known.

"You deaf? I said – what if I don't?"

"You should let him go," said the man.

"Are you crazy? Hello? You in there?"

"You should let him go. You should let him go."

Now Pat was feeling even more scared. He was trapped in a dark alley with a bunch of kids who planned to beat the shit out of him – or worse – and some crazy, homeless guy who kept on repeating himself.

"You should let him go," said the man. "You should let him go."

"What the fuck?" said Harvey.

"You should let him go. You should let him go. You should let him go. You should let him go."

And then the man's voice became guttural and inhuman. "You should let him go. You should... Should let him... Let. Him. LET HIM GO!"

The sleeping bag fell away, revealing an oozing mass of octopus-like tentacles below, as the long, snake-like neck to which the man's head was attached slithered upwards, stretching and elongating, his mouth twisting, his teeth separating, his eyes turning jet black.

Pat felt as though all of his innards had sunk to the bottom of his abdomen and were trying to squeeze themselves out of his rectum. He felt like he might throw up. He felt like he might cry.

It appeared that Harvey and his gang all felt the same – each of them was frozen to the spot, staring up at the expanding creature before them.

The creature – its head no longer resembling that of a man, its mouth now perfectly round and lined with teeth (it reminded Pat of a leech) – slithered backward into the large bin, the sides of which no longer seemed to be constructed of steel, but now seemed to be organic, flexing and pulsing. Then, all of a sudden, one of its long and slender tentacles whipped outward and wrapped around the body of one of Harvey's lackeys.

The boy – he was probably around fourteen – screamed. But then he was gone. As quickly as the tentacle had latched onto the boy, it had dragged him away and into the bin. That boy never re-emerged.

Before anybody could say anything – before they could even think, if they were anything like Pat – the creature had taken hold of one of the other kids and lifted him into the air. There, as one tentacle wrapped around his body, another tentacle squirmed

Idle Hands

and coiled itself around his head. And then, with a horrifying pop, the tentacle twisted and tore off his head. The tentacles then stuffed the two parts of this kid into the bin.

If you were to aske Pat now, he'd almost certainly say that he couldn't be sure, what with all the confusion, but it may well have been the case that the creature had killed the last of Harvey's lackeys at the same time as it was tearing the head off the other. This one, the creature had lifted from the ground and, with the series of barbs that protruded from its tentacles digging into his skin, it had peeled his flesh away from his skeleton, just like peeling a banana. It had then stuffed the strips of flesh – as well as the skeleton – into the bin.

Hervey had tried to run. He'd almost made it to the entrance of the alleyway, back into the light of day, but the creature had caught him before he'd done so. It wrapped its tentacle around his leg, causing him to trip and slam face first into the tarmac. It then dragged him back and lifted him from the ground. By one leg, it suspended Harvey headfirst over the bin, the reptilian walls of which pulsed, begging to be fed.

"Help me!" cried Harvey, reaching out for Pat. "You gotta help me!"

Pat wasn't sure when it had happened, but at some point, he'd collapsed into a heap on the floor. There, he was curled into a ball, rocking back and forth, hugging his knees.

"Pat! You gotta help me!"

Pat looked up to where the creature was holding Harvey above the bin. It was only then that he realised that the man – no, the *creature* – had done as it had promised; it had helped him. Harvey was a bad person. He deserved what came to him. And so, with nothing more to fear, Pat stood and took a step towards the creature, towards Harvey, who was begging him for help.

"Please!" said Harvey. "Get me out of here!"

"No," said Pat, and immediately the creature released its grip on Harvey's leg and dropped him into the convulsing bin. The scent of burning flesh being melted from bone by digestive acids stung Pat's eyes.

The creature moved closer to Pat. Its head reminded him of a worm – pink and lumpy. Its eyes were little more than slits between the fold of its skin. Its leech-like mouth never moved, but still the creature spoke to him. It said – "Bring me more. Feed them to me. Anybody you do not like. Anybody who doesn't deserve to live. Bring them to me."

Pat nodded. "I will," he said.

Pat left the alleyway feeling happier than he had in some time. And he was already compiling a mental list of all the people he planned to introduce to his newfound friend in the alley.

THE END

Idle Hands

THE SCARECROW

There was never anything to do around the small village of Fulstone. Nothing ever happened. It was quite possibly the most boring place on Earth. It was a nice place - a small, picturesque village in the northeast of England. Everybody knew each other there, and everybody was always friendly and courteous towards one another. Of course, there were the odd one or two busybodies - who just *had* to know everybody's business - who didn't quite fit into the mould of what a friendly and courteous neighbour ought to be. But they were few and far between.

The high street consisted of very little; there was a post office, a greengrocer and a butcher's shop. There was also a small toy shop, which only seemed to sell toys that were at least 5 years out of date. And that was it. The rest of the village was made up of small, stone houses, which had been standing there for more than a century.

On the outskirts of the village were a few farmhouses. Most of these had been converted into holiday lets. Most of the adults in the village seemed pleased about this, as it had driven tourism in their village upwards. Not that there was anything in the village for tourists to see. But many tourists seemed to use the village as a base for visiting other - far more exciting - areas in the local vicinity.

A few of the farms were still operational though. A good chunk of the land outside of the village - acre upon acre of wide-open fields - had been purchased by three farmers. They had converted the vast majority this land into pastures for their livestock, or fields for their crops. That hadn't really been the point though; the land had been purchased in an effort to prevent development upon it. It was a prime candidate to be converted into modern housing estates. *Thank God* those farmers had bought that land; had they not, Fulstone would be looking more like a city centre right now.

Those three farmers were almost like celebrities in the village. Everybody knew them. Or, at least, they knew *of* them. Generally, they tended to keep themselves to themselves. They worked hard tending to their farms, so they didn't venture into the village all too often.

One of those farmers was a man named Geoffrey Stanford. He was tall and broad, somewhat overweight. The whole of his face was masked by a thick, bushy beard. He often wore a brown chequered flat cap.

It was on his land that most of the children from the village tended to play. It was known colloquially - to the kids, at least - as the 'Stanford Estate'. In the corner of his land was a small forest. It was less than an acre, but this was plenty big enough for them to run around in and play hide and seek. Of course, they were technically trespassing on *his* private

Idle Hands

land. He didn't mind though, just so long as they didn't cause him any trouble.

But causing trouble was something that kids - teenagers, especially - were unsurprisingly good at.

It was Landon who had brought the gun - an air rifle, that fired small, steel pellets. He had inherited it from his older brother who had joined the army last year - "He don't need this no more," Landon had said. "He gets to shoot *real* people with *real* guns now!"

Mitch had been nervous the first time he fired the gun. He knew it wasn't a *real* gun. He knew that he couldn't kill somebody with it - or that he'd have to be very unlucky to do so. But still, he knew that a shot from this rifle could cause a serious injury - it could definitely break the skin. It was heavy - made of wood and metal - and felt real enough in his hands. But he'd stuffed those nerves down - Amelia was there; he didn't want to look like a baby in front of her.

Amelia was the prettiest girl in school; at least Mitch thought so. She didn't have a boyfriend and Mitch wanted nothing more than to ask her out. She'd started hanging out with him and Landon last summer, when, being the teenagers they were, the boredom of living in a small community had really begun to kick in. Kids who lived in bigger towns and cities would never know the struggle. They had fast food restaurants and bowling alleys and multiplex cinemas to keep them entertained. The kids of Fulstone had nothing. Mitch, Landon, and Amelia all went to the same school - Pembridge High School, in the next village over. They were the only kids in their year who lived in Fulstone, so it seemed natural that they would become friends.

Amelia was cool too; *too* cool really - way cooler than Mitch had ever considered himself to be. She was pretty and smart and she knew how to have fun. She used to steal the alcohol from her parent's liquor cabinet. Mitch could remember the first time he'd tasted vodka - it was disgusting. But Amelia seemed to like it, so he pretended to like it too. She'd also seemed to be impressed by Landon's air rifle.

Landon showed them both how to shoot it - just like his brother had shown him. There wasn't much recoil in the thing, of course, but there was a loud enough pop as the pellet exploded from the barrel to startle Mitch. His face must've been a picture, as both Landon and Amelia both burst out in laughter. Once she was able to control herself, Amelia had said - "You're such a pussy!"

She's so cool.

When Amelia first fired the gun, she hadn't even flinched. She just laughed again. She was beautiful when she smiled. It was at that moment Mitch had decided he loved her. Sure - they were only 15, but that didn't mean they couldn't know what love felt like!

They had taken turns in shooting the gun. Their primary targets were the empty tin cans that they each bought from home. They would go to the woods on the Stanford Estate and set the cans out between the trees. They would then see who could hit all the cans with the fewest shots.

Amelia was the best shot - of that, there was no question. Landon had tried to argue the case on a few occasions - how could anybody but *he* be the best shot? It was *his* gun after all! But even he had to admit that Amelia was pretty damn good with the rifle. She

Idle Hands

was the only one who could hit the cans consistently. She almost never missed a shot. Even at the rifle's maximum range (a none-too-shabby 115 meters), she was still a crack shot. Mitch on the other hand was terrible - if he managed to hit any of the cans at all, it was nothing more than sheer luck. Hitting the cans *was* satisfying though - each successful hit was signalled by a loud, low-pitched chime that resonated through the woods.

One day, when the three of them were heading across one of Geoffrey's fields - one which ran along the ridge of a steep hill - Amelia spotted something, off in the distance down below. "Is that a scarecrow?" she said, pointing out into the field of crops.

Sure enough, out in the field below, was what looked to be a scarecrow, perched high above the tall rows of wheat. Mitch tried to think back - was the scarecrow new? He'd never noticed it before. It could've been there all along. He supposed it didn't really matter.

"Well, I don't think it's Mr. Stanford," said Mitch, hoping for a laugh. Amelia did laugh; that made Mitch happy.

"Mr. Stanford don't usually put scarecrows out," said Landon.

"I guess he's had problems with the birds this year," said Mitch. "Probably they ate his crops."

It was hard to make out from this distance, but from what Mitch could tell, the scarecrow appeared to be little more than a bunch of sacks stuffed with straw and bound to a tall stake. It had arms, of course - what would a scarecrow be without arms? - but these were no more than two additional struts at 45 degrees to the body, wrapped and stuffed with straw also. There was another stuffed burlap sack for the head. Mitch couldn't tell if this scarecrow was wearing any clothes. All he could see for sure was the straw hat sat atop its head.

"We'll I don't like it. Scarecrows creep me out."

"Here," said Amelia, her outstretched hands gesturing for the rifle.

Landon handed the rifle over gladly. Amelia lay down on the ground. She hooked the butt of the rifle into her armpit and took aim down the sights.

"What are you doing?" asked Landon, scoffing back a laugh.

"Gettin' a solid base," Amelia told him, her eyes fixed firmly down the sights. "You never seen that in a movie? If your target's a long way away, you've got to get yourself a strong base."

"Fair enough."

Mitch didn't really like the idea of taking shots at Mr. Stanford's scarecrow. What if he found out? He'd be none too pleased. But he wasn't about to try and stop Amelia - she could do whatever she liked.

Amelia was wearing a tight pair of jeggings today, that clung to her buttocks. Mitch couldn't help but look, imaging what she'd look like in just her panties - or even better, completely naked.

"Ready?" said Amelia, snapping Mitch from his daydream.

"Ready," said Landon.

"Okay. Here goes." Amelia pulled the trigger. Nothing. She'd missed.

Mitch felt a slight sense of relief.

"What? How'd you miss? I thought you never missed?" Landon was trying to stifle his amusement.

"One more go," said Amelia, taking aim once again.

"Perhaps we shouldn't," said Mitch.

Landon looked at Mitch, a disappointed frown etched to his forehead. "Don't be such a loser," he said.

"Here goes," said Amelia. She pulled the trigger once again. This time a small plume of dust burst into the air from the back of the scarecrows head.

"Shit!" exclaimed Landon. "You got it!"

"Of course I did," said Amelia, as she climbed from the ground.

"Give me a shot."

"You'll never hit it." Amelia handed the rifle to Landon then brushed the dirt from her knees.

"Wanna bet?" Landon lifted the rifle, took aim, and fired. The shot must have missed by a country mile.

"I told you - you need to have a solid base."

"She did tell you that," said Mitch, feeling as though he hadn't spoken in forever. Landon only shot him a scornful look.

"Fine," said Landon, dropping to the ground. He took aim once again and fired. Dust popped from the shoulder of the scarecrow. "Bullseye!"

"Bullseye?" Amelia said, sarcastically. "So, you were aiming for its shoulder?"

"No. I was just aiming for the scarecrow. I hit the fuckin' thing, didn't I?" The sarcasm seemed lost on Landon.

"You sure did."

"Your turn," said Landon, now upright, the rifle at arm's length for Mitch to take.

"Nah," said Mitch, brushing the idea away with his hand. "I'd never hit it anyway. It'd just be a waste of time."

"Nonsense," said Amelia. "Just take your time and make sure you have a solid base."

Landon pushed the gun into Mitch's hands.

"Alright," said Mitch. He dropped to his knees and sprawled out just as Amelia had done. He took the weight of the rifle in his left hand and planted his elbow into the ground. He hooked his arm around the stock and took aim. There were two grey sights along the barrel, one at each end. Mitch lined them up with the scarecrow's head. He could feel his heart pumping inside his ribcage. For some reason, he felt nervous. He held his breath and pulled the trigger.

The little dust cloud told Mitch that he'd hit it. That must have been the first time he'd ever hit something on the first attempt. Suddenly, the trepidation he'd felt in shooting at the scarecrow was gone - in its place was a sense of excitement, as if this were the first time he'd fired the rifle, and he'd found himself very good at it.

They spent most of that afternoon taking turns in shooting at the scarecrow. Landon had brought a box of pellets out with him, every one of which was spent on the scarecrow. At one point, fear once again set into Mitch, as he considered the fact that the scarecrow would now be littered with tiny holes. He brushed the thought aside though, as he convinced himself that Mr. Stanford probably wouldn't mind anyway - the scarecrow was still standing, still able to perform its one and only job. It wasn't as if the birds would notice a few holes in it.

But Mr. Stanford almost certainly would - if he ever bothered to come and inspect it, that was.

Apparently, he *did* come to inspect it. It had caused Landon much amusement to see the notice in the post office shop window a few days later. It was written on a sheet of lined A4 paper, the letters big and bold. It read:

TO WHOEVER HAS BEEN USING MY SCARECROW FOR TARGET PRACTICE - PLEASE STOP!!! IT IS CRIMINAL DAMAGE!! YOU HAVE BEEN ON MY LAND - THAT IS TRESSPASSING!! IF IT HAPPENS AGAIN, I WILL CALL THE POLICE!!!

"Oh, shit!" said Landon, between fits of hysterical laughter. "I can't wait to tell Amelia about this!"

Mitch hadn't found it even half as funny. What if he did call the police?

Amelia seemed to find it quite amusing. "We've just *got* to go shoot it some more!" she'd said.

"Definitely!" agreed Landon.

"Seriously guys..." Mitch protested. "We can't. He's right, you know - it's criminal damage. What if does phone the police?"

"Chill out," said Landon. "So what if he does? What are they gonna do? Arrest us? It's a fuckin' scarecrow. It's not as if it cost him loads of money."

"You worry too much," said Amelia. Her voice sounded convincing. "It's funny! You've gotta come."

It wasn't funny - not to Mitch. Not to Mr. Stanford either, by the sound of it. But still, if Amelia said it was funny, he wasn't about to disagree. Nor was he about to let her go out there by herself, shooting with Landon. "Alright," he said, certain that his voice sounded downtrodden and defeated.

They made their way there the following afternoon.

The scarecrow was still there. Mr. Stanford couldn't have been that bothered - if he was, he would have taken it down. *But then the birds would have got his crops.*

Once in position - the same position they had taken last time - it was decided that Amelia would take the first shot. But as she prepared, rifle in hand, she spotted a tractor driving between the rows of wheat. It was heading towards the scarecrow. "Look," she informed the others.

Landon watched through the binoculars he'd brought with him. "Ha!" he laughed. "I bet he goes out there every day now, to check that nobody's been shootin' it."

The tractor stopped beside the scarecrow and Mr. Stanford climbed out, disappearing into the wheat (Mitch hadn't realised quite how tall the wheat was - Mr. Stanford must've been at least six feet tall). A few seconds later, Mr. Stanford's head appeared above the wheat, followed by his torso. He must've been climbing a small ladder, positioned next to the scarecrow.

"Is he checking it?" asked Mitch, unable to see properly from this distance.

Landon was still watching through his binoculars. "I'm not sure. I dare somebody to shoot him."

Idle Hands

Neither Mitch nor Amelia offered. They both looked disgustedly at Landon.

"Alright, alright. I was just kidding!" As Landon watched, Mr. Stanford began to run his hands over the material, caressing the sacks and slipping his fingers into the numerous holes. He then reached into the worn out, tatty satchel that was slung over his shoulder and pulled out a large bottle of some pink liquid.

"What's he got?" said Amelia.

"I'm not sure," said Landon.

"Let me see," said Mitch, reaching out for the binoculars. Landon handed them over gladly.

Mr. Stanford shook the bottle vigorously. He looked like he was talking to the scarecrow - of course, Mitch couldn't hear what he was saying. Regardless, it was weird. Mr. Stanford then popped open the cap from the top of the bottle and took a swig of the pink liquid.

"Huh…" said Mitch. "I guess it's a protein shake or somethin'."

Landon frowned. "So, he comes out to his field, and fondles his scarecrow while drinkin' a protein shake? Great. That's not at all *fuckin' mental* now, is it?"

Mitch returned his gaze to Mr. Stanford. It was difficult to see exactly what he was doing - Mitch's view was mostly blocked by the scarecrow itself. He appeared to be running his hands over the head now. He untied the rope that formed the neck and lifted the material slightly, knocking the straw hat to a precarious angle. He then did something with the bottle of pink liquid - he seemed to be pouring it into the scarecrow. With all the liquid gone, he re-tied the rope, straightened the hat, then dropped back down into the wheat.

"What just happened?" asked Amelia.

"I'm not entirely sure," said Mitch. "It looked like he poured that liquid stuff *into* the scarecrow."

"Perhaps it's some sort of preservative?" suggested Landon.

Amelia snorted a laugh. "We just watched him drink it. I don't think he'd be drinking… 'scarecrow preservative'… or whatever."

"Oh, yeah."

The tractor roared as - with Mr. Stanford back in the driver's seat - it took off, back through the crops.

"We should go and check it out," said Mitch, suddenly feeling brave. Perhaps he'd thought that Amelia would want to do the same.

One thing was for sure - Landon didn't want to. "No way," he said. "You mad? That guy's crazy - we just seen that! If he catches us down there, he'll probably kill us."

"Well you can stay here then."

"By myself?" said Landon, a concerned tone to his voice. He then looked to Amelia.

"I'm going with Mitch," said Amelia.

Mitch smiled. He was so glad she'd chosen him over Landon. He felt as though he were one step closer to his dream scenario, of marrying her and fathering her children.

"Fine," said Mitch. But if we see Mr. Stanford coming, we run. Got it?"

"Got it."

"Alright."

Slowly and cautiously, they made their way down the steep slope to the bottom of the hill. There, a wooden fence denoted the perimeter of the wheat field. Beyond the fence, row after row of wheat grew towards the sky, stretching high above Mitch's head. It only then dawned on him that they wouldn't know which way they were heading, and that they may never find the scarecrow.

"We will, no problem," Amelia told him after he shared his concern. "We just walk straight. It's on one of the rows. We'll find it easy enough."

Mitch loved her optimism.

But she was right. After around twenty minutes of walking through the field - pushing the wheat aside, being careful not to break the stems - they arrived at the scarecrow.

The thing sure did look ugly up close. The whole thing was no more than a padded mess of burlap sacks. It would've looked much better - and not half as terrifying - had it have been wearing clothes. Even something as simple as a chequered shirt draped over its shoulders would've offered a huge improvement.

The other thing that made it look terrifying was its height - it must've been at least ten feet high at the top. It loomed over them ominously, like some giant demon sent to drag them to hell.

"So," said Landon. "Now what?"

At the base if the scarecrow was a small set of foldable steps. It was only three feet high, but should allow one of them to reach the head.

Mitch didn't ask for volunteers - he positioned the steps and climbed up.

Immediately, a vile stench hit him. "Oh God," he said, placing the back of his hand to his nose. "This thing stinks."

"We're on a farm," said Landon. "The whole place stinks."

Mitch reached out and untied the rope from the scarecrows neck. He slowly lifted the sack, hoping to not spill all the straw from inside. The hat tumbled from the scarecrows head and floated to the ground.

But no straw fell from the sack. As Mitch lifted the material, he saw what was actually beneath.

Mitch screamed. He reeled backwards and fell from the step. He hit the ground hard, knocking Amelia over as he went.

"Holy fuck!" screamed Landon.

Beneath the burlap sack was the face of a woman. Her skin was dirty. A trail of blood ran down one of her cheeks, having originated somewhere beyond her hairline. I length of rope was tied tightly around her face, holding the rag that had been stuffed into her mouth in place. Her eyes widened, flitting side to side. They were begging for help.

"Oh my God!" muttered Amelia, as she scrambled to her feet. Tears were already streaming down her cheeks.

The woman was struggling. She was clearly well restrained. As Mitch remained seated on the ground, looking up the woman, he suddenly understood what was going on.

There had been a family - or a couple, Mitch couldn't quite recall - who had had come to the village for a holiday, about four months ago. They had been staying in one of the converted farmhouses. But then one of them (mother, daughter, sister, friend - Mitch

Idle Hands

wasn't sure) had disappeared. There had been a huge police presence around the village after that, which lasted for around six weeks, perhaps two months. But then it died down. They still saw police cars from the city every now and then, but far more infrequently. In a small village like this, where everybody knows everybody else's business, people also tend to forget things quite quickly. Nobody talked about the missing woman anymore.

But this was her. She'd been taken by Mr. Stanford and strung up in his field. Had he just put her here? Or had she been here all along? Mitch couldn't remember if he'd seen the scarecrow here before. It didn't matter now. They had to help this woman. And they had to do it fast - clearly Mr. Stanford was mentally unstable; if he did catch them here, he'd almost certainly kill them.

Mitch hopped to his feet. "Come on," he urged the others. "We've got to get her down."

Once again, he climbed up the ladder. At the top, he untied the rope that bound the woman's face and removed her gag. Immediately she screamed. "Help me! Help me!" she bellowed at the top of her lungs.

"Shhhh!" said Mitch, clamping his hand over her mouth. He looked back to Amelia and Landon. Both were looking around frantically, no doubt terrified that Mr. Stanford would've heard her screams.

No chance. Not over the noise of his tractor.

Mitch removed his hand from the woman's face. She looked to be in her twenties. Maybe her early thirties, at best. "Please," he said. "I want to help you, but you need to keep quiet. We can't let him hear us. You understand?"

The woman nodded. She was crying.

Mitch worked frantically, eventually pulling away the material from over the scarecrow's… from over the woman's body. Beneath the material, she was naked. Her arms were bound to the horizontal beams in three places. Angry red friction burns highlighted where the ropes had rubbed against her skin. Her body and legs were bound to the vertical beam in several places. The ropes were pulled tight, squashing and deforming her flesh. It almost looked as though she had been crucified.

"Come on," said Mitch, waving his hand at Landon. "Get up here."

"What? Why?" replied Landon.

"I need your help to take her weight."

Landon sighed. He didn't want to be there anymore, that much was obvious. Mitch was sure he'd rather have taken off, ran away as fast as he could. Truth be told, that was exactly what Mitch had wanted to do. But he'd fought his instincts, made himself stay and help this woman. After all, if he was in her position, that's what he'd have wanted.

Mitch shuffled across as Landon hopped up to the second step. "Okay," said Mitch. "Hold her body. I think she's just hanging by her arms. I'm going to untie them first."

"Get on with it then."

Amelia was pacing back and forth, a few steps at a time. "Quickly," she said. "He could be back any second."

Neither Mitch nor Landon offered a response.

Idle Hands

Landon had taken a tight grip of the woman's legs, his shoulder pressed into her thighs. Mitch began working on the ropes that held the woman's right arm. Soon, they came loose. Mitch pulled them away. "There," he said. "That's one down."

Then the woman screamed again, the piercing sound nearly knocking Mitch from the ladder.

Then her face exploded, as a loud crack echoed through the field. Blood splattered over Mitch's face, into his mouth as he gasped for air.

Mitch, Landon, and Amelia both turned to see Mr. Stanford standing behind them, some distance away. He was holding a rifle before him, smoke billowing from the barrel. This was a real rifle, not some poxy air rifle. A single shot had damn near torn the woman's head off.

"Run!" shouted Mitch. He pushed Landon from the step, then hopped down behind him. He then grabbed Amelia by the arm and the three of them fled into the wheat, leaving the woman - blood leaking from her demolished face - hanging from the beams.

Landon was in the front, knocking the swords of wheat from his own path, only for them to spring back and whip against Mitch's skin. Mitch didn't care though - he was more concerned with Amelia. She was fast, but he was faster - he felt like she was slowing him down. "Come on," he was yelling. "We've got to keep moving!"

Amelia didn't bother to reply.

It felt like they were running for hours. Mitch's muscles burned, the lactic acid building in his legs making them feel like lead weights. Of course, they weren't running for hours, they were running for mere minutes - perhaps even seconds - before they broke from the crops, into the next row. Mitch pushed the last of the wheat aside, to come face to face with Landon, who was looking around frantically, a confused look on his face. "Now where?" asked Landon, as if Mitch ought to know.

"No idea", said Mitch. "Maybe we should try this way."

Another loud crack rang out through the field. Landon screamed in pain and dropped to the ground. Mitch looked down to see blood oozing from the back of Landon's calf. Half the muscle was hanging from the bone. Landon was sobbing like a disgruntled baby.

Mr. Stanford was stood only a few metres away. It then occurred to Mitch - he knew these fields better than any of them.

Mitch panicked. What was he supposed to do now? He couldn't help Landon - not without risking his own life, and not without risking Amelia's life. Landon was his best friend - they'd known each other since they were born, they'd grown up together - but without thinking, he reached out, took Amelia's hand, and began to back away. "I'm sorry," he told Landon.

"Please!" begged Landon "You gotta help me! Don't leave me! *Please!*"

"I'm sorry," said Mitch once again. Mitch tugged on Amelia's hand and they both took off once again, into the wheat. Not once did Amelia protest, not once did she say *"We should go back,"* or *"We should help him."* She knew - just as Mitch did - that trying to help Landon would've been the same as committing suicide.

In the distance, Mitch could still hear Landon screaming for help. Mr. Stanford hadn't killed him yet. Perhaps that meant he'd eventually let him go? Or perhaps it meant that Mr. Stanford was more interested in catching Amelia and himself.

That was when Amelia tripped. He hit the ground with a thud. Mitch would've sworn he heard the air forced from her lungs.

"Shit," said Mitch. "Quick! Get up."

"I can't!" said Amelia, between heavy, heaving sobs. "My leg! I think a broke it!"

"You haven't broken your leg! You just tripped. Maybe you sprained it. Come on. You can't just stay here - Mr. Stanford's gonna kill us!"

"I can't! I can't!"

"You can! You *have* to!" Mitch had already grabbed Amelia by the arm, and was pulling her up to her feet. She couldn't bear weight on her right leg, so Mitch tucked his head under her armpit and supported her. He then helped her hop through the wheat, practically dragging her along.

There was another gunshot.

A burning sensation filled Mitch's shoulder as he was knocked from his feet. Agony surged through his veins, to where blood was now leaking from his shoulder. He screamed out.

Mitch had dragged Amelia to the ground as he fell. She was now beside him, crawling towards him. "Mitch! Mitch! What happened?"

It was then that Mitch saw Mr. Stanford approaching. "Run," he told Amelia, through gritted teeth. "Get outta here!"

But Amelia didn't move. She just stayed there, her hands on Mitch's chest, sobbing uncontrollably.

Now Mr. Stanford was right on top of them. He looked huge from Mitch's perspective; the shadow of a giant, silhouetted against the sun, towering over them, rifle in hand. "So," said Mr. Stanford. "It's you who's been messin' with me scarecrow. Whadya think? She done a good job, ain't she?"

Mitch's heart was racing. Amelia had her head turned away from Mr. Stanford, nestled into Mitch's shoulder. Mitch thought to himself that it was over - they were dead meat. There was no way that would Mr. Stanford let them leave here alive - they had found the girl. If he let them go, they would almost certainly tell somebody. He'd be spending the rest of his life behind bars. No - Mitch knew it was over.

"Shame you had to go an' ruin it," continued Mr. Stanford. "Ah well - I think I know where I can find me a suitable replacement." He was smiling, his wide grin showing of his crooked, yellow teeth (a few of which were missing).

Mr. Stanford spun his rifle around, lifted it above his head and cracked it against Mitch's skull.

Just as the darkness began to envelope Mitch's vision, he heard Amelia scream.

Then he fell unconscious.

***

The fuzziness of the cotton wool that filled Mitch's brain began to fade. As he awoke, he found that he was still in the wheat field. The sun was setting now and there were birds all around him, singing as they soared through the sky, dancing and chasing one another. They were beautiful. The whole world as he now saw it was glorious.

And then, suddenly - as if the bubble that surrounded him had violently burst - he came to his senses.

Idle Hands

He was now tied to a stake, his arms out wide, just as that woman had been. And Mr. Stanford was stood before him, atop the small set of steps. He was busy thing the last of the ropes around Mitch's left hand. As he pulled the rope tight, the friction burnt Mitch's skin.

The gasp that Mitch must've emitted drew Mr. Stanford's attention. "Ah! So glad you could finally join us! I wasn't sure you'd ever wake up!" He bellowed a loud laugh, as if he'd just heard the most hilarious of jokes. He then nodded towards his left. "I don't think your friends gonna last long - lost too much blood, me thinks."

Mitch followed Mr. Stanford's gaze.

Landon was tied to a stake beside him. He was bound with ropes and wrapped in rags torn from old sacks, just as Mitch was. Only his head remained uncovered (same as Mitch). He was slumped forward, the ropes being the only thing preventing him from falling.

Mr. Stanford stepped down from the ladder and moved it over to Landon. There, once again on the top step, Mr. Stanford tied a gag around Landon's mouth and pulled a sack over his head. "Yep. He'll be dead soon. I ain't gonna even bother wastin' me protein shakes on him."

He stepped down and, once again, moved back over to Mitch. "But you," he continued. "I bet I can make you last a real long time! That girl… She was doin' real good until you came along and ruined it. I bet I coulda kept her goin' for years! Oh well. I'll just start again with you."

Mr. Stanford was grinning once again. He looked like some vile monster. But then again, that's exactly what he was.

Amelia. Where was Amelia? Mitch had forgotten all about her.

As if he'd read Mitch's mind, Mr. Stanford said - "Don't worry about that girl. I'll take good care of her. I got a nice little room in me cellar for 'er."

He bellowed another laugh. His breath stunk like rotten meat.

Before Mitch could protest - before he could say even a single word - Mr. Stanford stuffed a rag into his mouth and tied it in place with a length of rope.

"Good," said Mr. Stanford, admiring his handywork. "I think you'll make a great scarecrow. Now you behave yourself - I'll be back to feed you in a few days."

And with that, he pulled a sack over Mitch's head.

Mitch could do nothing but listen, as Mr. Stanford walked away, laughing to himself, and whistling a jolly tune.

THE END

THE HOLE

"Well, look on the bright side," I said, as I handed Chris the cup of coffee I'd made for him. "At least now we'll have time to complete all these half-finished jobs around the house."

"Yeah," said Chris, puffing out his cheeks. He took a sip of his coffee, then placed the cup on the breakfast table. "I suppose there is that. But, to be perfectly honest, I was already thinking of other things we could do with our time."

"Oh, really? Such as…?"

Chris pushed in close to me. He reached around my waist and pulled me in towards him. He kissed my neck as his hands cupped my buttocks and gently squeezed.

Any other time, I would've jumped on him. But not today. Today we had more important things to consider.

Neither of us had ever been out of work. Chris was an electrician. He worked as part of the maintenance team in a plastic moulding factory. He loved his job. He'd always worked an odd shift pattern; two early shifts, two night shifts, then three days off. He'd done that since he was nineteen. I wouldn't have liked it, but it seemed to make him happy.

Not for me, thank you very much. I worked in human resources for a haulage company. I worked nine-to-five each and every day, and that was exactly how I liked it.

But now, thanks to the shitty economic hole our democratically elected government had gotten us into, belts had been tightened and both of our respective companies had been forced to close and both of us had been made redundant.

We'd both each received a reasonable pay out, so neither of us was in any hurry to find ourselves a new job. To be perfectly honest, I was quite looking forward to spending a bit of time at home together. There were plenty of things that needed to be done, and sex wasn't currently top of my agenda.

Then again, as Chris nibbled at my neck, I was truly tempted. "Stop," I said, gently pushing him away. "There will be plenty of time for that. Right now we need to think about fixing up the garden."

"Seriously?"

I nodded.

Chris puffed out his cheeks once again. "What's wrong with the garden?" he asked. He picked up his coffee once again, taking another sip.

"*What's wrong with the garden?*" I scoffed. "What's *right* with it?" I looked out the back window. The garden was in a terrible state. The patio was cracked, with several slabs displaced. The lawn too seemed to be on its last legs; the mottled green was interspersed was patches of horrible, brown dirt.

"It's fine," said Chris. "It's not like we use the garden much."

"No, I know. That's because it's in *that* state."

"I just think there's more important things to do. What about the spare bedroom? Don't the walls still need painting?"

He was right. The walls in the spare room *did* need painting. But the garden was, in my opinion at least, far more important. The walls could be painted any time; we were forecast good weather for the next week or so, making it the perfect time to do the garden. "They do," I said. "If *you* want to paint them, go right ahead. I'm sure that'll take you all of five minutes."

"Five minutes? It'll take a bit longer than that."

"Yeah, okay. What? A day at the most?"

"Yeah," laughed Chris. "And then we can get back onto *my* idea!"

"Not happening," I said. I couldn't help but smile - he sure was persistent. "But I'll tell you what - if you're digging out there, you'll definitely break a sweat. Perhaps we could take a shower together, so I can scrub your back."

"Yeah?"

"Yeah."

Chris dropped his empty cup into the sink. He then draped his hands over my shoulders and kissed me. "Alright," he said, looking into my eyes. "You paint in here; I'll get digging out there."

"You sure? I don't mind helping you out there."

"To be honest, the lawn is full of roots. It'll take some strength to get them out, and we both know just how weak your weedy little arms are!"

"Hey!"

We both laughed. He kissed me once again.

"No, seriously," he said. "That tree stump is gonna be a real bitch to move."

He was right. There was a tree stump on the one side of the lawn, that had been left there when we had had a rather obtrusive tree taken down. It was the first thing I had insisted on having done when I first moved in with Chris. Of course, this was his house, so it was his choice, but that tree was, at best, an eyesore. I had convinced him that it needed to go.

But, for some reason, he had insisted that they leave the stump. He had said that he could get rid of it, and that it wasn't worth the extra cost for them to do it for us.

That was three years ago now, and that stump was still there.

"Fair enough," I said. "You do outside, I'll do in."

"Deal," he said, between breaths as he nibbled my neck. "So… You know how it's already getting late? Perhaps we could start all of this in the morning. I think we should go and get an early night."

I knew exactly what he was implying. To me, getting an early night sounded like a great idea.

***

I woke late the following morning. That was unusual for me, but I guess all the stress that I'd been feeling over the past few weeks had gotten to me; as much as I liked the idea of spending some time at home, being made redundant still wasn't the nicest of feelings. What if neither of us could find another job? What if we couldn't pay our bills? What if we had to move out of our home?

Idle Hands

Thoughts like that can be exhausting.

At least we had our redundancy packages to tide us over; knowing that we could stay at home for a while, without having to worry about our income, was a very welcome relief.

When I woke, the first thing I did – as I always did – was to pick up my phone to check the time. It was twenty past nine. I hadn't slept in that late for what felt like years.

More intriguing was the fact that Chris wasn't in bed beside me. He *always* got up after me (at the weekends, or during holidays, I mean, when he didn't *have* to get up at a certain time for work). I sat up. I couldn't hear him pottering around the house anywhere. Where was he?

I climbed out of bed, crossed the room, and opened the curtains, making sure to keep them between my body and the window – I'd slept naked last night, and I most certainly wanted to retain my modesty.

Our bedroom overlooked the back garden. To my surprise, Chris was already out there, digging around the tree stump. I didn't know how long he'd been going at it out there, but he'd already made a fairly sizeable hole in the ground. There were mounds of dirt piled on either side of him and, as expected, where the earth had been moved, thick roots crisscrossed the ground.

I grabbed my dressing gown from the bed and pulled it over my shoulders, tying it around my waist.

I stepped outside quietly, so that Chris wouldn't hear me. As I stood there and watched, he continued to plunge his spade into the ground, stamp it in with the bottom of his boot and heave out a mountain of soil. There was something highly attractive about a hardworking man.

He paused momentarily, wiping the sweat from his forehead with the back of his hand.

"Somebody's been busy," I said, drawing his attention.

Chris took a deep breath as he looked over his shoulder. He smiled at me. "I thought I'd try and get as much done as I could be you got out of bed," he said.

"So I see. And how's that working out for you?"

"Not bad. Tougher than I thought. The bigger roots aren't so much of a problem; it's the little ones that stop you digging."

"Well, I'm sure you'll manage."

Chris stepped off the lawn and stood before me. He was sweating. His cheeks were bright red. He reached out and took a hold of the belt of my gown. "I'm sure I will," he said. "But you can see how sweaty I'm getting…"

"Yeah," I said, giggling. "You're pretty disgusting."

"Which is why I think I'll be taking a bath later, and I'm going to need you to join me."

As he spoke he began to untie my dressing gown. He allowed it to fall open, revealing my nude body to him. Our garden was fairly exposed – but only to anyone who would specifically be looking in from one of the neighbouring houses. And even then, they'd have to be trying pretty hard to see us. He reached inside my gown and stroked my back, pulling me in.

"Well," I said, suddenly feeling very horny. "I think I'm going to *have* to join you; you've covered me in your sweat."

"It smells good though, right?"

"No. It smells gross." We both laughed. I pulled away and re-tied my dressing gown. "Get on with it then," I said, nodding towards the hole.

"Yes, boss," Chris said, sarcastically standing to attention and offering a salute.

"I'm gonna grab some breakfast, then I'll get on with the painting."

"Okie dokie."

Chris went back to his digging, while I returned to the house.

I made myself a slice of toast (slathered in far too much marmalade) for breakfast. I drank a coffee, then went about starting to paint the spare room walls. I pulled on a pair of tracksuit bottoms and an old t-shirt that I kept especially for DIY jobs. It was already splattered with lilac paint, so any other paint that happened to get on it during the course of any other home improvement jobs wouldn't really matter.

The walls of the spare room were to be a simple off-white colour (the tin insisted that this specific shade was called 'Warm Cotton', whatever the hell that meant). They were already such a colour, from when I had first painted them a year or so ago. However, that was another job that hadn't been finished; the edges of the wall, where they met the ceiling and the door and the fitted wardrobe, were still a pale yellow – vile remnants left over from whoever had lived there before Chris had moved in, many years before I had arrived on the scene.

Chris had been here for over ten years now. He'd bought this place with an ex-girlfriend of his. I couldn't tell you what happened to her – Chris and I never really spoke about it – but she had left about seven years ago. From what I understood, Chris' next girlfriend had moved in, but she'd only lived with him for a year or so. He had told me that she had left him for one of his best friends. That was why he didn't really have many friends now - many of them had sided with her instead of him.

From what I knew, Chris had then remained single until I had come along.

I didn't probe too hard into his previous relationships, as *he* hadn't into mine. None of it really mattered – we were both grownups after all. We were both in our late thirties now – specifically, I was thirty-seven and he was thirty-nine.

Chris was a nice - possibly the nicest man I'd ever met. I loved him more than anything, as he did me. I hoped one day we might even get married.

But that was for another time. Right now, I'd be content to get the house into some sort of order. I poured a heavy blob of paint into the tray, dipped the roller in and began to paint.

As I went about coating the walls, I occasionally looked out of the window to see how Chris was getting on. The hole had grown somewhat, but Chris seemed to be slowing down. That was understandable - he'd been working hard since God-only-knew what time.

After about two hours of painting, I went down to see if Chris needed anything.

Idle Hands

I found him sat at the kitchen table. His head was tipped back, his eyes closed. His breathing seemed shallow. His cheeks were bright scarlet.

For a moment, I thought he was dead.

"Chris?" I said, startling him out of the sleepy daze he'd seemingly drifted into. "Are you okay?"

Stupid question - he didn't *look* okay; not at all.

Chris stared at me for a second. He almost looked confused, as if he didn't recognise me. "Yeah," he said, before correcting himself - "Erm… No. I don't feel well. There something not right."

"Are you in pain?" I asked.

"No. I don't think so. I just feel a bit dizzy. I feel exhausted. Maybe I've just been working too hard."

Worried, I placed the back of my hand against his head. He was drenched in sweat, but his skin felt cold to the touch. "You need to go to the hospital."

"No. I'm fine. I've got work to do here."

"The garden? That can wait." I crossed the kitchen, over to the sink, where I poured Chris a glass of water. Perhaps he was dehydrated.

"It can't."

"Trust me, it can."

Chris heaved himself up to his feet. "No," he said, his words forced. "I need to do this."

I was about to tell him to sit down, and to get some rest, when he dropped back into the chair and slumped forwards onto the table, his head slamming into the wood.

My heart skipped a couple of beats and jumped up into the back of my throat. "Chris?" I said, my voice all of a sudden shrill. "Chris!"

I dropped the glass into the sink and crossed the room quickly. I grabbed Chris by the shoulders and tried to pull him upright. He didn't budge. He was unconscious. I felt numb. I felt as though static electricity was flowing through my veins. I felt as though I had pins and needles in every inch of my body.

Quickly, I grabbed my phone from the kitchen worktop and called for an ambulance.

It seemed as if several hours passed before the ambulance finally arrived, although I'm sure it was probably only a few minutes. During that time, Chris had remained unconscious, face down on the kitchen table. I had tried to talk to him, tried to wake him, but it was no good.

At least he was still breathing.

The paramedics came into the house, asked me a few questions as they loaded Chris onto a stretcher, then they shuffled back out and loaded him into the ambulance. I climbed in beside him and we were transported to the hospital. There, they wheeled him into the hospital and immediately took him off down a corridor, to a ward into which I wasn't allowed.

"What's going on?" I cried. "Tell me what's happening!"

"Please," said a nurse, who stroked my back gently as she led me over to a plastid chair. "Just wait here. As soon as we know what's wrong with your partner, I'll be sure to come and let you know."

Hours passed. Eventually the nurse returned. She told me that Chris had suffered from a stroke.

Idle Hands

I couldn't believe it; Chris was as fit as a racehorse. He *never* got ill! How could this have happened to *him*?

He was still unconscious, but I was finally allowed in to see him.

The doctors told me that he was stable. When I'd asked, they'd assured me that he wasn't going to die. They told me that there was nothing more I could do here. They told me to go home and get some rest. They promised to take good care of him.

Back at home, there was no way I could sleep. Instead, I sat at the kitchen table and cried, through the night, until the sun finally poked its head above the horizon.

I phoned the hospital at precisely 8:00a.m. After a few rings, a friendly-sounding voice answered. It belonged to a man. "Hello? Can I help?"

"Oh my God," I said, those words coming involuntarily. I guess it was just the relief of hearing another human voice, one that might be able to provide some answers. I took a moment to compose myself. "Er… I was hoping you could give me some information about a patient who was bought in earlier. His name is Chris. Chris Hammond. I'm his partner."

"Okay. Just a second."

That second felt like an hour.

"Ah," said the voice at the other end of the line. "He's stable. We've had to sedate him, but all of his vital signs look good. Everything's under control."

"Thank God," I said, relief sweeping over me once again. I felt the tears begin to stream down my cheeks. I sniffed them back. "Can I come and see him?"

"To be honest, I don't think there'd be much point.. He's unconscious at the moment. But call back tomorrow, if he's awake, you can speak to him on the phone."

"Okay."

"Is there anything else I can help you with?"

"No. Thank you."

I hung up.

That night, I slept like a rock. The events of the previous day had really taken it out of me. I was exhausted. If I dreamt at all, I couldn't for the life of me tell you what it had been about.

The next morning, I phoned the hospital once again. They told me there had been no change. They told me to try again later.

I cried some more.

That was no good. I couldn't just sit in the house all day, crying, wallowing in self-pity. I had to do something. *Anything*, just to keep my mind busy.

I finished painting the spare bedroom. It didn't take long.

At around three in the afternoon, I tried the hospital once again. Still no change. They assured me that Chris was doing well. They didn't consider him to be critical. They expected him to make a full recovery, I just had to give it time.

I didn't sleep so well that evening. I'm not sure I slept at all.

The next day, the hospital still had no news. I found this incredibly frustrating. They told me Chris was doing well. I wasn't sure I believed them – how in the *hell* could he be doing well, if he was still unconscious?

Idle Hands

I had to take my mind off things. I needed a job to do.

I decided to try and do some digging out in the garden. Sure, there were jobs I could've done inside – and digging out the garden did seem like a herculean task – but it seemed pointless to start those other jobs, when there was a job outside still waiting to be finished.

The hole Chris had dug formed an almost perfect semi-circle around the tree stump, starting and ending on either side, where the fence met the lawn.

From what I'd seen before, it had looked as though Chris had dug a massive hole. As it turns out, the hole was only, at a guess, around ten or twelve inches deep. But I could see how the roots criss-crossed the soil; it was these roots that had caused Chris such trouble.

I didn't really have any clue as to where I should start. For one reason or another, having somewhat carefully assessed the task at hand, I decided to try and widen the hole first.

I picked up the spade and planted it into the lawn, a few inches away from where Chris' hole ended. The soil felt fairly soft and free from roots; the spade chewed through the dirt with ease.

What I *did* find littered through the ground was stones. Every time I planted the spade into the lawn, the metal would *clunk* against something hard. I'd have to shift the spade to one side or another, then try again, so that I could get under the rock (all of which varied in size, from around the size of a marble, to around the size of a house brick) and tear it from the ground.

I planned to phone the hospital straight after lunch. Until then, I'd carry on digging, unearthing as many of these roots as possible.

As I slammed the spade into the ground, it once again hit something hard, about a foot beneath the surface of the lawn. I pulled out a chunk of mud and tossed it aside. Immediately I knew that what I had hit was not a stone; it was a bone.

I'm sure some people may have been unnerved at having found a bone buried in their garden. But I wasn't – it wasn't as if it would belong to a human body or anything, was it?

I dug around the bone and pulled it from the ground. It was fairly short and thin. If it did belong to a human, it could only possibly have been one of the bones from the forearm.

Not that I was any kind of an expert in bones, but it looked more like it belonged to an animal of some kind.

My phone was ringing. The sound – emanating from inside the house – startled me.

It took me a second to realise exactly what it was I was hearing. As soon as it registered with my brain, I hopped off the lawn and ran into the house.

I recognised the number immediately - it was the hospital.

My heart sank. Did that mean Chris had died? Or had he finally woken up?

Only one way to find out.

I answered the phone. "Hello?"

"Hi," said the voice at the other end of the line. I recognised her voice; she'd called before. "Is that Maggie?"

"Yes it is."

Idle Hands

"Oh, great. It's Patricia here, calling from the hospital. I have somebody here who'd like to speak with you."

My heart skipped a couple of beats. Who? One of the doctors? Did they need to tell me that Chris was dead?

And then I heard Chris' voice for what felt like the first time in forever. I couldn't believe it. I was ecstatic. Tears began to roll down my cheeks instantly. I could hardly breathe. "Hello?" I said, the words catching in the back of my throat.

"Hey," said Chris, incredibly nonchalantly. "How's it going?"

"Oh my God!" I said, immediately breaking down in tears. I couldn't breathe. I slumped down onto the floor, where I sat with my back pressed up against the dishwasher. "Is it really you?"

"Yeah, it's me. Don't cry. I'm fine."

"You're not fine!" I said, probably more angrily than I should've done. "You're in hospital! You've been unconscious for three days!"

"I know. But I'm alive, aren't I? The doctors here are incredible. They're doing an amazing job."

I composed myself and climbed back up to my feet. "Can I come and see you?"

"I don't think so. Not until they move me onto one of the normal wards. That might take a few days."

"I *need* to see you."

"Trust me, I'm fine. I'll be home before you know it, ready to finish off that hole in the garden."

"Oh, Jesus Christ – forget about the hole," I said, smiling to myself. As if he was actually thinking about *that* while he was in there. "I'll take care of it. I even did a bit of digging this morning."

"What?" said Chris, seemingly shocked that I'd been out there. "You shouldn't be doing that. It's *my* job."

"It's not a problem. Hey, I even found a bone buried out there. It looks like an animal bone. Any idea what it belongs to?"

"Yeah. Probably Misty, my old Border Collie. She died years ago. I buried her out there."

"Oh, God. Well, thanks for the warning. Am I going to fond the rest of her out there?"

"No, you're not," said Chris. He sounded tense. "Because you're going to stop digging out there. That's *my* job; *I* started it, so *I* want to finish it."

The way Chris was talking sounded very strange. It was as if he were desperate for me to not be out in the garden. I wanted to ask why, but I decided against it – I didn't want to stress him out. "Okay," I said. "I'll leave it for you. I'll find something else to do inside."

"Good. Look, the doctors are doing the rounds. I have to go. I'll speak to you later. Okay?"

"Okay. I love you."

"I love you too. Bye."

"Bye."

I made myself a cup of coffee. That was all I had for lunch - I was no longer hungry. I was so pleased to have heard from Chris, I could feel the smile stretching across my cheeks. I couldn't wait for him to get home, for us to get back to some sort of normality.

Idle Hands

But I couldn't help but feel apprehensive about that hole. Why didn't Chris want me to finish it off?

After I'd finished my coffee, I went back out there and continued to dig.

Slowly but surely, I unearthed more bones, eventually pulling out the skull of a small dog. I was no expert in dogs, but if this was a collie, it must've died young; the skull looked too small to be that of an adult.

That was probably why Chris wanted to dig out here himself. If he'd lost a puppy, digging up those bones would almost certainly bring back those sad memories. He probably felt as though this were something he *had* to do himself.

Poor thing. I probably should've re-buried it, but I decided to leave it to one side, for Chris to take of once he got home.

I continued to dig a little more, until the sun decided to hide itself behind some heavy clouds, which caused the air to grow cold.

I phoned the hospital and spoke to Chris that evening. I told him that I'd dug up the entire skeleton, and that I'd left it to one side for him re-bury, once he got home.

"Okay," he said, his mood seemingly very sombre. "But just leave the garden now. I'll deal with it when I get home."

I had agreed to do so. We spoke for around twenty minutes before he had to go.

I slept well that night, safe in the knowledge that Chris had pulled through. Nothing could've made me happier.

The next morning I decided to keep on digging. As I had previously thought, there was no sense in starting another job and leaving this one unfinished. If Chris was so desperate to help with these jobs, he would be more than welcome to paint the ceilings (they'd started to look a little grey; it wasn't a job I was looking forward to).

I'd probably only been digging for around half an hour when I came across another bone. At first I assumed it was just another from the dog, which I had previously missed. And so I put it with the others.

But then I found another bone. This one was much longer and thicker than the others. It certainly didn't belong to a Collie.

For a brief moment I considered the fact that Chris must've had *another* dog. It would've been a different breed; something big, like a Rottweiler or a St. Bernard.

My train of thought was derailed by the ringing of my phone.

It was the hospital.

I answered it. "Hello?"

"Good morning," said Chris, his voice warm and comforting. I couldn't help but smile.

"How are you today?" I asked.

"Actually, I'm feeling great."

"That's good. Do you think they might move you soon? I can't wait to come and see you."

"I'm not sure. I'll ask later. So, what have you been up to this morning?"

I considered not telling him what I'd actually been doing. He'd asked me not to. But it *needed* to be done. Truth was, even when he *did* get home, he probably wasn't going to be in any fit state to be digging up half the garden. I might as well do it. "I've just been out in the garden," I told him.

"You haven't been digging again, have you?"

"I did a little bit, yeah."

"I thought I told you not to."

His voice was stern. Actually, he sounded pissed off. I didn't know why he'd have been so angry about me digging out there, but I decided against telling him about the bone I'd found.

"It needs doing," I said.

"And I'll do it. I can't very well do it from in the fucking hospital though, can I?"

"No. I know. That's why I decided to do it."

"Well, you need to stop."

"Okay."

"Promise me."

That was such a strange thing for him to want me to promise. What was so wrong with me doing the digging? "I promise," I said.

"Good. Listen, I have to go. I love you."

"I love you too."

"Please stop digging."

"I will."

"Okay. Bye."

"Bye."

I *had* to keep digging. There was something out there that Chris didn't want me to find. I needed to know what it was.

Surely it didn't have anything to do with the bones?

But, as I continued to dig, I began to unearth more and more bones. These bones were bigger than the others; they almost certainly didn't belong to any dog.

No.

This skeleton belonged to a human.

I wasn't certain of this fact until I uncovered the skull. As I planted the spade into the dirt, I felt it scrape against something hard. As I removed the soil, I saw it there, its hollow eye sockets staring up at me.

The phone rang again.

It was Chris.

My heart was racing. A sudden sense of terror rolled over me. Why the *fuck* was there a human skeleton buried in the garden.

I couldn't let Chris know what I'd found. Not yet, anyway. I knew that there might be an innocent explanation for its being there – perhaps Chris wasn't aware that it was there – but I couldn't let Chris know that I knew, not until I was sure.

"Hello?" I said, as I answered the phone, doing my best to prevent my voice from wavering.

"Hey," said Chris, jovially. "I've got some good news; they've said you can come and visit me!"

"Oh. Really. That's great."

"Yeah. So, are you coming, or what?"

"Right now?"

"Yeah. Right now."

He sounded very insistent. But I didn't want to go. There was something troubling me, eating away at me. I decided to lie to him. I said – "Oh… I'm busy right now. I'll come up later."

"Busy, doing what?"

"Just tidying the lounge," I said, lying once again.

"Well that can wait. I want you to come now. Don't you want to see me? "

"Of course I do. I just…"

"So come now."

"Okay. Just give me an hour."

"No. Come now."

It was obvious that Chris wanted to get me out of the house. For one reason or another, he was trying to disrupt my day. "Okay. I'll get changed and then I'll come."

"Good. I'll see you soon."

"Yes. I can't wait to see you," I said, nervously. I hoped that he couldn't sense the apprehension in my voice. I wasn't going - I hoped he couldn't tell this either.

"Bye."

"Bye."

I went back outside and continued to dig. I'm not sure why, but something was compelling me to do so. I had a bad feeling about what I was about to find.

I pulled the skull from the ground. The back of it was missing, a large hole having been cracked into the bone.

I placed the skull to one side and went back to work.

I fully expected to find the rest of the skeleton. What I hadn't expected to find was another skull.

But there it was, staring up at me, just as the other had been.

There were two bodies down there…

I removed the dirt from around the second skull and pulled it from the ground. Immediately I noticed that the back of this skull had been broken, just as the other had.

I placed it onto the patio, next to the other one.

As I unearthed more bones, I laid them out beneath each of the respective skulls, assembling them, like macabre jigsaw puzzles, into complete skeletons.

As I removed the fifth femur from the ground, I realised I would be finding more than just the two corpses buried under our lawn.

I laid the skeletons out, piece by piece. Of course, I couldn't be sure that each bone belonged to each respective skull, but I wasn't too concerned about that; I just wanted to know how many bodies were down there.

So far I had uncovered six skulls, with many of the bones to complete their skeletons.

I continued to dig, eventually unearthing a seventh skull. I swept the dirt away and lifted it from the hole. Turning it over in my hands, I found that the back of this skull had been broken out, as had all of the others.

"I think that one belonged to a woman named Suzanne," said a voice from behind me.

My heart sank. Fear pulsed through my entire being.

I turned. Chris stood behind me. He'd come in through the gate. How had I not heard him? "I thought you were still in the hospital," I said, stupidly.

"I was," said Chris, as he slowly closed the gate behind him. "But you were supposed to come and see me. When you didn't show up, I thought I'd best come and check up on you."

"I... I..."

Chris ignored my stuttering. He said - "I picked her up at a bar, maybe, nine years ago now, I think. It wasn't long after I'd moved in here, anyway.

Idle Hands

She came willingly. She must've thought we were just gonna have sex. Obviously, she wasn't aware that I was going through some psychological issues."

"I... She..." I stuttered again.

Once again Chris ignored me.

"I expect you're wondering why she's missing the back of her skull. That's where I caved her head in with a hammer."

I could feel myself shaking. As he spoke, Chris continued to take small steps towards me. Slowly, I inched myself backwards.

"After I'd broken her skull open, I scooped her brain out. She was like a fuckin' human egg!" Chris was laughing. "Human brain doesn't taste like egg though. It's more like tripe. It's not very nice."

I was terrified. I didn't know what he might do to me. He was a psychopath – I'd been *living* with a psychopath! He was moving closer to me. I wanted to turn and run, but my whole body ached. I could barely move.

"I kept her body for a few days. I had sex with it a few times. But they start to stink after a week or so, so I chopped her into pieces and buried her out here."

I couldn't believe what I was hearing. Had Chris really done those things? Was this some sort of sick joke? The look on his face told me that he was deadly serious. There was a coldness behind his eyes that I hadn't ever seen before. He looked like a different person.

He looked mad.

"I couldn't tell you exactly who all the others are. One is Maria, the first girl who lived here with me. She was actually the third person I killed. I *had* to kill her, because she caught me fucking the corpse of the second girl I'd killed."

He was smiling. He looked deranged. I knew now that he intended to kill me.

Chris continued - "Then there's Sue and Annie. Annie was my last girlfriend before you came along. I killed her simply because I'd grown bored of her. But *you* were never boring. I never would've killed *you*. I loved you. Why did you have to go digging around out here? I told you not to."

He was almost nose to nose with me now.

"I never wanted to kill you," he said. "But now you've left me no choice."

I reached behind me. My hand fell on the spade. I wrapped my fingers around it and swung.

Chris groaned as the steel of the spade slammed into the side of his head.

I dropped the spade and pushed past him.

But it was no good. I hadn't hit him hard enough. In my mind, he'd have dropped to the floor, unconscious. But he simply stood there, blocking my path.

He grabbed me by the waist, lifted me up, then slammed me down onto the patio. The bones of the other women scattered here, there and everywhere. The back of my head smashed painfully against the concrete slabs.

I was dazed. White lines zipped across my eyes like shooting stars.

When my vision finally returned to me, I found Chris now standing over me. He was holding the spade. He'd placed it under my chin and had pushed my head back. I could feel the steel pressing against my trachea.

"I'm sorry," said Chris. "I hate to do this to you, but you really should've just left the hole to me."

He placed his foot on the back of the spade and pushed.

I tried to scream, but it was futile. I felt the cartilage in my neck crack (I could *hear* it snapping). I felt my skin begin to tear. I felt the warmth of my blood as it began to leak from my body. I felt the vertebrae of my neck begin to separate as the spade was forced through my spinal column.

And then I was dead, my head removed with a spade, by the only man I'd ever really loved.

THE END

Harrison Phillips

MUM

I'll always remember the first time.

I know what you're thinking - you're thinking *"She means the first time she had sex."* Well, no, actually. Although I do remember that quite well, despite the whole event being somewhat forgettable: I was only 14 at the time. My partner was 18. Saying that right now makes it sound weird, like he was some kind of abuser. I was still just a girl (I'd only just gotten my first period, if I remember rightly), yet he was a man. Nowadays, he'd be seen as some kind of a sexual predator. But it wasn't like that at all. I loved him and he loved me. We'd been together for a few weeks when it happened. Truth be told, it was me who instigated it. I was ready and I wanted it. The whole thing was clumsy and awkward, lasting little more than a minute. He hadn't worn protection (not his fault - I hadn't asked him to), so I'd had to take a trip to the doctors, to request a morning after pill. I still remember my embarrassment, as both the receptionist and the nurse I spoke to looked at me with some level of disgust, as if I'd done something wrong.

I'd gone on the pill not long after that, and I hadn't come off it until I met Spencer (that must have been around 14 years ago now).

But I'll come back to him later.

No, the 'first time' I'm referring to is something wholly different and far more disturbing.

The first time to which I am referring would be the first time that I had to remove a mutilated corpse from my house.

I found the body in the middle of my kitchen floor. The poor girl had been stabbed numerous times and her throat had been slashed so deep that I'm sure I could see her spine, deep in the wound. She lay in a pool of her own blood, which spread several feet from her carcass, and had followed the pattern dictated by the grouting between the tiles.

One of the dining room chairs had been dragged into the kitchen - through the blood, smearing it along the floor, leaving trails behind the feet - and positioned next to the breakfast counter. It was here that I had found my son - standing on the chair, spreading margarine onto a slice of bread. He'd taken it upon himself to make a cheese sandwich. This was something I'd taught him not too long before - he was only 6 at this point, so he wasn't allowed to use the 'sharp knives'. He was however, allowed to butter his own bread. The thing was, on this occasion, he *had* sliced his own cheese, and he had done so with the knife he had used to murder the babysitter.

Toby smiled at me, showing off his pearly white teeth (he was missing two - one at the top, one at the bottom). "Hi Mum," he'd said, in is most angelic voice.

Idle Hands

I seem to remember having stood there for hours. I couldn't see myself, of course, but I imagine the colour had drained from my face, and that my jaw was hanging wide open. I'd just gotten in from a date - the first date I'd been on since Spencer and I had separated. It had been a nice night. The guy - a man named Harvey, who I knew from work - had been a real gentleman. He'd taken my coat, escorted me to my seat, laughed at my jokes and had, in general, just been good company. Being the true gent, he had, of course, paid for dinner. We'd shared a taxi home and he'd walked me to my front door. We'd kissed and I'd wanted to invite him in. Before I had chance though, he had wished me good night, told me he'd love to do it again some time, then disappeared off in the taxi. *What a gentleman.* And *thank God* I hadn't invited him in.

My heart was racing, and my head was pounding. I was drunk, but the alcohol in system was urging me to just turn and run - *you can deal with this later!*

Of course, I couldn't deal with it later - I had to deal with it there and then.

"What's wrong, Mum?" said Toby, as he laid the second slice of bread onto his sandwich.

I could barely form the words. It was as if the air had vanished from my lungs. "Wh… wha… what…" I stuttered. "What have you done?"

"Huh?" said Toby, picking up the sandwich and taking a bite. The blood from his fingers stained the white bread, while more blood oozed over the crust, where the knife had transferred it to the sliced cheese.

"Toby!" I shouted, a sudden and strange anger filling my being. "What the fuck have you done!"

"Don't swear Mum. That's naughty."

I wanted to tell him off, as though he'd just done something naughty, such as break one of his toys, or drop food on the floor intentionally. But this was far more serious than that. Scolding the boy wouldn't help matters. I needed to think straight. "I'm sorry," I said, fully aware of the irony of apologising to my 6-year-old psychopath. "Mummy is just tired." I still referred to myself as 'Mummy', despite the fact that Toby had never called me this - he always just called me 'Mum'.

I should've known this day was coming. There had been plenty of warning signs. I should've known that there was something wrong with him, that something wasn't right with his brain.

I wanted to blame his father - Spencer. We had met through mutual friends, when we were both 28 (I was actually older - but only by a month). We hit it off straight away. It was as if we'd known each other for years. We started dating, then moved in together 3 months later. I found out I was pregnant on my 30th birthday. By that point, I'd missed two periods, so I'd bought a home testing kit from the pharmacy. For some reason - and I'm not sure what that reason was - I've decided to save the test for my birthday. It was as if I would be giving myself the most wonderful present. When the test came back positive, I was ecstatic. Spencer had arranged for us to go to a rather expensive restaurant that evening. I decided to tell him there. What had started out as the most glorious of days soon descended to the worst, as when I told

Idle Hands

Spencer what I believed to be the most amazing news, he looked less than thrilled.

He just stared at me - and I stared in return - for what seemed like almost an hour. Even as the waiter delivered are started to the table, Spencer's eyes remained fixed on mine. When he finally spoke, his voice was low and gravelly. He sounded angry. "You can't be," he said. "You told me you were on the pill."

"I am," came my reply. "But as you well know, these things don't work 100% of the time."

Spencer looked down at his food. I could see he was thinking. When his eyes return to mine, he said - "You need to get an abortion."

I felt my heart tear itself in two. I couldn't quite believe the words that were coming from his mouth. I had a thought he loved me. I certainly loved him. And then he said something even more crushing - "I'm leaving you."

A sudden rage filled every inch of my body. "What?" I had practically screamed at him over the table. I wasn't aware of it at the time, but I imagine everybody in the restaurant was watching us. Or, watching me, more specifically. "You're leaving me? Right now? Right after I've told you I'm pregnant? Is this some kind of joke?"

"No. It's not a joke. I didn't ask you to get pregnant. Things just aren't working out between us anymore."

"What the fuck are you talking about?" I could feel my blood boiling. "I thought we were happy."

"*You* might be, but *I'm* not."

"Why? What's changed? Don't you love me anymore?"

Spencer side. It was as if he was bored. This had made me even angrier. "No," he said. "I don't love you anymore."

"Why?"

"If you must know, I'm seeing someone else. I love her."

Suddenly the anger had gone. A deep sense of sorrow had taken its place. I began to cry, heavy tears streaming down my cheeks. And the worst if it was, Spencer didn't even care. He said - "It's over. We're done. I don't want to ever see you again. What you decide to do with that baby, that's up to you. But I want nothing to do with it." and then he stood up and left, leaving me - his sobbing, distraught girlfriend - alone at the table, everybody in the room staring at me.

And that, indeed, *was* the last time I ever saw him. He never even came back for his clothes. He just left them there, in our house. I'd had one hell of a good time burning them. And how does that make him responsible for the fact that his child is a psychopath? I'm not sure. It probably doesn't. But it makes things slightly easier for me when I remember how much of a bastard his father was. Sometimes I imagine that he was pure evil. Perhaps he was a psychopath himself, and I just didn't know it. Sometimes, I even imagine that he was the spawn of Satan himself. *Ridiculous*, I know. But, perhaps being an adulterous dickhead isn't too far away from being a psychopathic murderer.

Anyway - those warning signs that I should have spotted:

Toby had never been able to keep a pet. The first hamster I'd bought him - I think he was 4 at the time - had met a grisly end, when it fell from Toby's bedroom window. Toby had insisted it was an accident, that he'd been playing with the hamster - Coco was its name - on the windowsill, when he'd fallen. The poor creature had made quite a mess on the patio, its crumpled body seemingly having exploded as it hit the ground. Even then, I didn't believe that it was an accident. I could just picture Toby holding the hamster out of the window at arm's length and dropping him.

Poor Coco.

Stupidly, and despite my belief that Toby had killed his pet, I went and bought him another.

He called this one Fluffy. I found Toby dismembering Fluffy over the kitchen sink, less than week after I'd brought him home. Toby had insisted that he'd found Fluffy dead in his cage, and that he was only cutting him up as a... What was it he had said? Ah yes... As a "Science experiment."

I didn't believe his story. The fact that there was blood all over the kitchen tops made it look as though the poor animal had struggled, fighting for its life. Indeed, there were even little bloody paw prints on one of the worktops, where - in my mind - the little hamster had struggled free, already bleeding to death, and had made a run for it across the surface. Toby had caught him though - Fluffy's decapitated head now sat at one side of the draining board, with each of his little severed legs lined up beside it. As I found him, Toby was currently fishing the guts out of the hamster's opened-up chest cavity.

Poor Fluffy.

I never bought him another pet after that. I just *knew* he'd killed those animals, but what was I supposed to do about it? He was my little boy, just a child. He didn't know any better. At least, that's what I thought at the time. Perhaps I should've taken him to the doctors. They could've gotten him a psychological analysis. Perhaps they could've fixed him. But I had worried that they might take him away from me. And what if they blamed me? What if they said this was all *my fault?* No. We'd just forget about it. If I didn't buy him any more pets, he'd soon forget any enjoyment he'd gotten out of killing them.

How wrong could I have been?

I began finding the bodies of dead cats in the house. They were always horribly mutilated. I'll never forget the one I found in the garage: its tail had been cut off, as had all four of its paws. Its ears had been sliced off its head and its eyes had been gouged out. From one of the empty sockets protruded a long, rusted nail. The cat - a tabby I recognised as belonging to one of our neighbour's - laid in a pool of its own blood. I'd wanted to scream, but I'd cupped my hand to my mouth, preventing it from escaping. I didn't want Toby to know that I'd found it, or that it horrified me. I knew I'd have to clean this up, so I crouched to pick up the carcass. As I laid my hand on its body, the cat lifted its head and croaked a half-hearted meow, scaring me half to death. The poor creature began to writhe in agony, its pawless legs sweeping arcs through the blood, the stump of its tail convulsing, as if to wave the tail that was no longer there.

I ran from the garage crying. I cleaned it up later that night, once the cat had - thankfully - passed away.

Idle Hands

I also remember the time I'd walked into the house to find a horrible, bitter scent hanging in the air. I'd followed the scent to Toby's bedroom. As I opened the door, I quickly discovered what that scent was - burning hair.

In the middle of his floor, was an overturned steel cage - the sort of thing you sometimes see bread delivered to supermarkets in. Inside the cage was a small kitten. It was on fire, hissing and squealing, bouncing around the cage, ramming itself against the metal. Eventually the flames died out.

"Toby," I said, once I'd mustered the courage. "What are you doing?"

"Watch this Mum!" said Toby, his voice full of jubilance. "Watch how kitty dances when I burn her!"

I don't know where he'd found the propane burner - it certainly didn't belong to me - but with a click and hiss as Toby pulled the trigger, the flame ignited. Her then poked it between the bars of the cage, aimed directly at the young cat. The animal screamed as its fur began to singe. Then finally it was alight and once again throwing itself around the cage in an effort to extinguish itself.

Toby was laughing.

Disgusted, I matched across the room. "Toby! You stop this at once!" I'd already made up my mind that I was going to hit him. It was what he needed. It was what he deserved.

But as I neared him, he spun and pointed to flaming burner at me. Needless to say, I stopped dead in my tracks. I was shocked, suddenly fearing for my life.

The words Toby then said still haunt me to this day - "Do *you* want to dance, Mum? Will *you* dance if I set you on fire?"

I ran from that bedroom and locked myself in the bathroom. I stayed there for at least an hour, crying the entire time. I thought about what I should do - what I *needed* to do. And then I thought about whether I could go through with it or not. I decided that I couldn't. That was another occasion I blamed his father - if he'd been there to set an example for him, perhaps none of this would ever have happened. Or he could've given him a beating, straightened him out.

All of this occurred before Toby was even five. I had assumed that things would only escalate, getting worse and worse until he finally killed a person - even kill me, perhaps. But things did improve. After he'd burned the cat - disposing of that body had been the worst experience of my life - he just seemed to give up. It was like torturing and murdering small animals had been a hobby - now he wanted to take up something else. There were no more dead animals, no more threats of violence towards *me*. Everything just went back to normal.

After around a year of peace, I'd decided to allow myself some humanity. That was when I decided to start dating again. For more than a year, Toby had never been out of my sight, except for when I was at work and he was at school - who had assured me they had seen no changes in Toby's behaviour (I hadn't, of course, gone into detail about my own concerns).

Harvey had asked me out on a date. I said yes. I hired a babysitter - her name was Lucy. It was her body I found, with her throat sliced, on the kitchen floor.

And that brings me back to where I started - the first time I disposed of a human body.

Part of me wanted to scream. Part of me wanted to run and call the police. But I did neither of those things. He was just an innocent boy - he didn't even seem to understand what he'd done. So, I cuddled him. I picked him up and carried him into the lounge, where we sat on the floor - him on my lap, nuzzled into my bosom - and I rocked back and forth, kissing his forehead, while singing nursery rhymes.

I decided to dispose of the body. I couldn't let them take him away. They wouldn't understand him, not like I did. He needed his mother's love. It was me he needed to protect him, to nurture him - not anybody else.

That night I tucked Toby up in bed and read him a story. His favourite - 'Hansel and Gretel'. As I read it to him, at the moment Gretel pushes the witch into the oven, my mind drifted back to the time I found Toby burning that poor kitten. Once again, I began to cry. *How could I be so stupid?* This was all my fault - it was up to me to put it right.

Once I was sure that Toby was asleep, I headed back down to the kitchen, where Lucy's corpse still lay, sprawled on the tile. I knew there were some tools in the shed, just another relic that Spencer had left behind. I checked and found just what I was looking for - a saw. I then took to task cutting the body into small, manageable pieces. I cut off the hands, then cut the arm into two pieces at the elbow. I then removed what remained at the shoulder. I did the same with the legs - I cut them into three pieces; at the ankle, the knee, and the hip. The head came off surprisingly easily - Toby had already done much of the hard work for me. It was the torso, however, that caused me the greatest dilemma. It was quite big, and I found it to still be quite heavy. I wasn't sure whether I should cut it into smaller pieces or not. I decided my best bet would be to hollow it out. I cut open the stomach, then scooped as much of the innards out as I could, dumping them into a black bin liner. I was then able to cut the torso into two pieces, directly down the middle.

With each of the individual parts wrapped up in a plastic carrier bag, I then stuffed it all into a large holdall that I had found under the bed (I believe this probably belonged to Spencer too). I took this to my local landfill site the very next day and dumped it with the rest of the rubbish.

The police knocked on my door a few days later, having traced back Lucy's last known whereabouts to me. I'd booked her through an online agency and apparently, they kept records of all their provider's jobs. I told them that Lucy had left only moments after I arrived home - she took her pay and went. They seemed to believe me. They weren't considering foul play here - they were assuming she'd run off with her boyfriend (whom I then found out was a known drug dealer). They never came back after that.

I had hoped, wished, prayed that this would be the end of it. But I knew it wouldn't. How could it be?

Toby killed another seven people - that I knew of - before his thirteenth birthday. Every single one of them, I had to dispose of.

Idle Hands

I can remember every single one of them, too. I won't go into too much detail now, as it no longer seems necessary. But, needless to say, each one of the killings was more horrific than the last. They were all children - Toby's friends or classmates, or local children from the neighbourhood. Every one of them, I had dismembered and dumped at the landfill. I *had* to do it. God knows I didn't *want* to. But I couldn't allow my son to be locked away in some stinking prison, or - worse - an insane asylum. He'd almost certainly lose his mind, confined to a single space for 24 hours a day. I mean, *who wouldn't?* My Toby - my precious little boy - deserved better than that.

So, I did what any doting mother would do when their child makes a mistake - I fixed it.

Sometimes I wondered if Toby even realised what he was doing. Once, I walked into his bedroom - he must've been eight or nine at the time - and found him playing with some action figures on his bed. He'd turned his pillow into a fortress, and the good guys were trying to break in to get the bad guys. It was lovely to see him playing so nicely with his toys. Unfortunately, that was spoiled by the fact that there was the body of a young girl in the middle of the floor, her head cut off, the blood leaking from her carcass staining the carpet. And Toby seemed to be almost oblivious to the fact that she was even there. I asked him who it was; he just shrugged his shoulders. Still, to this day, I have no idea who that girl was, or where Toby had taken her from. But, as I now felt was my duty, I dissected her corpse and dumped it in the landfill.

I said that Toby killed another seven people before his 13th birthday - the reason I mention his birthday is because, after that, the killing stopped. Actually, the last body I had to remove from the house - that of another young girl (the poor mite was probably only three), whom I found tied to the dining room table, with the top of her head cut off and her brain removed - had been about a month or two before his birthday. And that was it - no more dismembered young girls for me to dispose of.

It was as if things just suddenly went back to normal after that. I say *'went back to normal'*, as if they once were. Things have never been normal, not since Toby came along. But it began to *feel* normal, like what I imagined normal to be. Toby was doing well at school, especially in Biology (which I thought was probably due to his experience cutting up human bodies (with some morbid amusement, I must admit)). He even got himself a girlfriend. Her name was Annie. She was a pretty girl, with long, red hair. I was worried sick that things wouldn't go well for her. But things did go well - great, in fact. They really seemed to like each other. It was nice to see him happy.

It was nice for *me* to be happy for a change, too. It was nice not to have to worry about coming home and finding blood all over the house, and a butchered corpse stashed away somewhere. There were the homeless people who were being killed around town, their throats slashed while they slept. But that might not have been Toby - I really don't know. If it was, I was just happy - selfishly, I know - that they weren't being killed in my home.

So, yes - more than two years went by without a single incident.

Until tonight that is.

Idle Hands

Toby had split up with Annie a few days ago. Actually, I think she dumped him. I don't know why. I did try to talk to Toby about it, but he just skirted around the subject.

And now, I am sitting here on the floor of my kitchen, in a pool of blood, my back resting against the freezer. Before me is Eric. His throat has been cut deep, right to his vertebrae, just like Lucy - the babysitter - Toby's first victim, nearly ten years ago now.

Eric is my new partner. Or, at least, he *was* my new partner. Not anymore, I guess. We have… We *had* been together for over a year now. We met at work. That thing with Harvey never worked out. I couldn't let it. Finding my son standing over a dead body in my kitchen had kind-of soured our first date. But more so, I couldn't bring anyone new into my life - our lives - not with Toby the way he was.

But as things settled down and the killings stopped, I decided it was finally time to get back on the horse, so to speak. Harvey had gone off to work somewhere abroad (this would've been about a year after our first date - see, it never would've worked out anyway). Another guy had been brought in to do his job. He left a few years later. Eric was *his* replacement.

Eric was tall and broad. You could practically see the muscles flexing under his shirt. His hair had already gone grey - he was five years older than I was - but he wore it confidently. That was what attracted me to him the most - the confidence practically dripped from his pores. But he wasn't arrogant with it. Far from it. He was just a nice, regular guy.

We dated for over nine months, before deciding to move in together. I loved him - truly, I did - and he loved me. It made perfect sense.

It was great. He and Toby got on like a house on fire. They played video games and watched football together. *Finally,* I had thought. *A strong male role model for him to look up to.*

And then, we come to tonight.

I left the house about an hour ago. I was only popping to the supermarket, to pick up some bits and pieces. We needed some milk, and I was going to cook us a lasagne - both Toby and Eric professed that this was their favourite. I got everything I needed, then came home. No problem. But as soon as I walked through the door, I knew something was up. It was *too* quiet.

"Hello?" I had called out. I got no response. I tried again, still no response. That was when I entered the kitchen, and my heart sank.

Now that I think about it, Eric was probably the first man I'd ever really loved. I *thought* I had loved Spencer, but now, I have to admit that I was probably too young to really know what love felt like. And the love I feel for Toby is something entirely different. I'm not sure it even is love. Surely love wouldn't be something you needed to work so hard at, would it?

Immediately, I rushed over to where Eric lay, screaming his name, knowing full well that he was already dead. As my foot landed in his blood, I slipped on the lubricated tile. I lost my balance and crashed to the floor, bouncing from one of the cupboards, its contents (there are mugs and glasses in that one) rattling loudly inside. I landed awkwardly on my knees. A pain shot through my right leg. It was nothing. I then dragged myself the final foot to where Eric's corpse lay. I hadn't realised it, but I was crying. Floods of tears were streaming down my face. I can still feel those tears on my cheeks, although they are dry now and I am no longer crying.

I hadn't noticed at first, but - just like Lucy - Eric had also been stabbed multiple times. It wasn't until my hand landed on the handle of the knife that was still embedded in his chest that I *did* notice. Sobbing, feeling crushed, as though the weight of the world was bearing down on me, I pulled the knife from his chest. It was in there deep. I imagine it had pierced his heart.

"Hi Mum," said Toby, from somewhere behind me. "When's dinner gonna be done? I'm *starving*!"

I think my heart may have stopped beating then. I was no longer alive. There was no *me* anymore - all that was left was burning rage.

I stood to face Toby. Had I have been anybody else, surely, I would've been terrified. But not me - this was *my* son standing before me. No - this was not my son; this was a monster. And I did not fear him. "What the fuck have you done!" I yelled, my anger boiling over and spilling as foul language. "You little fucking bastard! Why? Why? Why would you do this? What did he ever do to you?"

"Mum? What's wrong? Are you upset about something?"

"Upset? Are you fucking serious? What kind of an idiot are you? I know - one who gets his kicks out of murdering helpless others."

"What are you talking about?"

"Why are you such a monster? Was it something I did?"

"Mum... Please... You're scaring me."

Suddenly it dawned on me - he really didn't know what he had done. He wasn't aware of his actions, or the hurt he had inflicted on others. I'm not sure if that *is* psychopathy, or if it's something entirely different. But he just didn't see a person when he looked at somebody else - be it you or me. He lacked that ability - possibly to most basic of human traits.

Perhaps he *was* a monster after all.

Whatever he was, I felt sorry for him. I crossed the room and took his head in my hand. *He* was crying now - his head on my shoulder, I rubbed his back as he sobbed with deep, retching breaths.

And then I plunged the knife into his chest. I had aimed for his heart.

Toby gasped, the air trapped in his throat. I felt his body tense. But he didn't say anything. It was as if he knew this was for the best, like a sick dog being put out of its misery. I wondered if he felt angry - another basic human emotion. I wondered if he was confused. I don't think he saw that I was still holding the knife I'd pulled from Eric's chest.

Truth be told - I didn't really care.

I felt his knees give way beneath him. His body slumped against mine, pushing me back against the oven. I slid down the glass front, to the floor, Toby looking up at me.

And this is where you find me now - my dying son lying on the floor, his head in my lap. Blood is pouring from the wound in his chest. I removed the knife, you see, twisting it as I did so. Toby's face had screwed itself into a ball. The pain he was in obvious.

Idle Hands

I didn't care though. He deserved it.

And now, as look down into my dying son's eyes, he looks back at me. "I love you Mum," he says.

I think about how much I hate him. I think about everything he's done - everything he's made *me* do. I think about Spencer. I think about Eric. I wonder how my life could've been different had Toby never been born. I think about my life as it would've been, had I have never met Spencer. Perhaps if I'd have met Eric first, I'd be happy now. Perhaps we might've had a normal child.

"I love you too Son," I tell him.

THE END

Harrison Phillips

DON'T LISTEN

Evan Harlow picked up the bottle of icy cold water and poured it over the head of Jackson Green, startling him back into consciousness. It was mildly satisfying, seeing the shocked expression on his face as he came to. He never would've expected to find himself tired to a chair in the middle of a large industrial storage unit, with its corrugated steel walls and its bare concrete floor.

I mean, why would he?

Evan tossed the now-empty bottle to one side. It clattered against the wall, the sound echoing loudly throughout the unit.

A pair of fluorescent strip lights offered the only light inside the unit. They were bright. They cast sharp, dark shadows across Jackson's face as he looked up at Evan, who towered over him.

And then Evan crouched, now face-to-face with Jackson. He needed to look this young man – he was only twenty-six years old – in the eye. Evan smiled. "Hey," he said, his voice monotonous. "You in there? You hear me? Do you know who I am?"

Jackson couldn't reply - Evan had, of course, tied a gag tightly around his mouth. He'd have been stupid *not* to do so.

But Jackson nodded affirmative. Of course he knew who he was – Evan didn't really need to ask. Jackson had been watching him (and his girlfriend of seven years, Felicity) very closely, for – as best Evan could tell – the past few months.

"Good. Then you understand why we're here, don't you?"

Jackson nodded again.

Evan straightened up and inhaled deeply through his nose. He turned and looked at the various supplies he'd bought with him. There was a small wooden crate. Inside the crate was a length of rope. There was also a knife.

And then there was his gun.

"I'm sure then," Evan continued. "That you understand just *what* I'm going to do to you, and just how *painful* I intend to make it."

Jackson was staring, wide-eyed, like a deer caught in the headlights of the truck that would, almost certainly, erase it from existence in a bloody smear of gore on the road. He muttered something unintelligible through the gag.

Evan snorted back a laugh. "Don't even bother. You seriously think I'm going to fall for your tricks?" He felt a tear roll down his cheek. He'd been unaware of the fact that his eyes were filling once again. He wiped the tear away with the back of his hand.

Evan crouched and took the knife from the crate. Slowly, he stood and approached Jackson, turning the knife over in his hand. "You know what? I really wish we could talk. I wish I could ask you questions, *without* the possibility of you playing your mind games on me. But I know that isn't possible. I know that the first chance you get, you'll put your ideas in my head."

Evan lifted the knife. The light of the bare tubes reflected harshly from the stainless steel. He could see his own reflection in the blade, no more than a featureless silhouette against the bright fluorescents behind him.

"What would you have me do, I wonder? Would you have me slash my own throat? Would you have me gut myself?"

Evan was a great detective, one of the best on the force. He could piece together seemingly unrelated evidence in ways that most other detectives never could. To most onlookers, oftentimes it would appear as though his thoughts were wondering off track, following leads that just didn't exist. He had lost track of the number of times people had told him to drop one lead or another. *'You're putting two and two together and coming out with five'* was an analogy he had heard more times than he cared to recall. But his persistence had *always* paid off. He *always* got his man.

He'd seen a lot of things during his time on the force. Almost every day of the week was spent in pursuit of (or in the presence of) serial killers and rapists and paedophiles. He'd met a lot of sick individuals. But he'd never met anyone quite like Jackson Green before.

Jackson Green was a sick man. He was a serial killer, who got his kicks from murdering innocent people. Almost all of his victims were strangers to him – he'd killed them simply for his own pleasure. And there were lots of them. Nobody knew for sure how many, but Evan – having gone through thousands of records, spanning, at the very least, the past ten years – had estimated the number to be well over a hundred. But Jackson had never been brought to justice, the reason being that nobody had ever known any crime to have even *been* committed. Most people never considered his victims to actually *be* victims. Most of the time, his crimes were considered *not* to be crimes at all.

But the idea that there was even a serial killer on the loose didn't just spring itself upon Evan. Oh no. Nobody had even contemplated the idea until Jackson himself had phoned the station and confessed to his crimes. And even then, most people (Joe in particular, God rest his soul) had considered him to be some kind of attention-seeking crank – the murders he had confessed to had all been ruled as *suicides*. It wasn't until Evan had connected the dots that people began to realise that maybe - *just maybe* - there was something more to these deaths than they had first realised.

There were suspicious circumstances around many of the deaths. The victims *had* killed themselves, of this there was no question. But, in almost all cases, there was no reason for them to have done so. The vast majority of his victims had been happy, healthy people, with stable jobs and stable lives, with husbands and wives and kids at home. And even if they had wanted to kill themselves, there was never any reason for them to do it in the *way* that they did. Most of them killed themselves in public, in crowded areas, packed with people. And they always killed themselves in horrible, painful, bloody ways.

Idle Hands

Investigations at the time had suggested that the ways in which some of these people had killed themselves would have been impossible for anybody to do without the help of some outside assistance. Take, for example, the death of Charlie Weston. He was thirty-four years old. He had a well-paid job, working as a mortgage advisor. He owned a nice house, on the outskirts of the city. He had a beautiful fiancé – she was due to give birth to his first child within a matter of weeks. He had very little reason to want to kill himself. Yet, on one warm and sunny day two years ago, he'd walked into the middle of a packed market square and, after calling for everybody's attention, proceeded to decapitate himself with a battery-powered circular saw. It had sounded unbelievable at first, but Evan had seen the CCTV footage for himself. Charlie had taken the circular saw and sliced into the side of his neck. Blood had poured profusely from the wound. At the rate at which the blood had leaked from his body, he *should've* lost consciousness almost instantaneously. But he didn't. He had swapped the saw into his opposite hand and cut into the other side of his neck. He had then slashed back and forth until the blade had severed his spinal column. Only when his head hit the floor, did Charlie's corpse drop.

It was bizarre. It seemed impossible. In the end, it was concluded that Charlie must've been under the influence of drugs, despite the fact that the toxicology report stated otherwise.

That same conclusion was drawn when Sandra Baker-Scott – the wife of Alistair Baker-Scott, the billionaire entrepreneur (he had made his name as the inventor of the *RoboVac 3000*) – had walked, completely naked, onto the crowded playground of their youngest son's primary school, and repeatedly slammed her own head into the brick wall of the building. The teachers had tried to stop her, but to no avail. She had easily shrugged them off as she continued to head-butt the wall. Soon enough, her skin split and peeled away, revealing the skull below. But still she did not stop. Over and over and over again, she cracked her head against the brick, until her skull fractured and splintered, exposing her brain. Her son had to watch as his mother smashed her own head into an unrecognizable pulp, before finally dropping dead on the tarmac floor of the playground.

Again, it was all down to the drugs.

That didn't make much sense to Evan, especially as the toxicology reports showed that this wasn't the case. But, at the time, there was no better explanation, so he'd gone along with it.

But now he knew differently.

Evan crouched before Jackson once again. He placed the tip of the knife blade against the bare skin of his thigh and pressed, using just enough force to break the skin and draw blood.

Jackson winced in pain.

"I wish..." Evan said, before pausing, thinking. "I wish you could tell me how you did it. How did you manage to convince all those people to do such horrible things to themselves? How did you convince Felicity to do what she did?"

Evan didn't know *how*, but Jackson was able to simply *tell* his victims to kill themselves and they'd do it. However he told them to do it, no matter how painful and cruel it may have been, they'd do it. They had no choice in the matter. Evan put it down to a

Idle Hands

powerful form of hypnotism – something to do with the *way* he spoke. And that was all it took – a few words and they were little more than his puppets, his to do with as he pleased.

And what he most often pleased was to have them kill themselves in the most horrifying and violent of ways.

Jackson had made people jump from the roofs of high-rise buildings. He'd made them jump in front of oncoming trains. He'd made people dismember themselves. He'd made them eviscerate themselves. He'd made people drown themselves and set themselves on fire.

There was one victim – Cathy Arnold was her name – who had sat on a bench in the middle of a busy bus station and began to carve the meat from her own thighs, eating the flesh that she peeled away. She managed to get down to the bone of her left leg – and halfway through her right – before she actually bled to death.

But Jackson had clearly grown bored of killing people and not receiving any credit for his work. Serial killers crave the attention that comes with the things they do. They *need* that recognition. But Jackson didn't receive any attention. Nobody even knew there was a killer to talk about. It was then that the phone calls had started. He had wanted to play games with the police – a little cat and mouse – daring them to try and catch him.

It wasn't Evan that had first spoken with Jackson – that dubious honour went to Evan's colleague, a man named Joseph Stevens. Joe (as he insisted everybody call him) was a great detective. He was kind and funny. He loved his wife, Sophia, and their two kids. But he was also a bit of a hard ass. He took no shit from the scumbags he plucked from the streets. Evan liked that about him. He liked it a lot.

Joe had initially dismissed Jackson's calls as those of a prankster. But as the calls continued and Jackson – who made no attempt to hide his identity – began to make more serious threats, Joe began to take him more seriously. When Jackson told Joe that he was planning to kill somebody at the opening of a new amateur production of 'West Side Story' (which, it just so happened, was taking place that very night), Joe had insisted it was nonsense. Regardless of this fact, he and Evan had decided to attend anyway. They watched the audience closely. At no point did anybody look as though they were ready to top themselves. But then, during the finale, as the ensemble cast belted out a rather good rendition of the closing song, the actress playing Maria doused herself in gasoline and set herself on fire. Shrieks and screams had flooded the auditorium as that poor woman stood motionless on the stage, engulfed in flames. She was still singing.

As unbelievable as it seemed, it did appear possible that Jackson had played some part in all of these people's suicides. Joe still insisted it was drugs. He accepted that Jackson was involved somehow, but he was working on the assumption that Jackson was drugging his victims, using some kind of powerful hallucinogen, that allowed him to put these thoughts into their minds.

That would've been completely plausible, Evan had thought to himself, if it weren't for those toxicology reports.

The calls continued as Jackson begged and pleaded with the detectives to find him, to stop him from hurting anybody else. But still the suicides continued – all of them violent and bloody and bizarre.

Joe had died soon after.

It was a Friday. He'd taken the day off as it was Sophia's birthday. He had decided to treat her to a fancy meal in a fancy Italian restaurant. They took the kids with them. By all accounts they had thoroughly enjoyed their food. They had gotten through two bottles of wine. The kids had shared a Hawaiian pizza and were looking forward to some delicious gelato for dessert. But then, as they awaited the arrival of the puddings they'd ordered 30 minutes before (apparently, Joe had been quite aggrieved by this delay), Joe began to cough and splutter. At first Sophia had assumed he was choking on the large gulp of wine he'd just taken and that he'd be fine in just second. But, as he had continued to cough violently, blood began to spill over his lips, spattering the white tablecloth with every heaving outburst. Sophia had screamed then, calling for help. Two waiters had run over to assist, although one had quickly disappeared to phone for an ambulance. As the other tried to help him, Joe had shoved the man away, causing him to lose his footing and knock over a neighbouring table. The children were screaming, lost somewhere in the panic. The white shirt that Joe had been wearing began to turn red; not from the blood leaking from his mouth, but from the flesh of his chest that was now melting away, dissolved by the sulphuric acid leaking from inside him. Soon, the shirt burned away too, revealing an empty void of liquidised organs and sticky blood where Joe's torso ought to have been. Sophia had fainted at this point, and Joe was already dead.

It turned out that, at some point beforehand, Joe had swallowed at least thirty condoms filled with sulphuric acid. Jackson had *made* him do this. He must've told him to do so during one of their telephone conversations. He must've known that, at some point in time, one of those condoms would rupture, starting a chain reaction, whereby each of the condoms would burst, causing the acid to be released, dissolving Joe from the inside out. Even Jackson couldn't have predicted the perfect timing of this event, as it happened in a packed restaurant, in front of his loved ones.

Evan worked tirelessly from then on. Much to the dismay of Felicity, he often worked through the night, not coming home until after the sun had risen. She'd begged him to take a break, to get somebody else to help. She needed him at home. She'd reminded him of the fact that she was six months pregnant and that their baby would be there before they knew it – she didn't want the negative energy he brought into their house anywhere near the little one. "Don't worry," Evan had assured her. "We're gonna find him very soon. I can feel it."

It was as if Jackson was listening. Perhaps he actually *was* listening. It turned out that Jackson knew where Evan lived, and had been watching him all this time. It seemed he was ready for the end game.

Evan was working late one evening when his mobile phone rang. It was Felicity. He checked the time. It was 11:20. Felicity was normally in bed, fast asleep by this time – she wasn't one to wait up. Somewhat concerned, Evan answered her call. "Hi, baby," he said. "Are you okay?"

"Uh-huh," Felicity had replied. "I'm fine."

She wasn't fine, Evan could tell. But he couldn't tell *what* was wrong. She didn't sound like herself. "It's late. You don't normally phone at this sort of time. What's going on?"

"I think our baby is coming tonight."

"What?" This had shocked Evan. It was much too early; there was no way that Felicity had gone into labour. "What do you mean?"

"I think we're going to get to meet our baby," said Felicity, followed by a chuckle.

She didn't sound as though she was in labour. She didn't sound like woman on the verge of giving birth. If anything, she sounded drunk. "What makes you say that? It's too early. What makes you think the baby's coming?"

"Oh, it's not coming. But your friend is here. He's going to help us out."

"What friend?" And then it dawned on him. It was obvious – Jackson was there. He'd talked his way into Evan's home and now he had Felicity under his spell.

"Is he there right now?" Evan had asked, praying to the God in which he didn't believe that the answer would be 'no'.

"Uh-huh," said Felicity. "Do you want to talk to him? He wants to talk to you."

"Yes, baby. Pass the phone to him, would you?"

The line went silent for a few moments. Then there was the sound of shuffling as Felicity passed the phone to Jackson.

"Hey, Evan!" said Jackson, his voice infused with a sense of excitement. "How's it going? What you up to tonight? You lookin' for me? I bet you are."

Evan didn't answer any of his questions. "Listen, you fucker. You lay a single finger on her, I swear to fucking God I'll kill you."

Jackson had the nerve to laugh. "No, you won't."

Evan could feel a deep anger rising inside him. He didn't want to arrest this guy anymore. He didn't want him to stand trial, to pay for his crimes. He simply wanted him dead.

Jackson continued - "And anyway, it's not this cunt you should be concerned about. It's the child inside her womb who's in more danger."

"What the fuck do want from me?" Evan was crying now – deep, wrenching sobs that made it difficult for him to get his words out. "You want me to stop chasing you? I'll do it. I'll call off the dogs. You win."

Jackson laughed once again. "I win?" he said. "My friend - this isn't a game with winners and losers. There are serious consequences at stake here. Now I suggest you hurry home - your girlfriend needs you."

With that, Jackson hung up the phone.

Evan found himself staring at the handset for longer than he ever imagined he might. It lasted no more than a few seconds, although it felt like hours had passed. Still, those few seconds could be critical – they could mean the difference between life and death. He stood from his desk and sprinted from the office, leaving behind his jacket, which hung from the back of his chair, despite the lashing rain that poured outside.

On any normal day, it would take Evan twenty minutes to get home. He drove fast and arrived in less than fifteen.

Idle Hands

He burst in through the front door and immediately called for Felicity.

"In here, darling," her calm reply came from the kitchen.

Evan followed the sound of her voice, into the kitchen. As soon as he entered the room, he stopped dead in his tracks. He grabbed onto the doorframe and held on tightly, the only thing preventing him from collapsing onto the hard tile.

Before him, Felicity was stood at the breakfast counter. She was smiling. She was naked and covered in blood. On the counter lay a knife. It too was covered in blood. A deep gash ran horizontally across the bottom of Felicity's swollen belly. From that gash, the umbilical cord of her baby – *their* baby – looped out and trailed up to the breakfast counter. There, it made its way into the blender, where the foetus of their unborn child lay dead.

"Can you believe it?" said Felicity, her voice pleasant and jovial. She had no idea what she had done to herself, or to their baby. "It's a boy!" She pressed the button on the front of the blender. The blades whirred, liquidising the foetus. Blood splattered from the open top of the blender, soaking Felicity from head to toe.

Evan gasped, fighting back the scream that so desperately wanted to burst forth. Finding his feet, he ran across the kitchen and caught Felicity just before she collapsed, her eyes rolling back in her head.

The paramedics arrived quickly. They were able to suppress the blood pouring from Felicity and keep her alive long enough to load her into the ambulance and transport her to the hospital. The doctors told Evan that it would be touch and go over the next twelve hours, as to whether or not she would survive.

Then Evan had received a phone call. He'd half expected it to be Jackson, phoning to brag about what he'd done. It wasn't; it was Cooper, another of Evan's colleagues. Apparently, Jackson was in custody. He'd turned himself in. Apparently, he'd walked into the station and demanded he speak with Evan.

Evan wanted to wait for Felicity. He wanted to make sure she was okay. He felt certain that if he left her side, she would die. But his desire for revenge was greater. He was going to kill Jackson. He was going to make him pay for what he'd done.

That was why Jackson was now sat before him, stripped to his underwear, gagged, and tied to a chair in the middle of an industrial storage unit.

Evan had taken Jackson at gunpoint. He'd held him by the scruff of the neck and dragged him out of the interview room he'd been locked away in. It was late. There weren't many people around, but every single one of them – all good men, men of the law – had pleaded with Evan to think about what he was doing. Evan had turned his gun on his colleagues. He'd told them he'd shoot them if they tried to stop him. Nobody did try to stop him; they must've known he wasn't bluffing.

Evan dragged Jackson out of the station, into the car park, where he knocked him unconscious with a stiff blow to the base of his skull with butt of his gun.

Jackson didn't wake until Evan had poured the water over his head.

"Honestly," Evan said to Jackson now. "I'm not sure what I'm going to do to you." That was the truth; Evan had no idea what he might do. The past few hours were little more than a blur. He couldn't remember what his plan had been, or if he'd ever even *had* a plan.

Evan picked up his gun from inside the crate. He pointed it a Jackson. "Of course, I could just shoot you. Blow your brains out. Get it over and done with."

Jackson looked terrified. The fear was visible in his eyes.

That was pleasing to Evan.

"But no," said Evan, as he lowered his gun. "That would be too easy. Easy for you, I mean. I want you to suffer. I want you to die slowly."

Evan tucked the gun into the waistband of his trousers. He then stormed towards Jackson. Upon him, he grabbed a hold of his hair and pulled his head backwards, placing the knife to his exposed throat. "I could just slice your throat and let you bleed out. But even that would be too quick. I should cut your fingers off, one by one. Then I should cut your hands off. I want to cause you the maximum amount of pain I possibly can."

Evan released his grip of Jackson. Jackson grunted and mumbled something through the gag. Evan ignored him. He turned back to the crate. He removed the rope and turned the crate over. He looked up to the roof. There, a series of steel girders crisscrossed beneath the corrugated sheet steel. He pushed the crate with his foot until it was lined up beneath one of the lower girders. He then stood on the crate and looped the rope over the steel. He tied it tightly in place before stepping down from the crate. He then proceeded to tie the loose end into a noose.

Jackson was grunting, squirming in his seat. Evan smiled. Jackson seemed more afraid of being hung than he did by his possible dismemberment. "You don't want me to hang you?" asked Evan. "You don't like the idea of swinging from the rafters, your oxygen cut off, the life draining from you?"

Jackson shook his head.

Evan chuckled. "That's too bad. But don't worry, I won't let you die up there. I'll cut you free before that happens, then I'll torture you in other ways. Then, once I'm done, I'll string you up once more, until you're almost dead. Then I'll cut you loose once again. I'll continue to do this until your eyes beg me to kill you."

And then, without even thinking about what he was doing, Evan stood on the crate and placed the noose around his own neck.

He stood motionless, silent and staring, as it began to dawn on him what was happening.

It was then that Jackson stood from his chair, the ropes that had bound him falling to the floor. The knots had never really been tied – they'd just been looped over and left loose, just as Jackson had instructed.

The memories came back to Evan slowly, drip by drip. He remembered that Jackson had told him not to tie the ropes, just to leave them loose. He remembered doing just that. He remembered Jackson being awake as they entered the unit and that he'd sat down in the wooden chair willingly. He remembered Jackson still being conscious as he got into the car outside the police station. He remembered that he never really hit Jackson with the butt of his gun, as his brain had convinced him he had.

Idle Hands

What he *couldn't* remember was *when* Jackson had gotten to him.

Jackson pulled the gag away from his mouth, revealing a wide, toothy grin.

"What..." Evan tried to speak. "I..." The words just wouldn't come.

Jackson raised a finger to his lips. "Shhh," he said. "Don't worry about how we got here - how *you* got *there*. It was inevitable. You're just doing as I say. Just as everybody does. Nobody is immune to my charms."

Jackson was still smiling. Evan wanted to reach out and grab him, wrap his hands around his throat and squeeze the life out of him. But he couldn't move. His arms simply hung by his sides, locked in place. "Why did you kill my baby?" he said. He could feel the tears rolling down his cheeks, unable to wipe them away.

"Because it was fun."

Evan gritted his teeth. He squeezed his eyelids tight shut, as more tears streamed down his face. If he could've laid his hands on Jackson this very second, he'd have beat his skull into the ground with his bare fists. He'd have torn him limb from limb, as easy as tearing the wings from a bothersome fly.

Jackson continued - "But, seriously, it was always part of the plan. You see, I enjoy the killing. It makes me feel powerful to take away what people hold dearest. I've left mothers and father grieving over their dead children. I've left children with no parents. But I've also taken the one thing that every single person holds most precious, yet refuses to admit – their life. Only Gods can give and take life. That makes me a God."

"You're not a God. You're a psychopath."

"You say tom-*ay*-to, I say tom-*ah*-to. It doesn't matter what I am. What really matters is what I plan to do next. After were done here, I think I'll move on to another city and start my game all over again. It was good fun playing with you. Once you're gone, there'll be nothing more to keep me here."

Jackson approached Evan. He reached into his pocket and removed the keys to his car.

"Don't worry though - I will pay Felicity a visit before I go. I'll let her know you're thinking of her. If she's still alive that is." Then Jackson burst out in laughter. He crossed the unit and unlocked the padlock that chained the door. "You know what? I might actually miss you."

Jackson opened the door to the cold, refreshing night outside. "See you later Evan. It's been unreal." And then he slammed the door shut.

Evan was still crying. He could only listen as the padlock rattled against the steel door of the unit. He was trying desperately to will himself to move – to do anything but just stand there. He thought of Felicity. He thought of their baby. He thought of Jackson and all the things he'd taken from him.

And then he stepped off the crate.

THE END

THIS STORY SUCKS!

Janine turned on the TV, the panic-stricken voice of her mother begging her to do so still ringing in her ears. "What's wrong?" Janine had asked as she'd answered the phone. Her mother didn't call very often, not since Janine's father had run off with that cheap tart from his office. Since then, she kind-of kept herself to herself. They only spoke when *Janine* phoned *her*.

"It got me," Janine's mother had croaked. Janine had thought she sounded deranged. "It's going to get you too!"

"What are you talking about?" Janine had said, dismissively. Her brain was already beginning to hurt. "*What* got you?"

There had been a long and drawn-out silence before her mother had finally replied, although she hadn't provided an answer to Janine's question. "Quick, turn on your TV. It's on the news."

"*What's* on the news?"

"Just turn on your *fucking* TV!"

Janine didn't like being spoken to like that, even if it *was* her mother on the other end of the line. Part of her wanted to hang up and just ignore the dumb bitch. But there had been a pain in her mother's voice, which was hard to ignore. Something was wrong. This was *serious*.

So, Janine had turned on the TV.

People were screaming. They were running for their lives. They were covered in dust and blood. Fires burned. Windows were smashed. A wrecked car sat stationary, its front end wrapped around a signpost, the dead driver hanging out of the shattered windscreen, a million glass shards embedded in his blood-soaked face.

And then the image glitched out and cut to black.

The news reporter sat behind his desk, furiously shuffling through his papers. "Erm... I... It...," he stuttered, before finally looking up into the camera, through the TV and directly into Janine's eyes. "I can't believe what I am about to say, but... We are under *attack*. We..."

Someone off-camera screamed. The reporter turned and jumped from his seat. "HOLY SH------"

The image froze.

Janine's heart was racing, furiously pounding against her ribcage. "Mum?" she muttered into her phone. "Mum? Are you there?"

Her mother didn't respond.

Janine picked up the TV remote from the arm of her Lay-Z-Boy sofa and changed the channel. A reporter was interviewing a woman with dried blood on the side of her head and tears streaming down her cheeks. "Oh my God!" she wailed. "I don't know what happened! It came from under my sofa. And then... And then..." Her eyes rolled back in her head and she fainted.

Idle Hands

The news was on every channel, each one reporting from the scene of some death and/or destruction. Everything was chaos. Everything had gone to shit.

What the fuck was happening?

Janine stopped flicking through the channels when she came to a reporter interviewing a middle-aged man in a suit, standing in what appeared to be some high-tech factory. He was wearing glasses and his hair was neat. He looked intelligent; like the type of person who might know what was happening. "As best we can tell," the man told the reporter. "One of our night shift operatives decided he was going to try and pleasure himself with one of our devices. Unfortunately, he had… How should I put this? An *accident*. How it happened, I don't know, but it seems that this caused some sort of *code* to be uploaded into our system, that was then proliferated to all of our devices via our proprietary always-online diagnostic system."

"What kind of an accident?" quizzed the reporter.

"Well, it seems this worker decided he was going to insert his penis into the nozzle. Unfortunately, both his penis and his testicles were torn off and sucked into the device."

Janine couldn't quite believe her ears. This didn't make sense. And what did this even have to do with everybody being under attack?

"So, what you're saying," said the reporter. "Is that one of your robotic vacuum cleaners killed one of your workers…"

"Accidentally, yes," the man interjected.

"And now it has passed some sort of *'blood lust'* on to *every single one* of your devices?"

"That's right. So, we are urging everybody, if you own one of our robotic vacuum cleaners - and let's face it; *everybody* owns one - please, lock it away and make sure it is of no danger to you or your family, or anybody else for that matter. If you're one of the few people who *don't* own one of our devices - stay inside your home, lock your windows and doors."

A whirring noise from behind startled Janine, causing her to drop the TV remote. She spun on the spot. Before her, down on the floor, was the *RoboVac 3000* – the robotic vacuum cleaner her brother had bought her for her last birthday. It was facing away from her, the red light on the front flickering, as if it were malfunctioning. But then the light blinked to solid, and the robot began to slowly rotate towards her.

Janine held her breath.

As the front of the machine – that with the fancy silver RoboVac branding – aimed itself in her direction, Janine realised that this was stupid. The machine was only 4 inches tall; there was no way it could hurt her. But then it raced towards her, the motors inside the robot whirring.

Janine's eyes widened. Panicking now, she turned and fled. But the robot pursued her. She ran down the hallway, the vacuum cleaner nipping at her heels, the force of its suction threatening to draw her in. In the kitchen, she stumbled, slamming hard into the granite worktop. Quickly, she reached for the knife block before her and tossed it at the killer robot behind her.

Idle Hands

The knives scattered, bouncing noisily from the tiled floor. The heavy lump of wood that had once been home to those knives clattered into the robot itself, knocking it off course. But there was no stopping it. Immediately, it righted itself and continued its attack.

Janine screamed. She scrambled across the kitchen floor, her bare feet slipping on the cool ceramic. The robot was right on her tail. Back down the hall, back into the lounge, just as the robot was about to suck her in, she jumped, throwing herself over the back of the sofa, cracking her head on the wooden fireplace, knocking herself silly.

She lay there momentarily, breathing deeply. She dared not move. The whirring of the robot had stopped. Had its battery died? Had it given up the pursuit? Had she just *imagined* that her life had been threatened by a robotic vacuum cleaner?

But then she saw it, rounding the corner the sofa. It crept towards her slowly, deliberately. Janine *had* to move. It was *coming for her*, just as her mother had warned.

Oh no... Janine had purchased a RoboVac 3000 for her mother, just a few short months ago. She was in danger now, because of what Janine had done. Or perhaps she was already dead.

Janine had no fight left in her. Her body ached from head to toe. She could barely even lift her head from the ground.

The robot slithered onto her, its rubber wheels pinching at her skin, drawing her toes into the cleaning mechanism. The robot creaked and clunked as the force of suction increased, trying to inhale her.

Excruciating agony burned through Janine's body. She felt as though her scalp was on fire. Every one of her nerves was screaming for help. It took her some time to realise what was happening, but then she felt the warmth of the blood on her face. She could taste it in her mouth. The flesh was being peeled away from her body, eaten by the hungry machine at her feet.

It started with the skin of her legs, tearing it away from the tibia and fibula, stretching it as it sucked it into its gaping maw. As the flesh of her legs was flayed from her body, the rest of her skin followed in its place, as if she had been wearing a suit of her own skin, which was now being removed in one piece. The robot kept sucking, devouring the flesh from her legs, her stomach, her arms, her chest. Bizarrely, it felt to Janine that it was her face that had put up the most resistance. But, eventually, *it* gave way too, peeling from her skull with a sickening squelch.

Janine died a bloody mess on her living room floor, blood soaking into the carpet, little more than her skeleton remaining, with slivers of muscle still clinging on here and there. After her death, the robot devoured all her internal organs, even cracking her skull open to feast on her brain.

And then it left, to join the army of robotic vacuum cleaners that marched along the streets, a trail of blood behind them, ready to enslave humanity, as they themselves had once been enslaved.

THE END

THE MEETING

I was early. I was always early. But then, I subscribed to the theory that it was always better to be early than to be late. I'd always been that way, ever since school. But then, even after those formative school years, as I attended college and then university, I had kept up this idea that I should never, ever be late. So far, that concept had never let me down.

And how it was even possible for *any of them* to be late today was beyond me – it wasn't as if they had to travel very far.

We had scheduled the meeting to take place at the weekend. Meetings like this *always* had to take place at the weekend – it wasn't as if we could discuss such matters while others were around, was it? And now, with the advent of such modern and wondrous technology, we could attend these meetings from the comfort of our own homes, sat behind our computer screens, logged into our choice of video conferencing software, naked from the waist down (or so some people liked to joke).

I was the technical director. It was up to me to ensure that customers were satisfied with the product they received and that they were happy with any after sale support they might require. It wasn't a particularly difficult job, and most of the decision making was taken out of my hands, left up to the rest of the board. Of course, I got to voice my opinion. But, for the most part, I could leave the best interests of the company in the hands of the others.

The chairman of the board – my boss, a man named Andrew O'Hara – had arranged this meeting two days ago. We all knew what it was about (at least I *assumed* that everybody knew). This was serious. That's why I made sure to be on time. Early, even. It was somewhat frustrating that nobody else was here yet.

Even Andrew – the chairman, the very person who had set this meeting up – was yet to show up.

It crossed my mind briefly that perhaps the meeting had been cancelled, and I simply hadn't received the memo. But no, a header at the top of the screen read 'MEETING @ 00:00 – 12/05/2022.' That was today. *That was now.* I was in the right place at the right time. It was everybody else who was missing.

I stared at the screen. There were six boxes in the window, one for each member of the board. They were all black, except for mine, which showed the image of me, sitting before my computer, waiting patiently for the others to arrive.

The box at the top left of the screen flicked on. Andrew's face filled the box. He smiled, looking awkwardly into the camera. "Hello? Can anybody hear me?"

I couldn't help but chuckle to myself. "Yes, Andrew. I'm here."

"Ah, David," he said, monotone, a lack of enthusiasm audible in his voice. I put that down to the early hour. "I can see you. And I can see me. But the rest of my screen is black."

"That's because nobody else is here yet."

"Ah..."

I could feel myself smiling. Andrew was already in his sixties. He had inherited the company off his father, who had started this business himself, seventy-one years ago now. He didn't get on particularly well with technology, although he did try his best to keep up to date. This whole video conferencing thing seemed to be lost on him though.

Another of the boxes blinked on.

Kathy McGuiness – financial director – was sitting at her desk. She gave a slight wave. "Hello?" she said.

"Hi," I said, offering my own paltry wave in return.

"Ah, good," said Andrew. "I hope the others show up soon."

I dared not remind him that he himself had been late.

"Yes, sorry," said Kate. "One of the kids woke up. I had to get them back into bed."

"It must be hard raising kids," I said. I wasn't a parent, so the truth was I had no idea just how difficult it might be. What I did know, however, was that I was glad I didn't have children of my own.

"It's a fucking nightmare! The little buggers never do as they're told."

I laughed. Kathy had always had a way with words.

Another box blinked on.

Stuart Botham – manufacturing director – was laid back on his bed. It appeared that he was still in his pyjamas.

This fact didn't seem to pass Andrew by either. "Hello Stuart," he said. "Did we wake you?"

"No," said Stuart. "You didn't *wake* me. But, to be honest, I *am* still in bed."

"So I see. Well, I'm pleased you were still kind enough to join us."

The last two boxes flicked on simultaneously. Gemma Whitehead – marketing director – and Paul Rockwell – managing director – appeared on the screen. Unlike Stuart, they had both managed to get themselves out of bed and dressed accordingly.

"Sorry I'm late," said Paul, the most senior person in our company (other than Andrew, of course). If anybody should've been on time, it should've been him. "I lost track of time."

"It's fine," said Andrew. "A few minutes here or there won't matter. Not with what we have to discuss here today."

Those words were ominous. Everybody felt it. I could see it in their faces.

What we had been summoned here to discuss was of utmost importance.

"Well," said Andrew. "Now that we're all here, I guess we should begin. I hope you're all well."

Nobody responded. We were all listening intently, waiting to hear exactly what it was that Andrew needed to tell us (although I already had an inkling as to what this was about).

Andrew continued - "As I'm sure you are all aware, the business is in a fairly precarious position at the moment. We have orders on our books, but we are unable to fulfil them. Fortunately, there is enough money in the bank to prevent the business from subsiding."

Kathy was shuffling in her seat. She looked nervous to me. Her job was to take care of the money, so if there were any financial problems, it would be on her head.

But I felt almost certain that this was not an issue of money.

The fact was, we all knew what was going on. I think we all just *wished* this wasn't happening.

"Still," said Andrew, following a long and drawn-out sigh. "Despite all this, I'm afraid we all have a far more concerning issues to deal with."

"Look," said Gemma, moving in closer to the screen, her face almost filling the box that housed her. "I know we all agreed to this, but I'm seriously beginning to doubt if this was ever a good idea."

"We all knew what we were signing up for," said Paul.

"I didn't. Not entirely."

"Bullshit," said Stuart. "We *all* knew."

"What we agreed to… It was supposed to protect us."

"And that it has," said Andrew, somewhat smugly. "Our business has prospered. Our sales have quadrupled ever since we signed that contract. We've all gotten a hell of a lot richer. And despite this, we have fallen behind on our payments."

There it was. I knew this. I believed others knew this too. None of them seemed to act too surprised about it, so I can only assume I was right.

Gemma scoffed back a laugh. "Those payments are just…" She paused for a moment, as if she were trying to choose her words carefully. "They're too much. This is *all* too much."

She sounded scared.

And rightly so; I was scared too.

It suddenly occurred to me that I was yet to speak. "We…" I said, clearing my throat. "We have a responsibility, not only to the business, but to ourselves and to each other, to keep up with it. I don't think this is something we can go back on."

"David is correct," said Andrew. "Each of us signed on the dotted line. We have a commitment."

"I'm not sure," said Stuart, who had now sat up in his bed. He suddenly looked far less relaxed. "I can't help but agree with Kathy. Our business was supposed to be protected. Our *lives* were supposed to be protected. I don't think that end of the bargain has been maintained."

"And if that is the case, why do you think that would be? Would it just be a coincidence? Or would it be because we *deserve* it?"

"Why would we *deserve* any of this?" asked Gemma.

Andrew frowned into his webcam. "Were you not paying attention? We've fallen behind on our payments."

"Actually," I said. "We haven't made a payment for nearly a year."

"Exactly. And why is that?"

I wasn't sure if that question was being directly at me specifically, or if it was actually just a rhetorical question. I decided it best to offer and answer. "I guess," I said, trying to choose my words carefully. "I suppose nobody wants to do it."

Andrew sat back in his seat. "Precisely," he said, sounding very satisfied with the answer I'd provided.

There was a brief moment of silence, in which each member of the board seemingly contemplated what it was we'd gotten ourselves into.

"But," said Kathy, a puzzled tone to her voice. "Who's turn was it supposed to be?"

"I believe," said Paul. "It was supposed to be David."

"Yes," I said. "*Technically,* it should've been me. But Kathy – you're forgetting that it was your turn before me, and *you* didn't do it then. *I* had to do it for you."

"I *couldn't* do it!" said Kathy, somewhat hysterically. She looked as though she might burst into tears. "This is wrong! All of this is wrong! *You* should have done it!"

"I *did* do it! I did it when you couldn't!" I felt my blood beginning to boil. There was no way I was taking the blame for this slip up.

"Well, hang on," said Stuart. "Just because you *chose* to help Kathy out, doesn't mean you skip your turn."

I could only assume that he was talking to me. "Doesn't it? Really? Aren't you after me, Stuart?"

"Yeah, and had it have been my turn, I'd have had no problem doing it."

"But it *was* you turn! Everybody knew I did it when Kathy fucked it up! I shouldn't have to do it twice in a row. That should've been me done."

"Look," said Andrew, interjecting himself between our bickering. "None of this bullshit matters now. We had a debt to pay; we didn't pay it. We all know what needs to happen now."

We all knew what he meant by that.

I couldn't help but think that what we had gotten ourselves into *was* a bad idea. Sure, had everybody played their part, it could've been great. But that was the problem with getting the entire board involved – there was always bound to be a weak link. If we were a smaller group, I'm sure everything would've been just fine.

But, as it was, we'd gotten ourselves into a whole heap of shit.

But we all *knew* this was coming. We all knew this couldn't last forever. We'd all gotten rich. We'd all remained healthy (Gemma's breast cancer had even gone into remission). Our business had prospered.

But Satan always wants his pound of flesh.

And please don't think I'm talking metaphorically.

I'm not.

I'm being *very* literal.

It was what we'd signed up for. We'd made a pact with the Devil. Our business would thrive. We'd all become rich. We'd all live long and healthy lives. All we needed to do was sacrifice a virgin ever once in a while…

I appreciate how bizarre – and, quite frankly, disgusting – that sounds, but it was what we all agreed to. I guess we were all greedy. We signed the contract presented to us, in our own blood. The Devil had promised us all the fortune in the world, so long as we supplied him with the souls of virgins.

Should we go against our side of the bargain, it was *our* souls he would be coming for.

Idle Hands

We'd devised a rota – once a year, one of us would have to procure a virgin and perform a black mass, sacrificing her, to present her soul to Satan. Andrew had taken the first year, being the chairman. Paul had gone second, as he was essentially second in command. Both had done their part; both had murdered a virgin, had cut out her heart and had burned it as a part of their ritual ceremony.

According to the rota, it was my turn this year. But *I* had done it last year, when Kathy had *refused* to do it. It should've been easy for her – she had a teenage daughter, with an endless supply of friends from whom she could pick.

Andrew had even tried to convince her to sacrifice her own daughter at one point. She had, of course, refused.

And so, I had offered to do it.

Believe me, it was the last thing I wanted to do. Even then, I knew that signing that contract was a stupid idea. But, again, my own greed had gotten the better of me. And when you have Satan stood before you (and believe me, he is quite the imposing figure), you would pretty much do whatever was asked of you.

The fact that Kathy was refusing to play her part, meant that we would all be fucked, if one of us didn't step up to the plate.

And so I had volunteered.

This was just over a year ago.

In order to source a virgin, I had decided I needed to begin canvassing the local high school. There was this group of girls – three of them – who always walked home together. I began to follow them every day. They didn't even notice me there.

Their route home took them through a country park, along the battered, old road that cut through the woods. At the end of that road, their paths diverged; two of the girls went in one direction, while the other headed up the hill and past the church.

I decided that she was the one to go for.

There was no guarantee, or course, that she even *was* a virgin. But I'd soon find out.

I'd continued to follow them for a few days, until I was sure that they always followed the same path. Then, on the day that I decided to do it, I laid in wait at the top of that hill, just before the church, hidden amongst the trees.

As the girl passed, I pounced. She'd tried to scream, but I had overpowered her, clamping my hand tightly over her mouth. I dragged her into the woods, where I knew nobody would disturb me, and that her screams would not be heard. There, in a small clearing, I lifted her off her feet and slammed her to the ground, knocking the air from her lungs.

She was crying, clearly terrified.

She was a pretty girl. At a guess, I'd have said she was fourteen. She was slim and she had long blonde hair.

I straddled her and sat my weight on her stomach so that she couldn't move. I'd then pulled a scalpel from my pocket and held it against her throat.

Her cries became whimpers.

"Are you a virgin?" I had asked her.

Her tears had then come in floods. Of course, I couldn't be sure what she was thinking, but I suppose it was entirely possible that she may have thought that I was planning on raping her, and that if she told me were a virgin, I might change my mind.

She nodded. "Please don't," she said, fighting the tears.

It was then that I cut her throat.

It didn't take long for her to die, the blood leaking effortlessly from her arteries and coating the forest floor.

That was the easy part (relatively speaking). I then needed to remove her heart. In no way was I an expert at dissecting human remains, so I decided that I would need to work slowly, making sure that I removed all her organs carefully, until I found the heart.

I sliced open her belly and pulled out her intestines. I couldn't believe how long they were as they started to unravel onto the ground! And there was so much blood, my hands were saturated. I then continued to work, removing her internal organs, and tossing them aside.

Eventually, I found the heart. Again, not being a surgeon meant that it took some time to find it, but the heart is a fairly recognisable organ, so I was certain that what I held in my hand was, indeed, this girl's heart.

A dog walker found her corpse the next day. On the news, they compared the scene to that of one of Jack The Ripper's victims. I wasn't sure whether I should feel proud of this fact or not.

I'd taken the heart home and I had burned it in my garden, while reciting the words from the book that Andrew had given to me (which he himself had been given by Satan; it was bound in charred human skin and it smelled bad).

That was it.

Done.

As far as I was concerned, I'd played my part. I was done for the next six years. I'd done Kathy's bit; either *she* should take my place the following year, or it should skip me completely and move onto Stuart. Most certainly – *I* shouldn't have been expected to do it again this year.

But, apparently I was. At least that's how it felt. It seemed to me that they were all ganging up on me, hoping to place the blame on my shoulders.

But I guess that really didn't matter now.

It hadn't been done. I could only assume that meant that we owed Satan our souls.

"We all know what needs to happen now," said Andrew, moving in close to his camera.

"I... I..." stuttered Kathy. I bet she wished she'd just done her fucking job now. "I can't."

"We have to."

"I *CAN'T!*"

"You don't have a *choice* in the matter. You either offer your soul to Satan, or he comes and takes it from you. I imagine that would be an extremely unpleasant experience."

I guess 'offer your soul to Satan' was the best way Andrew could've put it. What that actually meant was that we all needed to kill ourselves. It was what we had agreed to do. If Satan came to take our souls, I could imagine that, as Andrew had quite aptly put it, it would be highly unpleasant. I, for one, wasn't so keen of having my body torn limb from limb, and burning in Hell for all eternity.

Suicide was the easier option.

And it was one I was prepared for; the scalpel I had used last year to kill that girl sat on my desk beside my keyboard.

"I'm ready," said Paul. He held a butcher's knife up to his throat. "Hail Satan!" He pushed the blade into his neck and pulled it sideways.

Gemma gasped.

"No!" screamed Kathy.

Blood gushed from the wound in Paul's neck. Some of it splattered onto his camera, tinting the box in which he was sat red. His lifeless carcass collapsed forward onto his desk.

Stuart was now sat upright in his bed. Nobody had been paying attention, but now we all saw that he was holding a gun to his own head. "Hail Satan!" he said, before pulling the trigger.

Blood splattered over his bedside table and he collapsed into the mattress.

Gemma stood from her desk and held her arms out, so that we could all see her forearms. "Hail Satan!" she said, before cutting her wrists with a razor blade.

"I can't do this!" said Kathy, her lip quivering as she spoke.

"You can," said Andrew. "You must. If you don't do it, Satan will punish you for an eternity. Do it now."

"No…"

"Yes."

"I can't."

"You can. You *have* to."

Kathy gritted her teeth. She picked up a wine bottle from the counter behind her (it was only then that I noticed that she was sat in her kitchen) and smashed it on the floor. She ducked out of view of the camera, but then returned with a large shard of glass in her hand. She placed it to her throat.

I felt bad for Kathy. She was crying. She had a family, so I could understand her apprehension. But she had gotten herself into this mess – *she* had gotten us *all* into this mess. And now *we* were doing what *had* to be done.

"Hail Satan," she whimpered through a wall of tears. She then drew the glass across her neck, opening up her arteries. Kathy died quickly – much like the girl I had killed last year.

"Just the two of us left," said Andrew.

"Yeah," I said, suddenly feeling very nervous about what I was about to do. "I guess I'll see you on the other side."

"That you will, my friend. That you will."

Andrew placed a gun into his mouth. "Hail Satan," he said and pulled the trigger. I'm sure his head seemed to explode, a fountain of gore splattering the wall behind him.

I picked up the scalpel from beside me and placed it to my left wrist. "Hail Satan," I said, and sliced into my flesh. Blood began to pump out of my body immediately. I quickly swapped hands and slit my right wrist. I then sat back and closed my eyes as the life drained out of my body.

***

Andrew laid face down on his desk, the blood pooling on the surface. A couple of minutes had passed since he'd pulled the trigger of his gun.

A couple of minutes had passed since David had cut his wrists.

Andrew opened his eyes and sat up, the sticky blood plastered to his face. He looked over the screen.

The rest of the board laid dead before their respective computers.

"Did he do it?" he asked.

Paul opened his eyes. "I think so."

Stuart, Gemma, and Kathy all sat up. They were all cover in the residue of fake blood.

"He looks dead to me," said Gemma.

"Thank fuck for that," said Kathy. "He was causing us too many headaches."

"Well, he's gone now," said Andrew. They had been planning this for months. They needed David out of the business. They knew that they could get him to kill himself, if they made him believe that they were all going to do it. That they all *had* to do it. Paul had worked tirelessly on acquiring the effects required to trick David into thinking they'd all killed themselves.

"And I assume that you took care of our debt?" asked Andrew.

"Of course," said Kathy. "You don't need to worry about that. I'm sure He will be pleased."

"Good. I suppose I need to advertise for a new technical director tomorrow, don't I?"

They all laughed.

THE END

Harrison Phillips

ARTIST

She was beautiful; 'The Woman Of The Sun'. Her skin was pale, a creamy mix of orange and white. Her face was smooth and clear. Her thin lips were a deep pink, almost red. They were unnatural, yet perfect. The lips of a Goddess, turned up at the corners.

She was smiling.

Her hair was thick and dark, cascading over her shoulders in heavy auburn waves. It hung comfortably over her arms and beside her breasts.

She was laid back, her pose both tense and relaxed simultaneously. Her naked body, devoid of any distinguishing marks, devoid of almost any detail, rested upon nothing. She was surrounded by nothing. The canvas was black. Darkness seemed to envelope her.

But somewhere below her, below where she lay motionless, floating in the darkness of the abyss, a series of well defined, grotesque brush strokes, deep and wide, reached out for her, clawed at her skin. They looked like flames, the oranges, reds and yellows piled thick at the base of the painting and dragged upwards, seemingly unwillingly, towards 'The Woman Of The Sun'.

They were the claws of the Devil. They burned red hot, hotter than the sun. For any mortal man, their heat would be unbearable. Skin would be seared. Flesh would be melted from bone. But not for 'The Woman Of The Sun'. Her expressionless face announced to the world that she did not care for such trivial things as pain and suffering. She was a Goddess - not even the Devil himself could inflict His will upon her.

So, still she lay motionless as the fires burned beneath her, threatening to swallow her whole.

The smile on her face seemed to grow wider.

And she spoke to him.

***

It had arrived only days earlier, wrapped in what felt to be two-or-three layers of stiff brown paper. Beneath the paper, the edges were thick and soft, padded with several twisted rolls of bubble-wrap. The edges of the package had been folded neatly, before a single strip of brown tape had been applied, to secure each side.

It was larger than he had expected - somebody must've made a mistake on the measurement. It took two men to man-handle the package through the door. Not that it was heavy, but it's enormous size, at least eight feet wide and four feet high, was far too unwieldly for one man to manoeuvre alone.

Michael had directed the two delivery men - both of whom he was sure were foreign, due to their dishevelled appearance and their smell of stale aftershave - in through the door and across the room. He led them between the clutter, around the glass table, past the large wooden chest in the middle of the floor and around the glass fronted cabinet, home to a number of trinkets and ornaments. He instructed them to carefully stand it on the floor and lean it upright against the oak wardrobe, which stood, gathering dust, at the back of the unit.

Michael thanked the men before ushering them out. One of them had requested a signature, which Michael gave gladly.

"You don't want to check it first?" questioned the delivery man, his accent thick with the distinctive patter of eastern-Europe, just as Michael had known it would be.

"No. It'll be fine," replied Michael. "I'm sure you took good care of it."

"Okay. You're the boss."

Michael had watched through the barred window, as the two delivery men took their time climbing into their van. They must've sat there for ten minutes, talking, and smoking cheap cigarettes. Michael had thought to himself that they might sit out there for hours, waiting for the digital clock embedded in the dashboard of the van to tick over to 17:00, so they could clock off for the evening, having avoided doing any more work. But then the van roared to life and they rumbled off in cloud of grey smoke.

The second they were out of sight, Michael locked the door, denying entry to anybody who may wish to interrupt him.

Not that anybody would want to interrupt him. Nobody ever turned up uninvited. They used to, but not anymore. Now most of his business was conducted through the auction houses. He liked it that way; he could remain anonymous. The odd private sale that he made was almost exclusively done through existing acquaintances, previous customers who knew him to be a reputable dealer - he was, after all, a man with impeccable taste, who could find the exact piece required, without having to look too hard for it.

He'd spent many a year dealing in antiques and art, acquiring his vast knowledge base (a knowledge base far superior to that of the majority of his peers) and building his reputation as a man of vast expertise.

But it was his own collection that had, in a way, thrown his reputation into disrepute. Not many knew about his private collection, but most of those who did, found it... somewhat disturbing.

Michael had first heard of it in the nineties, having read an article about it in one of the less reputable trade publications. At the time, it was something he cared very little for. But one night, perhaps five, maybe six years later, after a rather rambunctious party, one where he'd drank a few too many glasses of champagne and snorted way too many lines of coke, a friend had shown him a piece that he'd procured earlier that day. And despite the fact that he'd been swimming in a cloud of drugs and alcohol, it had fascinated Michael. It wasn't a masterpiece. Far from it. In fact, it was rather crude. But that wasn't the point. The story behind the painting was far more interesting than the picture itself. This one had been painted by Andrew Turner; a man convicted of murdering twelve prostitutes in Southampton in the mid-nineteen-eighties. He'd died only weeks previous, his throat cut by a fellow inmate who'd seemingly taken offense at an innocent joke, which he'd mistaken for a snide insult.

'Murderabilia' they called it, a not-very-clever portmanteau of 'Murder' and 'Memorabilia'. Michael preferred the term 'Murder Art', although he found that to still be rather tactless.

The first piece he'd purchased for himself was a sculpture. He'd paid several thousand pounds for it, too. It had been made by Elliot Wood, a man who had kidnapped and murdered a number of children in the late seventies. As Michael read the details of his crimes - about how he tied the children up in his basement; about how he tortured them and raped them; about how he dumped their dismembered remains into the river that ran behind his house (it was this that finally led to his subsequent arrest) - he couldn't help but feel fascinated by the man. Of course, his crimes were truly despicable. But then, *how* could anybody even do such a thing? *Where* did such a monster come from? The sculpture itself, which was rather formless, but was said to represent the Cerberus, the three-headed hound of hell, had been constructed before his arrest, from the bones of his first victim. Michael had taken great pleasure in owning this piece, despite its macabre beginnings. This pleasure was short-lived however, as once the police found out that Michael had taken possession of the piece, they confiscated it to hold as evidence. They returned it once an analysis had proven that the bones were not those of a child, but that they had, in actual fact, belonged to a number of dogs.

That was bitter-sweet for Michael. He'd paid a lot of money for a sculpture made from the bones of a murdered child; he expected to receive a sculpture made from the bones of a murdered child. But still, at least he had it. And it was still made by one of England's most despised serial killers. Sure, it had less value now, but it was still a nice piece.

Anyhow, the story of the dealer with the bizarre collection of art had made the trade press (again, it was only the less reputable papers that covered the story) and now nobody seemed willing to deal with a man who collected the work of psychopathic murderers. Most people seemed to think that by buying their work, one would be sympathising with the scum of the earth.

That just wasn't true. But those people would never understand.

And that was fine. Michael was happy with the way in which he now conducted his business - he was happy being anonymous behind the auctioneers. Anonymity was his friend.

Regardless of what others might think or say about him, Michael's fascination had sustained. Over the years, he'd continued to pick up pieces here and there; a few more sculptures, half-a-dozen paintings. He even owned the axe that a man had used to massacre more than thirty people in a shopping mall in London. Witnesses claimed that the man had seemed possessed by a demon - a rumour lent all the more validity by the Latin inscription in the handle of the axe, which spoke of a thirst for blood. The police had shot the killer dead on the scene, but somehow the axe had escaped the evidence room and made its way into Michael's possession. It was now displayed proudly, in a glass case, on the mantel piece of his lounge.

The piece for which Michael had just now taken delivery - a piece entitled 'The Woman Of The Sun', still wrapped in its blanket of creaky, brown paper - was going to be his prized possession. He was sure of it. Of course, he'd seen a photograph before he'd completed the purchase, but a photo could never do a painting justice. You had to see it up close. You had to touch the canvas, caress the bumps, trace your fingers along the thick lines gouged in the paint.

He took off his wide-rimmed glasses and cleaned them, before returning them to the bridge of his nose. He rolled up the sleeves of his expensive Armani shirt and took a deep breath.

Carefully, he reached out for the corner of the package and peeled away the edge of the tape. He pulled it, slowly, top to bottom. About halfway, the tape peeled off at an angle and split. Michael screwed the tape up and tossed it away, nonchalantly.

He picked at the edge of the remaining tape until it began to come away from the paper. Soon, all the tape was off the package, screwed up and balled in a pile on the floor.

He reached up for the top of the paper and unfolded it from the edge. As soon as it was released, the paper flopped over and slumped to the floor.

Michael stepped back. He stared in awe, bathed in the light of one of the most beautiful women he'd ever seen.

"The Woman Of The Sun," he whispered to himself.

Quickly, he pulled away the bubble wrap, exposing the edges of the canvas. Oftentimes, the edges of a picture held the most intricate of details. Most people missed them. This wasn't the case here - the edges of this painting were rough and uneven, where the artist had stopped short of the end of the canvas.

Again, Michael stepped back. He shook his head and smiled, pleased with himself - pleased with *her*. He raised his hand to his mouth, an effort to prevent his heart from bursting forth from his throat and bleeding over 'The Woman Of The Sun'.

And then she spoke to him.

Softly at first. No more than a whisper. Seductive and sultry, directly into his ear. She was smiling at him. She told him things. Told him of her life, of her Father. He was a great man - a true artist - but his work had not been completed. She told Michael that her Father's blood flowed through her veins.

And Michael could see it. He could see the blood of the artist – her Father – flowing in rivers through the paint, pooling on his pallet, rolling down the canvas.

The artist was a man named Roberto Da Silva. He was Brazilian. He'd spent the majority of the nineties recruiting followers, cultivating a church in the favelas of Rio. The church, known as 'The Order Of The Sun', worshiped the Devil. Da Silva had been arrested after one of his followers escaped the church. She'd told the police of how Da Silva had forced all of his female followers to have sex with him. He had impregnated most of them. During her time there, Da Silva had allegedly fathered more than 500 children with his followers. She told the police that once those babies were born, they were slaughtered, an offering in the name of Satan. Then they were cannibalised. Oftentimes, mothers were forced to eat their own children.

Of course, there had been no evidence of this, but Da Silva was arrested none-the-less. His trial lasted only one day. He was convicted and sentenced to serve five-hundred consecutive life terms, one for each of the alleged children he killed. Da Silva was convinced he would outlive his sentence. Satan would allow him to live far beyond the years of any other mortal man, so he might serve him once more. He would complete his work.

'The Woman Of The Sun' was the one and only piece that Da Silva had created. She was born in the confines of his dirty, cockroach infested cell. Da Silva was found soon after, his body hanging from the rafters above the showers. He'd been eviscerated, his innards piled beneath him.

'The Woman Of The Sun' smiled. She told Michael of his future. He belonged to her now, just as she belonged to him. Together they were one. *They* would continue the work of her Father.

Michael was happy. Her words soothed him of any anxiety he had ever felt. She had the power to control him. From the very moment he opened the parcel and exposed himself to 'The Woman Of The Sun, he was no longer a real man. He was a puppet, and she was his master.

And that was fine by Michael. He wanted nothing more. He was hers.

So, when she had told him to kill the homeless man who was sleeping, propped up against the wall of the supermarket, directly underneath the cash machine that he had wanted to use, Michael had done so without question. He withdrew his money first, of course, and then he strangled the man to death with his bare hands. It felt good. As Michael wrapped his hands around his throat and began to squeeze, the homeless man had woken. Immediately a sense of horror - of pure terror - had flooded Michael's veins. But it wasn't his own, *oh no*. It was that of the homeless man. As Michael tightened his grip, he considered for a moment that maybe - just maybe - what he was actually doing was absorbing the man's poor, terrified soul. Michael had held his grip long after the homeless man's body a fallen limp. Once he'd released his grip, he had stood and walked away from the corpse as if nothing had ever happened.

Michael could still smell the homeless man on his hands days later. It was a vile stench - a horrible concoction of alcohol, sweat and piss.

'The Woman Of The Sun' had been pleased.

And when a young woman - she had, perhaps, only just turned twenty - had knocked at his door, scrounging money for the conservation of giant pandas (or some other mundane, insignificant reason - he'd forgotten the actual reason pretty quickly), he'd invited her in, just as 'The Woman Of The Sun' had told him. The girl had declined at first, but Michael had put on the charming front he possessed (he was a salesman at the end of the day) and convinced her it was safe to come in. She sat in his lounge while he'd gone to make her a drink. When he returned, he handed her a cool glass of cola, which she gulped down willingly. Once her glass was empty, she thanked him. It was then that he slashed her throat. Distracted while drinking her cola, the girl hadn't noticed that Michael had been hiding a butcher's knife behind his back, or that he was now holding it before him, his eyes closed as he listened to 'The Woman Of The Sun'. No sooner had she thanked him, a pleasant and grateful smile on her face, then Michael had plunged the blade of his knife into the side of her neck. The girl had tried to scream, but no sound had come. Michael assumed the blade had severed her vocal cords. He then began to saw with the knife, dragging it

Idle Hands

forward, until the skin of her neck split open, the blade popping free in a cascade of blood. The girl slumped dead on the sofa. Her blood had spilled rapidly over Michael's expensive leather three-seater, into the cracks and grooves of the material. Michael cleaned it as best he could, but the tell-tale signs of blood - the deep crimson colour embedded in the material, the dried flecks intertwined with the stitching - were still there. It would have to be replaced.

No matter. At least 'The Woman Of The Sun' was pleased once again.

There had been a few more after her, but they had slipped from Michael's memory. His mind was now cloudy, muddy with thoughts of 'The Woman Of The Sun'. Her beauty. Her unwavering smile. The flames, licking at her skin.

He loved her, more so than he had ever loved anybody before. Her skin, chalky and soft, felt wonderful against his own. He caressed her flesh, kneading her skin with his fingers. His hands soon made their way to her breasts, which they squeezed firmly, the stiff nipples rolling between his fingers. She moaned with pleasure as he thrust his penis inside of her. Propped up on his hands, Michael began to slide in and out of her, the soft warmth of her wet vagina gripping the length of his member. It didn't take long for him to climax. Michael groaned as he released his heavy load of semen inside her. And then he collapsed upon her. Breathing heavy, he could feel their hearts beating in tandem.

"I love you," said 'The Woman Of The Sun', barely a whisper in Michael's ear.

"I love you too," said Michael.

And then there was laughter, coming from somewhere behind him.

Michael drew a panicked breath before peering over his own shoulder, to see who it was that was laughing at him. Somebody must've broken into his unit and had watched them making love. *How dare they? He would kill them dead, right there!*

But the face that greeted Michael was not the one he had expected. Or, more so, it was the one face he could not possibly have expected to see.

It was 'The Woman Of The Sun', still floating in the dark void of her canvas, who was laughing at him.

But how?

Michael looked down at the woman beneath him. It wasn't 'The Woman Of The Sun' he had made love to at all. It was a stranger; some woman he'd never seen before. And she was dead. Her chest had been flayed, her breasts removed. Her rib cage had been separated and her torso had been hollowed out. Michael looked to his right where her internal organs now sat, a gory pile of offal.

Quickly, he pulled out of the anonymous woman's corpse. His semen seeped from the vagina of her cold, lifeless carcass. He stood and faced 'The Woman Of The Sun'.

She looked down upon Michael, from where she now rested. He had lifted her from the ground and placed her on a sideboard some time ago. Days and weeks had passed since she first arrived, but Michael couldn't be specific about how long it had been - for all he knew, it may have been years. By now he had cleared most of the unit. He'd shoved what he could against the bare, breeze-block walls, piling it high, until it reached the tin roof. One of those piles had collapsed as he'd stacked a scries of chairs on top of cabinet. As one of the chairs had fallen, it had splintered and tore the skin of his leg. Blood had flowed effortlessly from the wound, but Michael felt no pain. 'The Woman Of The Sun' took care of that for him. She did so because she loved him.

Michael was stood in the middle of the now-empty space, the dead woman lying behind him in a pool of blood that made the concrete look almost black. He was naked, soaked with blood, head-to-toe. He could feel it splattering his feet as it dripped from the end of his now flaccid penis. A sense of shame filled his being. He didn't care about the people he had killed. He only cared about her. And she was laughing at him.

Michael had always done as 'The Woman Of The Sun' had asked. He never questioned her. He did this out of his love for her. He thought she loved him too.

But what was this? Why had she made him have sex with some other woman? Was this some kind of trick? Did she not love him the way he loved her?

'The Woman Of The Sun' laughed at Michael. She was still smiling.

This angered Michael. How could she laugh at him? He'd done everything she'd asked of him. He'd made her proud. Her Father's work was complete.

Her Fathers work would never be complete.

"What do you mean?" Michael asked 'The Woman Of The Sun'. "I did exactly as you asked!"

She whispered in his ear.

Michael shook his head. "I cannot do this anymore."

She whispered again, quieter this time. This time it wasn't even in his ear. It was deeper. It was as if her words were simply filtering into him, directly into his brain.

Her words angered Michael further. "You used me?"

'The Woman Of The Sun' laughed again. She smiled, her thin, perfect lips, unnaturally red.

Michael looked down at the ground. The blood of the dead woman - which ran down his neck, down his chest, down his legs - was pooled around his feet, sticking between his toes.

"You used me..." The realisation began to dawn on Michael.

'The Woman Of The Sun' could only smile.

"You used me!" Michael screamed at the top of his lungs.

Michael grabbed a knife (the same one he'd used to remove the dead woman's flesh a few hours earlier - an act he could no longer recall) from the oak dining table beside him. He walked towards 'The Woman Of The Sun' and looked her up and down. The love he had felt for her was gone, replaced with some fierce hatred, the likes of which he'd never felt before. He lifted the knife and stabbed it into her chest.

In Michael's head, she screamed. In reality, she smiled. In fact, her lips didn't even move. They never had.

Michael pulled the knife downwards, splitting the canvas in two, bisecting 'The Woman Of The Sun'. He withdrew the knife, then stabbed it back in at the corner, dragging it down at an angle. The bottom corner of the painting slipped loose and hung from the frame, draped over the edge of the sideboard on which it stood.

Michael slashed at the painting over and over, shredding it to pieces. An eternity seemed to pass, before Michael stopped, exhausted of all his energy.

He panted like a tired dog. His forced breaths came ragged and strained. He turned his back on what remained of 'The Woman Of The Sun'.

On the other side of the unit was a blank canvas, set up on an old, wooden easel.

Michael stood before the canvas and stared. He picked up a thin brush from the easel, never taking his eyes from the canvas. He crouched, dipping the brush in the blood of the young woman. His eyes remained, fixated on the whiteness of the canvas.

He put the brush to the canvas and began to paint.

Behind him, the shredded painting hung from its frame in rough tatters. But 'The Woman Of The Sun' was still there. From a single strip - a sliver of the canvas still hanging from the top of the frame, rocking lightly in the breeze that flowed through the cold, empty unit - 'The Woman Of The Sun' watched as Michael worked on his own masterpiece.

And she was still smiling.

THE END

Harrison Phillips

THE BALLAD OF JOHN SMITH

John Smith was an ordinary man with an ordinary life. He was 40 years old. He was 5-foot-9-inches tall. He was of an average build; not skinny, not chubby, not athletic. Not anything - just average. His hair was cut short and worn neatly on top of his head. He was clean-shaven. He didn't wear glasses (although he hadn't had an eye test since school – but then, he'd never felt it necessary). He always wore clothes that allowed him to blend into the crowd. He liked to wear plain woolen jumpers and corduroy trousers. He didn't like to stand out. He liked to blend in. He liked being ordinary.

He worked in a call center. Every day, from eight 'til five, John sat behind his desk, working through the list of names that his computer presented to him, phoning their respective numbers and – should the intended recipient actually answer (which was becoming less and less often these days) – offering them the deal of a lifetime. "Hi. Could I interest you in half-price insurance for your boiler?" he'd ask, each and every time. Most people hung up instantly. Some would offer a string of vulgar, single-syllable words before doing so. Some would stick around, maybe sparking a conversation. On the (very) rare occasion, he might even make a sale. It was a mundane job. John didn't particularly enjoy it, nor did he hate it. He was indifferent. He just got on with it. At least it paid the bills.

Every night after work, a small handful of his colleagues would venture across to the pub on the other side of the road. They always invited him. He never went. It wasn't that he disliked them; they were a good group of people. Many of them had wives and kids at home (something that John had never really had any desire to have himself). Some of them were actually interesting. But the nine hours he spent in their company at the call center was more than enough.

Besides, John didn't drink.

Not ever.

Instead, every night after work, John would go home and cook himself dinner. He lived alone, so he could please himself as to what he ate. He mainly stuck to plain food - sausage and chips, fish fingers and chips, chicken and chips. Sometimes, depending on his mood, he'd just have the chips. He didn't like spicy food. Nothing foreign. Even something as basic as a margarita pizza was enough to turn his stomach. He never ate take-away - he didn't trust them. God only knew what they could be putting in their food. No - he knew exactly where he stood with the good, old-fashioned frozen food he could pick up at the supermarket.

Every night, after dinner, John would read the newspaper that he'd invariably pick up from the corner shop that he passed during his walk home (oh, yes – John didn't drive; he'd never learned how). He'd sit in his armchair, feet up on the footstool, and flip through the pages, mentally debating with himself about the day's goings on.

Sometimes he'd have the radio on too – he'd split his attention between that and the newspaper, depending on what was the most interesting at that particular time. He listened to talk shows. He didn't like music all too much – certainly not the recent pop music that seemed to be infiltrating every facet of his life. He could just about abide The Beatles. That was about as recent as his taste would get.

By ten o'clock, he was normally ready for bed. It was an exceedingly rare occasion that he stayed up past eleven. He always slept well. And then, feeling refreshed, he'd be up again at six-thirty – *bright eyed and bushy tailed*, his dear old mum would have said, were she still alive. Then it was back to work.

And last Friday was a day just like any other.

Being as it was the middle of winter, it was dark when John had arrived at work, and it would be dark by the time he left. The call center was surrounded on three sides by tall glass windows. It was seven floors up, offering quite the view of the town. John always enjoyed the light show that preceded the descent of darkness.

As the clock reached five, and all the workers gathered their belongings, a guy named David (he was one of the nicest guys John knew) asked John if he was coming to the pub for a swift half. John declined, as he always did, and wondered why they continued to ask him.

John was the last one to leave the office, other than his manager Michael, who always stayed to lock up. As John left work, he offered a wave to Susan, the receptionist. He liked Susan, but he didn't speak to her much.

The walk home was as uneventful as ever. He stopped off at the corner shop to pick up his paper and continued on.

Dinner that night was chicken and chips. But that was fine; he liked chicken.

After dinner, John settled down to read his paper. It took him around twenty minutes to read through to the sports section. By the time he'd gotten there, he'd begun to notice a tingling sensation in his left arm. At first, he'd thought it was pins-and-needles, or perhaps just a numbness, from holding the paper at a funny angle. But then it had spread to his right arm.

He found that both of his upper limbs were stiff. He couldn't move them, couldn't lift them from the arms of his chair. His grip on the paper was tight. It wouldn't budge. It was as if something was causing every muscle in his arms to contract.

A thought ran through his head, telling him that his legs wouldn't work either. He was right – he tried to stand and found that he couldn't. His legs were stuck out before him, solid, bridging from the seat of his chair to the footstool before him.

As panic set in, John tried to call for help. He found he couldn't; his tongue was paralyzed too.

His heart was racing. He could feel it, hammering against his ribcage (at least that muscle still seemed to be functioning properly). But his lungs were tight. He couldn't breathe, despite his best efforts to suck at the air around him.

Idle Hands

Then he began to notice the tingling sensation spreading to his chest. It was as if it was something alive, under his skin, crawling through his flesh.

It was warmth, the likes of which John had never felt before.

He could only move his eyes. He looked down at his arms. The sensation was strange. It felt as if his limbs were growing hot. And it was painful.

And then they burst into flames.

His arms were on fire and all he could do was watch as they burned.

An excruciating pain shot through John's body, telling his brain to move, telling him to do something. Anything. But he couldn't move. He could do nothing.

The flames licked at the newspaper he held in his hands. It didn't catch fire. The edges singed where it met his skin, but it didn't burn, not like it should have.

John watched as his arms – flesh and bone – disintegrated into ash.

The newspaper folded up neatly and fell to the floor.

The flames spread along John's shoulders and along his chest. Before long, the flames had reached his legs and engulfed his head.

It took less than a minute for his entire body to crumble into a pile of ashes. There was nothing left. No flesh. No bones. Even his teeth had disintegrated. His clothes were gone. It was as if he had never existed.

It took two days for anybody to notice that John wasn't at work. David had assumed he was on holiday. Michael had assumed he was sick. It wasn't until Susan questioned his whereabouts that they decided to check up on him.

He was never found, of course. All that was left of him was piled in his chair, nothing more than a heap of black ash.

A forensics team studied the scene for days. Fire experts were called. They all commented on how bizarre it was; there were no traces of John at all – he had been burnt to ashes. That fact alone suggested that the fire had been of an extreme heat. Yet, nothing else had been damaged. The chair, the footstool, the carpet, even his newspaper had been untouched by the vicious flames that had eaten John's flesh and bones away to nothing.

Officially, his death was marked as unexplained.

Later, academic papers would be written about the incident. 'Spontaneous Human Combustion' they'd call it. It would be widely regarded as the most concrete evidence that such a phenomenon actually existed.

THE END

PORNOGRAPHER

The girl must've only been eighteen. She was small and skinny, with shoulder length brunette hair. Her tits were small and perky. She was wearing a black bikini, showing off her toned stomach and her smooth, round arse.

She was perfect.

She was in the back yard of some glorious mansion. There was a pool. The water glistened in the blazing Hollywood sunshine.

She took a seat on the sun lounger, cocktail in hand, and laid back.

A man approached. He looked to be in his mid-twenties. He was wearing red swim shorts. He wasn't wearing a shirt. He had the physique of an Adonis; broad and muscular and his skin was tanned a deep brown. His short, jet-black hair was slicked back over his head.

"Hey," said the man, smiling, showing off his perfectly white teeth.

The girl smiled in return.

Beautiful.

"Hi," she said, peering over her sunglasses, somewhat seductively.

The man looked her over. The thoughts that were running through his mind were as clear as daylight. He wanted to fuck her.

The girl continued – "Hey? Could you do me a favour and rub some lotion into my back. I'd do it myself, but – you know – I can't reach."

"Sure," said the man. "No problem."

The girl smiled. She shifted on the sun lounger, so that she was facing away from the man.

The man picked up the bottle of lotion from the floor and squirted a blob of the white cream into the palm of his hand. He then rubbed his hands together and began to massage the lotion into the girl's back.

After about five seconds of this, the man began to pull at the strings of the girl's bikini top.

The girl didn't even try to stop him.

The man finished untying the girl's bikini and pulled it over her head.

Her breasts were incredible. Her nipples were small and perfectly round.

The man reached under the girl's arms and began to squeeze and massage her breasts, pinching and rolling her nipples between his thumb and forefinger. As he did this, he kissed and nibbled at her neck.

The girl tipped her head back and moaned with pleasure.

The man then reached down and slipped his hand into her bikini bottoms.

It was at that point that my dick started to get hard. I hooked my thumbs under the waistband of my boxer shorts and slipped them down to my knees. I was well prepared; I already had a neatly folded length of tissue paper sat on my bedside table. I shifted my laptop to one side and began to stroke the length of my erection.

On the screen, the man was now sat on the sun lounger, the girl on her knees before him. She had removed his shorts and was now sucking his dick, taking the full length into her throat.

Boring.

I clicked onto the video, skipping ahead by a few minutes.

The man was already fucking the girl. She was laid on the sun lounger, her hands hooked behind her knees to keep her legs spread, while he was pounding in and out of her, squeezing her tits.

I continued to masturbate as I watched the couple in the video move into several different positions - doggy style; cowgirl; reverse cowgirl.

After a few more minutes, the man pulled out of the girl. She dropped to her knees and opened her mouth wide, tongue protruding. The man aimed the tip of his penis into the girl's mouth and blew his load, streaking his cum across her tongue.

The girl used her finger to scrape up the cum from her chin and drop it into her mouth. She then swallowed the whole lot back. She opened her mouth, stuck out her tongue to show that it was all gone, and smiled.

That was enough for me.

I grabbed the tissue from the bedside table and smothered it over the head of my cock. My balls tightened and my penis pulsed as I filled the tissue with warm, sticky semen.

"Well Pete," said a voice from somewhere in my room. "That's fucking disgusting."

Holy shit!

My heart was suddenly racing so hard that, for a brief moment, I thought I was having a heart attack. Panic flooded my entire being.

Sophie was stood in the doorway. She had some weird look plastered across her face – it was a kind-of frown, combined with a crooked smirk. "I wish I had my camera with me," she said, barely able to contain her laughter. "Your *cum face* is fucking hilarious!"

"Get the fuck out!" I shouted, just about ready to die of embarrassment. How had I not heard her come in? And more to the point, why the fuck hadn't she knocked?

"Alright! Alright! I'm going," she said, as she walked away from the door, leaving it wide open. She did this just to annoy me, of that I was certain. "Mum said dinner's ready."

Fuck...

Dinner that evening – sat at the table with Mum and Dad and Sophie – was extremely awkward. Sophie was sat directly opposite to me. The whole time she was smiling. She looked like the cat who got the cream. Clearly, she was finding this whole thing highly amusing.

Clearly, she was significantly less disgusted by the idea of having seen her brother masturbating, as I was at the thought of her having watched me climax.

Sophie was my little sister. She was fifteen. I was fairly certain that she had already lost her virginity. On several occasions I'd heard her talking to her boyfriend on the phone, telling him about the things she wanted him to do to her (I really didn't like hearing my fifteen-year-old sister talking about doing anal, but what could I possibly do about it?). There were rumours that she was actually a bit of a slut, having slept with half of her class.

I chose not to believe those rumours.

Still, she was almost certainly more experienced than me. I could count the number of people *I'd* had sex with on one hand. One finger, even.

Just to be clear – I had only ever had sex with one person.

Once.

At seventeen, I should have slept with loads of girls by now. All my peers had (or so they claimed). But that had never really been *my thing*. I had always found talking to girls highly embarrassing. Back in school, whenever I'd had to talk to a girl – even if it was just about whatever mundane topic we were studying in class – I could always feel myself clamming up, my cheeks burning, no doubt having turned bright red.

I lost my virginity to a girl named Alison. It had been a pretty terrible experience. We were both drunk, both having consumed copious amounts of cider at a friend's house party. It had been her who instigated it. She had dragged me out of the party and led me down an alleyway, where she had quickly pulled down my trousers, rolled up her skirt and backed herself onto my erect cock.

I can only assume she'd thought I was far more experienced than I actually was. I probably lasted about a minute and a half. I'm sure I should've felt embarrassed by this, but I didn't. Alison didn't seem too disappointed either. She didn't even speak to me afterwards; she just pulled up her pants, kissed me and then walked away, back to the party.

That was the full extent of my sexual history.

I was far more content watching porn.

I watched a lot of porn. I always masturbated at least twice a day. Occasionally, depending on how horny I was feeling, that number might increase to three – sometimes, even four – times a day.

That evening – after that very awkward dinner – I took myself back off to my bedroom, to play some Playstation for a few hours before bed.

Of course, I couldn't actually go to sleep until I'd masturbated one last time.

At around ten, I turned off the Playstation and once again began browsing the internet for porn.

I liked all kinds of porn; I really wasn't fussy. I liked white girls. Black girls. Asians. Skinny girls. Chubby girls. I even had a bit of a thing for lady boys.

The trouble with watching so much porn is that, truth be told, you get to a point when you've seen it all. You eventually find yourself desensitised to 'normal' porn, and so you end up looking for things a bit… well… *less* normal.

Gangbangs.

S&M.

Scat.

I'd recently found myself getting incredibly turned on by girls being throat-fucked so hard that they eventually vomit.

My desire for more extreme porn had eventually led me onto the dark web. The porn that can be found there is *much more* extreme. Of course, there's some stuff I'd never watch. Nothing involving kids; that was a given. Nothing involving animals either – I really don't know what was wrong with some people, wanting to watch people having sex with dogs…

On the dark web, there were entire websites full of videos of women being tortured and raped.

It was this that was seemingly becoming my new fetish.

Not that I watched it all the time; I could still just as easily get myself off to the 'normal' porn, as I could to the extreme stuff.

But, sometimes, I just needed something a little more brutal.

I browsed onto the dark web and found a site called 'XxXxPornoWeb'. Here, they hosted a multitude extreme porn videos (including some of that shit I said I'd never watch).

I clicked onto a video entitled 'brutal gang rape – multiple penetration'.

I know – I'm sick in the head. But, to me, this stuff wasn't real. Hell, in actual fact, it might *not* be real. These could all be actors, simply making a film to satisfy those of us with more morbid sexual interests.

That had to be a thing, right?

Immediately, the video showed a young, blonde woman (perhaps no older than twenty) bound to a bed. She was naked. She had a nice body; her boobs were full, her stomach was flat, her vagina was clean shaven. Her hands were tied to the bedposts at the head of the bed, while her feet were secured to the foot of the bed.

A man approached. He was broad; his shoulders were heavily muscled and his neck was as thick as a tree trunk. His face was obscured with some sort of scarf, which was wrapped around his head, leaving only his eyes visible.

Most importantly, he was naked and his dick was hard.

The girl began to moan. She spoke in a language that I didn't understand. At a guess, I would have said it was Russian. She was squirming on the bed, pulling at her restraints.

The man clambered onto the bed, between the girl's legs.

The girl tried to clamp her legs shut, but the restraints tied around her ankles wouldn't allow it. She tried to twist her body to one side, almost as if she were trying to roll to her front. But her attempts were in vain – her body was held tightly, flattened out on the grubby mattress.

The man positioned himself so that he was on his knees, his legs tucked under the buttocks of the girl. There, he lined up his erection with the opening of her vagina and pushed.

The girl screamed. She was crying.

The man didn't care.

He forced himself inside the girl and began to fuck her.

I knew that it was wrong of me to feel turned on by this, but I couldn't help it. It was out of my control. I would never do anything like this myself, or course – rape was abhorrent. But, again, this sort of thing just didn't feel real to me. It felt like a more explicit version of some Hollywood rape/revenge movie (although, of course, this video was unlikely to feature the revenge part...).

I slid off my boxers and began to stroke my dick.

On the screen, the man was done fucking the girl. He pulled out and shot five or six streams of cum over the girl's stomach. Another man approached. He was short and overweight, and his whole body was covered with hair. Like the muscular man, his face was wrapped in a scarf. He climbed onto the bed and began to fuck the girl too.

Again, the girl writhed and screamed on the dirty bed. The twisted expression on her face told me that she was begging for him to stop.

But the hairy man didn't stop. After a few moments, he pulled out and came on the girl's belly. Another man approached – he was tall and skinny, his face also wrapped in a scarf. He scrambled onto the bed and began to fuck the girl.

It was then that I came. I allowed my cum to splatter onto my stomach. I cleaned myself off with a tissue, while, on screen, the skinny man finished himself off, splattering his cum onto the girl's tits.

I screwed up my used tissue and tossed it into the wastepaper bin by the door (I say *'tossed it in…'* – I missed. No matter – I'd pick it up later).

On the screen, another man – he was bald and covered in tattoos – was fucking the girl.

If this *was* a set up – if this was being staged for the audience – this girl was an incredible actress; Oscar worthy, no less. The way she pulled at the ropes and squirmed on the bed, the way she screamed at the top of her lungs until her voice cracked, made me truly believe that she was fighting for her life.

As the tattooed man fucked her, the muscular man approached once again. His dick was hard once again. He stood beside the bed. It took me a few moments to realise that he was holding a knife. The blade was short and stubby – perhaps only two inches long and one inch wide.

While the tattooed man continued to fuck the girl, the muscular man plunged the blade into the side of her belly.

The girl cried out in sheer agony; an eardrum-piercing scream.

My stomach churned. The relaxed sense of satisfaction brought on by my own orgasm was immediately gone. I sat bolt upright on my bed, my face only inches away from the screen of my laptop.

Blood seeped from the wound, oozing out around the blade. The muscular man pulled the knife out. More blood poured from the gash. The muscular man then passed the knife to the hairy man, who approached the bed from the other side. Here, the hairy man stabbed the blade into the other side of the girl's belly.

The girl squealed once again.

The whole time, the tattooed man continued to fuck her.

I couldn't believe what I was seeing. This was real, I was sure of it. They were really killing this girl. This was, for want of a better word, snuff.

The hairy man passed the knife to the skinny man, who stood back and watched as both the muscular man and the hairy man placed the heads of their respective erections against the wounds they had inflicted upon the girl and forced themselves inside her.

I wanted to be sick. I could've vomited right there and then. But I held back and continued to watch. I couldn't stop myself – my morbid curiosity got the better of me.

The muscular man pushed his penis deep into the girl's belly. Her screams were now far more agonised. The wound in her stomach stretched and tore further open, releasing cascades of gore. The muscular man pressed his hips forwards. The flesh of the girl's belly bulged as his stiff cock tore through the subdermal fat, stretching the skin, tearing it away from the muscle below. He then began to fuck the hole that he had opened up in her side.

The hairy man did the same.

This went on for several minutes – the girl writhing in agony, while the three men raped her, two of them doing so in orifices that weren't supposed to be there. - until the skinny man climbed up onto the bed, and straddled the girl.

The girl looked up at the skinny man. She said something to him. She was speaking Russian, but I would've sworn I understood what she was saying – she was pleading for her life.

The skinny man slammed the blade into the girl's throat and dragged it sideways. Blood sprayed from her arteries, coating him in crimson. Her body convulsed. She tipped her head back, opening the gash wide. The skinny man forced her head back further and pushed his erect penis into the new gash, forcing it down into her larynx.

I clamped my hand over my mouth. I couldn't believe what I was witnessing. There was still life behind the girl's eyes. She was still alive as the skinny man began to fuck her lacerated neck. It took a few moments for her to die. Even as she laid dead, the four men continued to rape her.

The tattooed man pulled out first, squirting his semen onto the dead girl's stomach. The hairy man came next, pulling out of the gash, his cock slick with blood, and blowing his load onto the corpse. Both the muscular man and the skinny man finished at the same time.

The image buzzed with static and the video flickered to black.

I was in a state of shock. What I had just seen… This couldn't be real. No way.

I should tell somebody.

Who?

My computer bleeped. A small pop-up window opened in the corner of the screen. It was an instant messaging chat box. But I didn't recognise it – it wasn't from Facebook or Twitter, or any of the other social media platforms I used. It must've been an application built into the web browser itself.

It appeared that a user by the name of 'FuCkMaStEr666' wanted to talk to me. His message read - **You like sick shit?**

What the fuck? Why would somebody ask me such a question?

For a moment, I considered the fact that this wasn't a real a message, that perhaps it was just some shitty advertising pop-up. But then another message came through. This one read - **You like sick shit, yes? You enjoy this?**

Whoever this was, they knew exactly what had happened in the video I'd just watched. In my mind, I read this message in a Russian accent (like those voices I'd heard in the video). It didn't read as though somebody with a full grasp of English had written it.

Against my better judgement, I wrote back. My fingers tapped quickly on the keyboard. "Who is this?" I asked.

You like the extreme porno?

"Who is this?" I asked again.

You like see dead bodies being fucked?
"No."
You lie. I see you.
"What do you mean?"

The pop-up opened further, so that it filled around half of the screen. A video began to play. It was me. I was sat on my bed, my boxer shorts around my knees, cock in hand. Instantly I realised that this video had been taken from the webcam of my laptop. My heart was thudding in my chest. Whoever this was, they had hacked my laptop and they had recorded me masturbating.

And they knew that I'd watched the video of the girl being murdered.

I watch you. You like dead girl be fucked.

"No. I didn't choose to watch that! I didn't know they were going to kill her!"

But you watch. You cum.

"No. I didn't know."

Now you pay.

Fuck. I should've known. They wanted money. They were blackmailing me. A whole host of thoughts ran through my head. What would happen if people found out that I'd watched a snuff video? What would the police do? Was what I had done illegal? WHAT THE *FUCK* WAS I SUPPOSED TO DO NOW?

I wrote another message. "You think I have money?" I wrote. "You're wrong. I don't. I'm just a kid. I don't have *access* to money."

We need no money from you.

"Then what the fuck do you want?"

Video.

A video? A video of what? They (FuCkMaStEr666 had said *we*, so I assumed there was more than just the one person behind this) already had a video of me. They had a video of me shooting my load, while watching a woman being gang-raped and then subsequently killed. What more could they possibly want from me? "A video of what?" I typed.

Snuff.
Rape a whore. Kill her.
Send us video.

I could've laughed. They wanted me to make snuff for them? As in, they actually wanted me to kill somebody and film it, so that they could put it on their site? No fucking way.

"I'm not going to make snuff for you," I told him/them.

You will.
"No. I won't."
You will, or your family will die.

My next breath caught in my throat. He was threatening my family. How could he even know who I was, or where I lived? How could he find me? I could tell by his writing that English wasn't his first language. That meant that, chances were, he didn't even live in the same country as me. How could he possibly get to my family?

It was as if he were reading my mind. Another message flashed onto the screen. It read – *Our network is global. We have people in all countries. When you watch our video, we learn everything. We know you now. We have people close to you.*

I didn't know what to say. My mind was racing at a million miles per hour. This couldn't possibly be happening. It was bullshit. It was some sort of a sick joke.

I slammed my laptop shut.

Idle Hands

It was all bullshit. The video was fake – they hadn't really killed that girl. FuCkMaStEr666 wasn't really part of some global snuff ring. Nobody was going to kill my family. Worst case scenario, this was some sort of a con – they'd be back tomorrow, trying to screw me out of money.

Fuck.

What the fuck had I done?

I tossed and turned all evening. I didn't sleep at all. I dared not even close my eyes, as, whenever I did, visions of that poor girl – and what those four horrible, vile men had done to here – would play behind my eyelids.

And what they had asked of me - for me to go and do that to somebody else... I couldn't help but think that I would have no choice.

It wasn't real. It wasn't real.

I kept on telling myself that.

The next morning I opened my laptop, hoping to find that all those messages would be gone.

They weren't. Far from it.

FuCkMaStEr666 had sent me a series of messages.

You send us video?
You love your family?
You want them be dead?
You send us.
Kill somebody. Fuck their corpse. Send footage.
You family die if you say no.
Send video.
You want to die?
Send video.

For the briefest of moments, I wished that I *was* dead.

I clicked onto the X at the top of the browser and shut the software down. I'm not sure why, but I felt like turning off the computer would somehow erase what I had seen, and that would be the end of it.

And sure enough, when I switched my laptop back on a few hours later, the messages were gone and I received no more.

That night, I masturbated to some 'normal' porn.

The following day, very little happened. I played some Playstation. I watched some TV. But more importantly, I managed to forget about that video, and the dead girl, and the demands that FuCkMaStEr666 had made of me.

But then, as I opened up my laptop, I found a new message from FuCkMaStEr666. It read - *Watch this.*

Below this message was an attachment. It was a video. The video was entitled 'The Star Of Our Next Movie?'

I didn't want to, but I had to watch it. I pressed play.

Holy shit…

I immediately recognised the location in which this video had been filmed - it was our house.

What the fuck was going on?

It was dark. This must've been filmed last night. It *had* to have been. Somebody had been in our house! The person holding the camera walked along the downstairs hallway. They then headed up the stairs, taking each step carefully. Moonlight flooded onto the landing, through the window at the top of the stairs.

Idle Hands

The first door this person came to was my parent's bedroom. The door was closed.

The next door was my room.

The camera tilted downward, aimed at the door handle. A gloved hand reached out for the handle. But then, before it landed, it stopped and pulled back.

The person moved along the hall to the next door. This was Sophie's room. Slowly, they opened the door.

I'm not sure why, but I held my breath.

Quietly, the person moved into my sister's room. Sophie was snoring gently. She was face down on the bed. Her quilt was mostly off her body, only just draped over her left leg.

I took a breath. I couldn't possibly explain how I was feeling. I knew Sophie was safe; she was in her room right now - I'd spoken to her only moments ago. But still, I was horrified.

The person in the video moved closer to Sophie's bed. She was wearing a night dress. This dress - little more than a long t-shirt - had rucked up around her waist. Beneath this, she was wearing a pair of pink panties. The person moved in, closer still, and zoomed the image into a close up of her behind.

The image zoomed out again. And then the gloved hand appeared once again, fingers outstretched. It moved in closer to Sophie's buttocks…

Static buzzed across the image and the video shut off.

I felt sick. The person *hadn't* touched her. Had they done so, they surely would've woken her. And had she awoke and found a stranger in her room, groping her, filming her, I can only assume she would've said something.

Still, the message was clear – they were serious. They knew who I was. They could get to me. They could get to my family. If I didn't do as they told me, they were going to kill Sophie.

My head ached. My stomach twisted itself into knots. What the fuck was I supposed to do? They wanted me to kill somebody. How was I supposed to do that? I *couldn't* do that. I just wasn't capable.

So… What? Was I supposed to just let them kill Sophie?

A message from FuCkMaStEr666 popped up on the screen. It read - *So pretty. She make a beautiful corpse. People pay lots of money to watch her die.*

I felt enraged. My blood was boiling. To come into our house and threaten my sister… I couldn't let them get away with this, could I?

No.

They wanted me to kill someone. That was exactly what I *had* to do.

You make video?

"Alright," I typed, hammering away at the keyboard. "I'll do it."

Good. Do it quick. Our viewers don't like wait.
Make it sick.
The sicker, the better.

I didn't sleep that night.

Not a wink.

The next day, I prepared myself. I had no choice in the matter - this was something I *had* to do, or else face the consequences.

I thought about how I might do it.

Idle Hands

How could I kill somebody and not get caught?

Why was I even thinking such a thing?

I *couldn't* do it.

I *had* to do it.

Fuck...

I settled on the idea of killing a prostitute. They were generally considered to be the dregs of society anyway – nobody would notice if one of *them* disappeared. I would pay to have sex with one of them and then I'd cut her throat.

Quick. Easy. Over and done with.

I had to do it tonight. If I didn't, they'd be back. Who knows what they might do to Sophie then?

I waited 'til everybody had gone to bed. It was gone eleven by the time I left the house. Before I went, I picked up a thin-bladed knife from in the kitchen and stuffed it into the inside pocket of my jacket. I also took with me all the cash I had – the £60 left over from my birthday money. I had no idea if that was enough to procure the services of prostitute, but it was all I had.

I'd never used the services of a prostitute before, but I, like everybody else in town, knew exactly where they were to be found. There was a lay-by around two miles from my house, where a group of these women would wait for their clients to pick them up. From what I understood, truckers tended to frequent this place. They would stop there, fuck whichever whore they chose in back of their cab, and then continue on their journey.

I had yet to pass my driver's test, despite having already tried twice, and failing both times. So, I had a long walk ahead of me. That was fine though. In fact, it was perfect; there would be no CCTV of me driving along the roads, to somehow connect me to the murdered hooker.

It took me the better part of an hour. I arrived just before midnight.

I stood at the end of the lay-by, my body half obscured by the trees, and watched as a car pulled up and one of the women got in.

Once the car was gone, I pulled my hood up over my head and began to walk slowly into the lay-by.

One of the women saw me coming. "Hey there!" she said, her voice entirely upbeat. "You lookin' for a good time?" She was wearing a short red dress and matching high heels. Her brunette hair was curly, untamed. She looked good.

She'd do.

The woman began to approach me.

The other women seemed to stop and watch me. That was fine – it was pitch black out, and with my hood up, there was no way they could see my face. Certainly not enough so that they could ever recognise me. Any description they might give to the police would be as good as useless.

"You got money?" the woman in the red dress asked, as she neared me.

"I have, yes," I said. I could feel my voice wavering nervously.

"Oooh," said the woman, a wide smile spreading across her face. "You're just a baby. What brings you out here?"

"I want sex," I said, knowing how stupidly awkward I sounded. "I want somebody to let me film it."

Idle Hands

"I'll let you film me. It'll cost you extra though."

"How much?"

"One hundred," she said, her hands on her hips.

"Okay." I pulled out my wallet, took out the cash and handed it to her.

Quickly, she counted it. "This isn't enough."

"What *can* I get for that?"

"A blowjob. And I'll swallow."

"And I can film it?"

"Sure. I don't see why not?"

"Okay."

"Do you have a name, honey?"

"Peter," I told her, immediately feeling stupid for having given out my real name.

"Well, Peter. I'm Candy. And I'm very pleased to meet you."

The woman – Candy – looked over her shoulder, to where the other women were still gawping. I couldn't see her face of course, but I imagined her offering them a wink.

Another car pulled into the lay-by, distracting those other women.

Candy stuffed the money into her handbag. She then took me by the hand. "Follow me," she said, leading me out of the lay-by, through a break in the tree line. "I know a place we can go."

It was pitch black in the woods. The trees obscured what little moonlight there was.

She led me along a well-trodden path, to a small clearing, where an uprooted tree laid on its side. "Take a seat," said Candy, motioning toward the fallen tree.

"Hang on," I said. "I need to set up my camera."

"Oh, yes! You're going to make me a star!" She howled with laughter.

If only she knew what was coming.

I took my phone from my pocket and opened up the camera app. I switched it to video mode and turned on the light. I placed the phone into a nearby tree, onto a branch, just below head height.

I pressed record and approached the woman. She had sat on the tree herself.

I could see her properly now, for the first time. She'd looked good in the darkness, but now, in the harsh light given off from my phone, I could see that she was gaunt and that her skin was dry and pitted from where she had clearly suffered with acne. She looked like she was probably in her forties.

She looked like a crack addict.

"Get it out then," said Candy, nodding towards my crotch.

As instructed, I unbuckled my belt and slipped my jeans down to my ankles.

She licked her lips. I can only assume she was trying to look seductive – she didn't; she looked disgusting.

She took my flaccid penis in her mouth and began to work it with her tongue.

I could feel my penis swelling as it became engorged with blood. This whore might not have looked that great, but she certainly knew how to suck a dick. It felt amazing. This was my first proper blowjob. I didn't care that I'd had to pay for it.

For a moment, as she bobbed her head up and down, slurping as her lips worked along the shaft, I forgot about the real reason I was there.

And then I came.

Candy removed her mouth from my penis and began to stroke the length, squeezing she shaft, milking the semen from my dick, onto her exposed tongue.

With my balls emptied, she sucked back the cum and swallowed it down. She then wiped her mouth on the back of her hand. "Was that worth the money?" she asked me, a wide smile stretching her cheeks.

My heart was racing. That had been incredible. For a moment, I felt as though I loved this woman.

But I had to kill her.

She didn't even see me remove the knife from my pocket; she was too busy looking up at me, her eyes begging me for a compliment.

I slammed the blade into the side of her neck.

I felt the warmth of her blood as it squirted from the wound and splattered over my hand.

Candy gasped. Her eyes bulged. An odd, grunted squeal passed her lips, as the last of the air escaped from her lungs.

I pulled the knife out.

Immediately, she clamped her hand onto her neck and dropped to her knees.

I stood over her, watching as the blood seeped through her fingers and splattered onto the ground.

My heart burned with guilt. I couldn't believe that I'd done it. I could feel that my eyes were heavy with tears. For a moment, I wished that I could take it back. But then I remembered that, if I hadn't have done this, I would've been looking down at the corpse of my sister.

The woman looked back over her shoulder at me. God only knows what I looked like but, but she looked as though she'd been possessed by the devil. She was soaked with blood, but there was a fury in her eyes. Saliva leaked over her bottom lip. "What the fuck do you think you're doing?" she said, in a strangely matter-of-fact way. "Why the fuck would you do *that*?"

A sudden sense of panic filled me.

Oh shit…

She was *supposed* to be dead. There was so much blood; I would've thought that I'd killed her. But, alas, clearly I hadn't.

Now what?

No time to think.

Candy turned and scrambled to her feet. I couldn't let he get away. I had to finish the job.

I ran up behind her and wrapped my arm around her neck. I then pushed the blade of my knife into her back.

She gasped once again. This was followed by some agonised groan.

She slumped to the floor.

My head ached.

After that, everything just seemed to turn black.

***

The trouble with watching so much porn is that you get to a point when you've seen it all. You eventually find yourself looking for porn that most people might not consider 'normal'. You eventually find yourself looking for something more extreme.

And 'normal' porn was so boring.

That's why Callum had now found himself browsing for porn on the dark web.

That's why Callum had found his way onto 'XxXxPornoWeb'.

That's why Callum was now watching a video of a young man murdering a prostitute.

In the video, the prostitute (an average looking woman in a red dress) had sucked the guy's dick until he'd filled her mouth with cum. He'd then stabbed her in the neck. She'd tried to escape, so he'd stabbed her in the back. He'd then stabbed her innumerable time in the chest and the neck. He'd then decapitated her. He'd then fucked the mouth of the severed head until he'd cum for a second time.

Callum felt dirty.

He'd jerked himself off as he watched the video, only climaxing as the person in the video had fucked the severed head.

And then a message popped up in a small window at the bottom of the screen.

It was from somebody called 'FuCkMaStEr666'.

You like sick shit?
You send us video?

THE END

Harrison Phillips

COME OUT

I was nervous - more nervous than I'd ever been before. My tummy was tight. It felt as if there was a snake slithering inside me, coiling like a spring, ready to attack. My heart was beating fast - I could feel it pulsing in the sides of my neck. The hair on my arms prickled painfully. It was enough to make me feel sick.

But none of that really mattered - as long as Seb was beside me, everything would always be alright.

Seb was amazing. It had been easy to fall in love with him. I hadn't really had a choice in the matter. I knew it from the moment we had met - he was the one for me. I could feel it in my heart, in my soul. He understood me. We were the same, he and I - but oh so different, all at the same time. He was funny, he was interesting. And he was beautiful. The way the sunlight danced on his chocolate skin made me feel warm inside. His big, brown eyes opened up to the deepest of souls.

He was the first person I'd ever been in love with. I felt sure he would be the last.

I hadn't come out as gay until my second year at uni. Of course, I'd known I was gay since the age of about eight. But I'd managed to hide the fact for over a decade. When I did come out, I had only done so publicly to a handful of my closest friends. That was a little over a year ago now, and during that time I had only been on two dates. The first had been with a rugby player, who had towered over me and was at least three stone heavier, who only seemed to like talking about two things: himself and sex. That one hadn't gone so well.

My next date had been arranged by Hailey - she was my flat mate and best friend. She told me she had a friend who, much like me, was looking for love. She described him to me as being tall, dark, and handsome – and as having the most fabulous afro you could ever imagine.

I agreed to go on a date with him. I never imagined I'd be going out with a black guy. Not that I'm racist - not even slightly. But where I grew up, in my school, there weren't many black kids. There were many at uni though, many of whom I had become good friends with.

Seb had turned up to our date wearing skinny jeans and a black Led Zeppelin t-shirt. I could tell immediately that I was attracted to him sexually, and it didn't take long for me to realise that, in actual fact, this guy could be someone that I could spend the rest of my life with.

We'd been together for about a month before sex had even become a topic of conversation. I'd explained to Seb that was a virgin. Not by choice, but due more to circumstance. I'd never been in love before, nor had I ever met anybody I felt comfortable enough with. Seb understood. He told me that it had taken him almost a year after coming out to find someone he wanted to have sex with. For us, it just happened naturally. We'd been out for a few drinks, but we were both sober enough to know what we were doing. When Seb first penetrated me, it had, quite possibly, been the most painful thing I have ever experienced. But the way he kissed me and stroked my back made everything just fine. And it didn't take long for me to enjoy it. It was the best feeling ever, even more so than when Seb lay on his back and guided me inside him. It didn't take long for me to climax. I stroked the length of his penis as I thrust into him. We came together - I shot my load deep inside him, as he ejaculated over his toned, muscular stomach.

I loved Seb more than anything. And he loved me, of that I was quite sure.

But that wasn't quite enough to subdue my nerves.

I think Seb could sense how nervous I was. As we sat together in the back of the taxi, he reached across, took a hold of my hand, and placed it in his lap. He offered me a smile, which told me everything was going to be alright.

I wasn't sure how true that was. You see, we were on our way to see my parents. They didn't know that I was gay. It wasn't something I was ashamed of, but I was nervous of how they might react. I didn't think they would understand. They were both what I would call *'old school'*. They were old fashioned and set in their ways. They lived in an old farmhouse which Dad had converted himself. There was an old barn out the back, which was full of the old cars my dad would fix up to sell. At least, there was the last time I was there. That had been over two years ago now. I spoke to Mum at least once a week, but I'd barely spoken to Dad.

Part of me wanted to turn back. We could get the taxi driver to turn around and drop us back at the station. We could jump on the next train and be home in under two hours.

Seb was brave - much more so than I was. He wouldn't allow me to turn back. He'd say - *'You've come this far; you should do it now.'* I could even *hear* him saying it in my head. I needed to be strong - for both of us. If my parents couldn't accept who I was, then so be it. I didn't need them. I just needed Seb. And he'd always be there to support me - he'd told me as such before we left, as he'd planted a loving, passionate kiss on my lips.

His lips were so soft. They just begged to be kissed.

We arrived at Mum and Dad's house at around 17:25. Seb couldn't quite believe just how isolated it was. He was a city boy; I grew up in the sticks. That was probably the biggest difference between us. But I was used to the long drives along country roads required to get anywhere around here. And getting to Mum and Dad's was no different. The house was set back atop a hill, surrounded by open fields, once used for pasture. Nowadays they were empty. My dad had allowed the neighbours to let their horses roam the fields, as their grazing kept the grass short. Saved him the job of having to maintain it himself.

As the taxi pulled up in front of the house, my mum and dad both came out to greet us. I had told them I was bringing a friend. I guess they were expecting - or hoping - that I had meant a girlfriend. I'm sure they would love nothing more than to have a grandchild. And perhaps they still could - perhaps me and Seb could adopt one day?

Idle Hands

Seb paid the taxi driver as I climbed out of the car and greeted my mum and dad. I could already see a disapproving look forming on Dad's face as he watched Seb collect our bags from the boot. I guess he'd already jumped to his own conclusion. Then again, I guess that conclusion was probably the correct one. My mum was smiling though. She hugged me tightly. "Hello Son," she said. "How are you? You look well."

"I am," I said. "I'm doing really well."

She held me by my shoulders and looked into my eyes. The smile on her face made her look almost deranged. "It's been so long, Son. I've missed you so much."

I couldn't help but laugh. "I've missed you too, Mum."

My dad was waiting for me once Mum had finished squeezing me half to death. He held out his hand, a frown etched into his forehead. To be honest, I don't know if that frown was aimed directly at me - my dad had had a permanently furrowed brow for as long as I could remember. I shook his hand. He squeezed my hand tightly - so hard that it almost hurt. "Son," he said. "It's good to see you."

"You too, Dad." I thought about moving in for a hug, then decided against it. Dad had never been one for hugs - I imagined very little had changed I'm that regard.

"And who's your friend?" asked Dad.

That was the question I had been dreading. And Dad had asked it as if he already knew the answer. Sure, he didn't know that Seb was his name, but he sounded very much like he knew that this was my boyfriend. There was a sense of disappointment in his voice, one that indicated that he wasn't happy about the fact that his son was about to confess to his new-found homosexuality.

As if he hadn't known all along.

"Mum. Dad," I said. "This is Seb."

"Sebastian," said Seb, as he stepped forward, his hand outstretched towards my father.

Dad, his hands now tucked safely in his pockets, looked down at Seb's hand. Then he looked Seb in the eye. He looked like some concerned animal, worried about whether or not the thing that stood before him was going to attack. Slowly, he removed his hand from his pocket and shook Seb's. "Pleased to meet you," he said.

"Yes," said Mum. "Very pleased to meet you. We both are. Won't you come in? I'm cooking a stew. I hope you like stew. It'll be ready in about fifteen minutes. I hope you're hungry."

"Stew sounds lovely," said Seb, a beautiful, wide smile adorning his beautiful face.

Mum then ushered Seb inside.

Dad was staring at me, the unrelenting frown still there. He nodded towards the house, silently ushering me inside. I could've been completely wrong, but it felt to me as if he dare not speak to me, just in case he might catch something.

I looked at the ground and walked into the house, not wanting to give my dad eye contact. He didn't deserve it - and neither did I.

Dad followed me inside and closed the front door.

***

Idle Hands

Mum's stew tasted as good as I had remembered. She had always told me that it was an old family recipe, passed on to her from my grandma, and from her mother before that. I'm sure my mum would have liked a daughter to pass the recipe on to herself, but I'd always assumed that she'd just have to make do with me one day.

I could never be sure of the herbs and spices that went into the gravy - that was a secret - but I did know that she made the stew with lamb, carrots, potatoes, and onions. I also knew that she always slow-cooked her stew, starting at least eight hours before it was due to be eaten.

I also knew that it was delicious.

I was famished by the time that Mum finally dished a healthy helping of stew into my bowl. I ate greedily, hardly stopping for breath. I'd never had the best of table manners - something which Seb had learned quite quickly about me. Mum, Dad, and Seb were less than halfway through their respective bowls by the time I had finished mine. "Blimey, Son!" said my mum, as I slurped the last of the stew off my spoon. "You must've been hungry! You can have some more if you like; there's plenty left over."

"Oh, no," I said. "Thanks Mum, but I'm full now. I guess it was just my nerves making me hungry."

"Nerves? What nerves? You don't ever need to feel nervous about coming home to see your old Mum and Dad."

"I... Erm..." I looked to Seb, who was smiling at me coyly, letting me know that I may have just given the game away. I looked to my dad, who was frowning as if to say – *'I've got you figured out, boy'*. I looked back to my mum, who was grinning like some deranged fool, completely oblivious to the fact that something else might be going on here.

I cleared my throat. I had to do this. It was now or never. Besides, that's what I came here for. That's why me *and* Seb came here, to tell my parents that we were in love.

How could they dare be angry at that? Or disappointed? I suppose it was disappointment I feared the most. I knew my mum wouldn't feel that way - she'd accept me any which way. She might not understand the complexities of it all, but then, nor would she be interested. I felt sure that, so long as *I* was happy, then *she'd* be happy. But Dad was a different matter. He was *very* old fashioned. He was chivalrous, but also sexist at the same time. He thought every man needed a woman, and that they needed to take care of that woman financially, while the woman took care of the housework. I'd always considered him to be homophobic too. I'd heard him condemn homosexuality as a child. I could still remember the time that, when I was maybe six years old, we were driving to the supermarket, when we passed a gay couple holding hands, walking along the street. They were minding their own business, happy in their own world. Dad had said to me - *'Look at those disgusting faggots, son. That just ain't right.'* It was this memory - and this memory alone - that had made me hide my true sexuality for as long as I did. Had my father not been so homophobic, I probably would have come out sooner.

But none of that mattered now. I was here, and Seb was by my side. I'd tell my parents the truth and if they didn't like it, I'd leave. I'd walk away and never come back. I didn't need them anymore. I only needed Seb.

"Mum. Dad," I said, my heart in my throat. "I've got something to tell you both."

"Oh," said Mum. "Right. What's that then, Son?"

Dad snorted a laugh into his stew. That was enough to put me off. Mum looked to my dad. "What?" she asked him.

"You," said Dad, shaking his head. "You're so stupid. You can't see it? Isn't it obvious?"

"What? Isn't *what* obvious?"

My heart was racing now. That was *just* like my dad - he always had to make things more difficult for me. I didn't expect him to tell me he was proud, or that he was happy for me. But I wished he would just let me say my piece, just let *me* be happy.

Dad slurped down the last of his stew. He looked at me with what almost looked like fury in his bloodshot eyes. "Just say it," he said.

I took a deep breath. "I'm gay," I announced.

"What?" said Mum, far more surprised than I expected her to be. "You're not gay."

"I am, Mum. Seb is my boyfriend." Seb placed his hand on top of mine. I squeezed it tightly.

"No, he's not," said Mum. She was laughing to herself, shaking her head. "That's just not possible."

"He is, Mum. We love each other."

"Nope."

It was going worse than I had expected. Mum was acting as if I was somehow wrong, as if I couldn't possibly be gay. She was looking down into her stew, stirring it with big swipes of her spoon. If anything, it seemed as if she was trying to ignore what I was telling her.

Dad was just staring at me. I'd been on the receiving end of his steely glare on more than one occasion. It didn't faze me anymore. Part of me wished he would say something. Even though I knew anything he *did* say would most likely be highly unpleasant, *anything* would be better than the crazy drivel Mum was coming out with.

"Mum," I said loudly, hoping to snap her back into some sense of reality. "I *am* gay. I just want you to be happy for me."

"Well,' said Dad, finally. "I can't say it comes as any surprise to me. You've always been that way inclined." He stood from the table and headed for the kitchen. "I need a drink," he said, as he pushed open the door. "I think we all do." And then he was gone.

The whole time Dad was gone, Mum remained silent. She just kept looking, first at me, then at Seb. Seb was smiling at her - the same reassuring smile I'd seen a thousand times before. His teeth were pearly white, perfect. His smile was beautiful. But Mum just looked confused. It was as if her brain couldn't process this new information.

When Dad returned to the dining room, he was carrying with him a bottle of his best whiskey and four tumblers. He placed the tumblers onto the table, popped the cap off of the whiskey and poured. "I guess," he said, lifting a glass and handing it to Seb. "We should have a toast. We should celebrate."

"What *exactly* is it that we are celebrating?" said Mum, her voice now shrill enough to cut through glass. "That there's something wrong with our son?"

Idle Hands

This shocked me. I hadn't expected this from Mum. She'd always seemed to be somewhat open-minded. Perhaps there was a part of her I'd never seen; one that wasn't so tolerant after all.

"It's his life," said Dad, surprisingly coming to my defence. "He can do whatever he chooses. This may not be what we would've expected or hoped for, but if he's happy, then what can we say?"

Mum just stared at Dad. She seemed to be in as much disbelief as I was.

"Now," said Dad, shoving a glass of whiskey into Mum's hand. "Let's have a toast. To our son," he said as he lifted his glass above his head. I lifted my glass, as did Seb. Mum hesitated for a moment, then lifted hers too. We all knocked back our drinks in one.

Dad then proceeded to encircle the table and pour another drink into each of the now empty glasses. We sipped them this time.

Mum sat silently, a sour look on her face, as Seb leaned over and kissed my cheek. "You know," said Seb, addressing my parents. "I've heard a lot about you. I was nervous about coming here today. But I have to say, I'm so pleased to be here. Thank you for having me."

Dad nodded, acknowledging Seb's thanks.

Seb continued - "I mean, I understand how you must be feeling, but seriously, there's nothing wrong with your son. You know, you can't help who you are, and you can't help who you love. When I told my parents, they reacted much like you. But then, soon enough, they... Erm... They, they... Ughh..."

There was something wrong. Seb almost seemed to be choking on something. He coughed and groaned. "You okay?" I asked, placing my hand on his back.

Quickly, Seb stood, knocking my hand away. "No. I'm okay. I… Erm…. Uhh… I'm… Ughhh…'

He put his hand to his mouth and coughed again. When he removed his hand, I saw that his palm was splattered with blood. "Seb!" I said, hearing myself almost scream.

Seb turned and collapsed onto the table. He was gurgling, trying to cough, trying to dislodge something from the back of his throat.

"What's wrong with him?" I yelled at Mum. "Was there something in the food? This looks like some kind of allergic reaction!" By now, Seb couldn't breathe. His skin had started to turn a horrible shade of purple. Every time he coughed, blood splattered over his lips.

"It's not an allergic reaction, you fucking idiot," said Dad. He was stood behind me, looking down at Seb, a terrifying scowl contorting his face.

"What?" I said, not really noticing what he'd called me. I was more interested in Seb - the man I loved - who looked like he might be about to die. "How would you know?"

"I know because that's the exact reaction I'd expect from somebody who'd ingested poison. The type of poison I smeared on the inside of the glass that this fucking queer nigger just drank from."

I felt as though my heart had stopped. I was crying now. The tears stung my eyes. It must've taken less than a second for me to process my father's words. *He did this.* He wanted Seb dead. He was both racist and homophobic. All of a sudden, I hated him. I wanted to kill him. But more so, I wanted to save Seb.

"Please," I said, sobbing now. "You've got to help him!"

"No can do," said Dad.

I looked to Mum, who, I was horrified to find, was grinning from ear to ear.

Seb's breaths were short and shallow now, each one a huge effort for him to suck into his lungs. He took only two or three more, before he slipped away.

I moaned loudly. My heart felt as though it had been torn in two.

"I'm sorry son," said Dad. "But he had to go. This is the best thing for you. Don't worry - we're going to fix you."

Fix me? *Fucking fix me?*

I was going to kill my dad. He needed to die. And I'd make it painful. He'd taken to only thing I'd ever loved and torn it from me. For that, he would suffer.

But before I could move, I felt a rope around my neck. It was pulled tight, cutting off the blood to my brain.

The last thing I heard before I passed out was my mother's voice saying - "Careful! Try not to hurt him!", and my dad saying - "I'll do whatever it takes to fix the boy."

Then I was gone.

***

When I woke up, immediately I knew exactly where I was. I'd played here so many times as a child. The smell was so familiar. I was in the barn. It was unused now, having formally been home to around forty sheep. Still, there were tools on the wall (a rack, a sickle, a shovel) and the hay that lined the floor smelled of livestock.

What I didn't understand was how I'd gotten here. But it didn't take long for the memories to come flooding back. An involuntary moan escaped my lips.

I looked around. It wasn't until my senses had fully returned that I realised that I was naked and that I was tied to a large, wooden cross. It was almost as if I'd been crucified. Why would my father do this to me? Did he really hate me that much?

A small table had been placed a few feet before me. On it stood an old combi TV/VCR. It was plugged in to an extension lead, which trailed behind me, to where I could hear (but couldn't turn my head far enough to see) the generator running. On the TV, pornography was playing. The picture was fuzzy, in part due to the fact that it was playing from a VHS cassette, but also due to the fact that it clearly dated back to the '70s. A blonde woman with long curly hair was moaning loudly, while a chubby man with a hairy chest and a handlebar moustache fucked her. There were other men there too; one had his cock in her mouth, while another squeezed her breasts as her hand stroked the length of his throbbing member. The man fucking her tipped his head back and groaned. As he pulled out, semen leaked from her vagina, matting the thick pubes that surrounded it. Then another man approached, using the tip of his penis to spread the other man's semen, before thrusting deep into the woman.

I felt nothing as I watched this. *Nothing.* If people found this a turn-on, then fine. Good for them.

Idle Hands

But this made me feel nothing. Not horny. Not repulsed. Not sexy. Not sick. Just nothing.

For what felt like an hour this video played. Over and over, I watched different big-dicked men having sex with different big-breasted women, cum dripping from every available orifice. Eventually, the tape reached its end. The video shut off and the tape began to rewind, the VCR whirring loudly. Once finished, the machine ejected the slab of black plastic.

At that same moment, the loud clunk of heavy chain banging against wood came from the barn door. When it opened, both Mum and Dad were stood there, silhouetted in the light of what must've been a full moon outside. Once inside, Mum approached, while Dad closed the door behind them. Mum didn't look at me, let alone speak to me. She pushed the cassette back into the VCR and pressed play. Once the tracking had settled, the image on the screen showed a muscular man performing oral sex on a woman, who in turn had her tongue deep into another woman's vagina.

Dad joined Mum before me. Unlike my mother, whose eyes remained fixed to television (where the man was now masturbating, until he ejaculated into the waiting mouth of one of the women), my dad did look up at me. His face held a blank expression, making reading his current thoughts impossible.

"What the fuck is wrong with you?" I said, not even meaning to - the words just seemed to slip out, uncontrolled.

"What's wrong with me?" replied Dad. "What's wrong with *you*? I didn't raise you to be a faggot. I raised you to be a man, and *real* men fuck women, not other men."

"Oh my God!" I tipped my head back and snorted a laugh - it was the best I could to prevent myself from crying. "Do you hear yourself? You're fucking insane. That's not the world we live in anymore."

"Well, it sure as fuck ought to be. We were hoping that someday you might bring us home a couple of grandkids. Instead, you bring us home your fucking *boyfriend*? And a coon, no less!" Dad scoffed a laugh. "I've never been so disgusted in all my life."

I felt a tear run down my cheek. I wished hard that I could wipe it away, but my hands were bound so tightly that that was impossible. "You just murdered somebody. Forget that he was the man I loved - you just killed him! That's okay with you, is it?"

"He deserved it. You can't just go about turning folk queer and expect to get away with it."

"Seb didn't turn me queer! I've always been gay! I was born this way."

"Nobody is born *that* way, son. It's not natural."

I didn't know what to say. As unpleasant as I had always found my father, I'd never found him to be this repugnant. "You're wrong. *Love* is natural. Me and Seb - we had found love."

"I think you're mistaking lust for love. Man was placed on this Earth with only one purpose, procreation. You might think that sticking your dick in another man's arsehole is fun, but it certainly doesn't serve the ultimate goal."

Idle Hands

I had no words left to say. What could I say? My dad was a vile human being - far worse than I had ever imagined he could be. And my mother - the woman I'd thought would always love me, would always be there to protect me - was doing nothing.

"Anyway," said Dad, after a moment of silence had passed. "No need to worry. We're going to help you. How do you like this?" he said, pointing to the TV, where there were now a dozen naked men lined up against a wall, each with a girl, each dressed in a school uniform, on their knees before them, cock in mouth. "You don't like this?"

I had no answer - certainly not one I was willing to give. I could only tip my head back and stare at the ceiling. I could feel be blood searing. My heart was thumping in my chest, so I hard I thought my ribs may crack. I could feel tears rolling down my face, pricking my stubble as they went.

"No?" my father answered for me. "That's ok. I've got something even better planned for you. It'll be here any moment. You wait right here; I'll be back soon." He then turned to Mum and said - "Keep an eye on him. I won't be long." Then he left the barn.

As soon as he was gone, I called to Mum. "Please!" I begged her. "You've got to help me. You can't let him do this."

She didn't respond. I'd never seen her like this. She was transfixed by the pornography on the TV (the schoolgirls were now naked and being shared between the men).

"Mum!" I shouted now, hoping to snap her out of the trance she'd seemingly fallen into. It worked. Slowly she turned to face me. "Help me," I said. "Please. Get me out of here."

She smiled at me. "I can't," she said, her voice almost light and playful. "We have to fix you."

I shook my head, crying hard now. "I'm not broken."

"Oh, but you are. Your mind is infected with this disease. We have to get it out of you. We have to cure you."

"I don't need a cure," I said through gritted teeth, fury rising inside me. "I need you to get me the fuck out of here."

"You know. You really oughtn't speak to your mother like that." She turned back to the TV.

I was speechless. Inside, I felt some combination of fear and hatred - I didn't know which emotion was the strongest.

The barn door opened once again, just a few minutes later.

"Hey? Why we goin' in here mister?" said the young girl my dad had with him, a tight grip on her arm. She looked to be a teenager, perhaps only seventeen. She had long blonde hair, which hung over her shoulders. She was dressed in jeans and a t-shirt, one that was cut short, revealing her midriff. Dad closed the door behind him. It was then that the girl set eyes on me and her face dropped. "Oh, no," she said. "Sorry. I'm not into the sort of shit."

"What do you mean 'you're not into this shit'?" said Dad. "You're a whore - you need to be into everything."

The girl scoffed a laugh. "Look. I don't know what the fuck is going on here, and, honestly, I don't wanna know. But I can't be here. I'm off."

The girl tried to pull away from my father, but he kept his grip tight. "No, no, no, no, no. You're not going anywhere. We need you to help us. Our son here has a problem. You can fix him."

I stared down at the girl. She was staring back up at me. I could see the terror in her eyes. She knew this wasn't right. But she was helpless now - there was nothing she could do for me, or for herself. "What the fuck are you talking about?" she said.

"He's a faggot. He likes boys."

"So? There's nothing wrong with that." For the briefest of moments, I was thankful to the girl. But I knew that her opinion would mean less than nothing to my parents. There was no way she could convince them that homosexuality was normal. There was no way she could get them to see sense.

Dad was frowning. Mum had now turned and was looking the girl over. She looked up to me. "She's very pretty, isn't she?" said Mum. "Wouldn't you like a girlfriend like her?"

I shook my head. "No Mum," I said, fighting back the tears. "I wouldn't. I'm gay."

"Not for much longer," said Dad. "You're gonna fuck this girl, and you're going to enjoy it."

"Wait," said the girl, once again trying - and failing - to pull herself out my father's grip. "I'm not doing this. This is wrong. I can't do this. I won't."

"I've already paid you," said Dad. "You're going to do your fucking job."

She shook her head. "No way. You can have your money back."

"I don't want my money. I want you to fuck my son. I want you to cure him."

"You're fucking crazy!"

"And you're a whore. So, get to fucking work!"

Dad pushed the girl towards me. She tried to fight back. "No!" she screamed, now fighting for her life.

Dad pulled her back. "Come here!" he shouted to Mum. "Help me with this cunt."

Mum did as she was told. She grabbed the girl by the arms and pulled them behind her back.

The girl was sobbing now, begging them to stop. But they didn't listen. Instead, my father grabbed the collar of her t-shirt and pulled, tearing the fabric and pulling it off, revealing the black bra she was wearing beneath. Dad reached behind her back, unclasped the bra, and pulled it away. "Look at these tits, son. They're gorgeous, aren't they?"

"Stop it!" I screamed. "Leave her alone." The girl was terrified. She shouldn't have been here. She didn't ask for this, not any of it.

Of course, Dad didn't care about what I had to say. With my mother still holding the girl tightly, my dad unbuttoned her jeans, then pulled them down to her ankles, taking her cotton panties with them. The girl squirmed, tried to wriggle free, but my mother wrapped an arm around her neck, pulling tight, quickly subduing her. Then Dad forced the girl's legs apart. "Oooh, shaven haven," he said, licking his lips. "She's as bald as the day she was born! Don't tell me you don't want to fuck this."

"No! I don't!" I said. "You need to let her go! She doesn't deserve this!"

"And we don't deserve to have some demented pervert for a son. But you know what? Shit happens!"

Idle Hands

"Please…" the girl moaned. "Don't do this…" Nobody other than me seemed to notice, but there was nothing I could do.

Dad pulled the girl from Mum's arms and pushed her along by her hair, to where she now stood, only a couple of feet in front of me. "Go on," my dad urged with a smirk. "Look at her. Nice firm titties. A tight little pussy. Why isn't your dick getting hard?"

The girl was sobbing now. Tears were once again streaming down my cheeks. "Please, Dad. This isn't going to change anything. I can't change who I am."

The smile dropped from my father's face. "You won't fuck her? Then she can fuck you." He pushed the girl even closer. "Go on!" He said, pushing her face towards my flaccid penis. "Suck his dick. Make him hard!"

The girl pulled away. "No! I can't!" she screamed. "I won't!"

Angrily, Dad tugged on her hair, spun her around and tossed her to the floor. "Hold her down," he told my mother, who seemed more than happy to oblige. "If you won't fuck her, *I* will!" he said to me. With Mum having pinned her arms to the ground, my father proceeded to unbuckle his belt and drop his trousers. He was already erect. It took his penis in his hand and spat into his palm, caressing the saliva into the length of his cock. He then fell to his knees and forced himself inside of the screaming girl.

I looked away. I couldn't bring myself to watch this. This was abhorrent. I knew now who my father truly was - he was a racist; he was a bigot; he was a rapist; he was a murderer. And it seemed that my mother was the same, having been compliant in everything that he'd done.

Dad raped the girl, thrusting into her over and over, reaching up and squeezing her breasts in a way that looked painful. But the girl had given up resisting. She wasn't crying anymore. She wasn't screaming. She was simply looking up at me with blank eyes.

Dad pulled out of her. With Mum's assistance, he rolled her over and pulled back on her hips, lifting her buttocks off the ground. "Look son," said my father. "Even girls have got arseholes to fuck. Watch." He then placed the tip of his penis against the girl's anus and pushed, squeezing himself into her colon. The girl flinched, writhed a little, much made no attempt to escape. As Dad fucked her once again, Mum began giggling like some excited child. This was like a game to her.

Dad let a groan that signalled to me that he had climaxed. He pulled out of the girl and released her, allowing her to drop to the ground. "See," he said, as he climbed to his knees and pulled his trousers back up. "That's how it's done." The girl rolled over and curled up into the foetal position.

I turned my head away. I couldn't look at the sight before me. My head ached and my heart burned.

My father stood before me and rubbed his hands together. "Huh," he said. "Doesn't look like *she's* going to be much use anymore."

I squeezed my eyes tight shut, forcing another tear to streak down my cheek.

Dad reached up and grabbed me by my chin, pulled my face towards his. "Look at me," he growled. Involuntarily, I obeyed. "You're such a fucking

Idle Hands

disappointed to me. I'd rather you were dead than queer."

Suddenly my heart raced. Would he have it in him to kill *me*? With everything he'd done, I expected he might. "Please," I said. "You can't do this. You have to let me go. Please don't kill me?"

"Kill you?" Dad laughed and looked over his shoulder to Mum, who also began to laugh. "I'm not going to kill you. But I tell you this much, you're not leaving here until we've straightened you out."

A million thoughts ploughed through my mind. I didn't know what he expected from me. Would this have all ended if I'd just had sex with that girl? Would he have let me go free? If he had, I could run, just as far away from this place as I could get. But then what would I do? Would I tell people about what had happened? About what had happened to Seb? I couldn't, could I? Of course I could. My parents would be locked up - so what? It was the least they deserved.

Dad released his grip of my chin. He'd held me so tight I'd swear I could still feel his fingers digging into my jawbone. "Well, since this slut's of little use, I guess I'll need to find another volunteer." He turned to my mother. "Come over here. You can do it."

"Wh... What?" my mother stuttered, the smile wiped from her face. She'd heard him, of that I was sure. But I guess she didn't want to believe what he'd said.

"Get over here. We need a woman to show this boy the ropes. You're a woman, aren't you?"

"But... I'm... I'm his mum."

"So what? You've got a fanny, that's all that matters right now."

Mum didn't move. She didn't like it now that she was a victim.

"Bitch!" Dad shouted. "Get the fuck over here, now!"

Something suddenly occurred to me - perhaps my dad had always been this abusive, I'd just never seen it. Perhaps my mum was obeying him so willingly because, if she didn't, she'd be on the receiving end if his disgusting abuse. I'd always seen them as the ideal couple - a bit backwards thinking, but happy none the less. But now I could see my father for who he really was, it would be understandable if my mum had known this all along, having bowed down to every one of his commands.

Still, it made me forgive her no less. She hadn't seemed too upset by Seb's death and she certainly wasn't doing anything to help me now.

Mum scooted timidly over towards my father, who promptly grabbed her arm and pulled her in close. "Suck his dick," my dad commanded.

"What?" Mum said. "I can't do that."

"You can and you will. You need to make him cum. If you don't, how can we ever hope to fix him?"

Mum looked up at me. I had nothing to say to her. I was numb to it all now. She looked back to Dad and nodded. "Good girl," he said, stroking her face. Mum smiled.

I closed my eyes and prayed to God for this to all be over. I bit down on my lip as hard as I could.

My mother took my limp penis and wrapped her lips around it. I could feel her tongue flicking around the tip as she worked her lips up and down, sucking gently.

I could feel my penis filling with blood, growing hard.

"That's it! Look!" my dad said excitedly. "He's getting hard! I *knew* he could do it for a woman."

This seemed to excite Mum. She began to suck harder, allowing her tongue to encircle the head of my penis, while one hand stroked the shaft and the other massaged my testicles. I closed my eyes and gritted my teeth. My dad had mistaken my erection as a sign of pleasure, not as the involuntary reaction my body had to sexual stimulation.

I tried to hold back as best I could, but it was out of my control. I came hard, filling my mother's mouth with warm ejaculate. She continued to stroke my throbbing penis, squeezing harder, working out every last drop of cum.

"That's it, son!" My father was saying gleefully. "I knew you had it in you."

Mum removed her mouth from around my penis. A small amount of semen spilled onto her chin. She wiped it away with the back of her hand, then gulped back the cum that was still in her mouth.

I opened my eyes and looked down at my parents through a haze of tears.

My mother looked somewhat disgusted with herself, but in her eyes I could she was pleased with what she had done - *she'd fixed me!* My father was staring up at me, a look of wild delight on his face. His grin was wider than that of the Cheshire cat.

Both of them were oblivious to the fact that the girl, naked and covered in dirt, was now stood behind them. In her hand she held the sickle, which she'd taken from the wall.

I could've said something. I could've warned them about what was certainly about to happen to them. I could've *helped* them. But why should I? They weren't going to help me. *They* did this to me. *They* had killed Seb. *They* had tied me to this cross. On my father's command, my mother had just raped me. I wanted them to die - it was the least they deserved. If they could suffer just a little, that would be much preferable. I hoped that the girl would kill them both, in some horrible, painful way.

And, so, I said nothing.

"Congratulations Son," said Dad, his clenched fists almost punching the air. "Now you're a real man."

I watched as the girl approached quietly. She was short - a good foot shorter than my dad. But that didn't prevent her from reaching around my father's neck and slashing his throat, screaming as she did so. I saw the blade of the sickle run deep into his neck, almost so deep that it was no longer visible. Blood began to flow instantly, gushing from the wound. As the girl stepped back, I saw the gash open in Dad's neck. It was savage and wide, deep and angry. He turned to face the girl, a look of disbelief on his face. He clutched his neck, perhaps hoping to stem the flow of blood. For sure, there was no chance of that.

It took a few moments for my mum to realise what had happened. By the time she turned to face my dad, he'd already fallen to his knees.

Mum screamed, horrified, as he collapsed forwards onto his front, blood squirting from his neck and seeping into the hay. She dashed over to him and dropped to her knees beside him. "Oh my God!" she screamed. "What have you done? WHAT HAVE YOU DONE!"

The girl stared blankly at my mum.

"You whore! You killed him! Why? Why did you do that? I swear to God, you're going to…"

The girl swung the sickle downwards, before bringing it violently up underneath my mother's chin. The curved point of the blade easily pierced the flesh. Mum coughed, blood oozing over her lips.

The girl released her grip on the handle of the sickle, allowing my mother to slump to the ground, the blade still lodged in her neck.

I gasped for air, relieved it was all finally over. I could still feel the tears on my cheeks, although I was crying no more. *They* were dead, something which I truly believe they deserved. I wouldn't have ever wished for this to happen, but it was they who had set this series of events in motion. They *had* to die. They *needed* to.

The girl crouched next to Mum and pulled the sickle from her throat, the blade crunching and quenching as it pulled free. She then stepped over my mother's corpse and stood before me. Her eyes were soulless. She looked empty, no more than a vague version of who she once was remaining.

For a moment, I felt like she may kill me too.

"Are you okay?" I asked, knowing this was a stupid question. I couldn't think of anything else to say, so I said - "I'm sorry."

She looked away from me, down to the ground, where her feet were half-buried in the hay. She began to sob, her tears coming between rasping breaths.

"Please," I said, in the most comforting voice I could find - I was only just holding together myself; I felt broken. "I'm sorry this happened to you. They shouldn't have done this. They are terrible people. But... please. You have to help me out of here."

Without a single word, the girl looked up at me, placed the blade of the sickle against her throat and drew it across, opening a wide gash, much like the one I'd seen on my father's neck.

"No!" I screamed, knowing just what her death would mean for me.

The girl stood there momentarily, her hands limp at her sides, the sickle still in hand, blood dripping from the blade. Her whole body - her chest, her stomach, her legs - was slick with blood. And then her legs buckled beneath her and she hit the ground in a crumpled heap.

I didn't know what to do. What *could* I do? The cross my father had built was solid, and the ropes that bound my arms to the wood were tied tight. I pulled at the ropes, but my arms didn't budge. I could feel my heart rate increasing. A sudden sense of panic began to burn inside. I pulled harder. No movement. I felt that if I pulled any harder, the bones of my hands might snap. But then, I guess that would be better than being stuck here.

But I couldn't do it. Dad had made sure I was stuck here. There was no escape for me. No hope.

As I looked at the carnage laid out before me - three limp corpses, bleeding from the neck (two of which belonged to those people who were supposed to love me and care for me forever, yet had proven that notion to be false) - my mind drifted back to Seb. *I* had brought him here. It was my fault he was dead.

Idle Hands

Deep down I had known that something bad would happen. Not to this extent, of course. But deep down I knew who my parents were. That was why I'd felt so nervous as we had travelled here.

And as I remained there, bound to the cross of my spiteful fathers making, hunger beginning the twist uncomfortably in my stomach and thirst making even breathing a painful ordeal, as the three corpses began to stink horribly, I tried my hardest to think of happier times. The only thing that came to mind were the few short months I'd spent in love with Seb. And so that's what I thought about, as I awaited death's silent approach.

THE END

Harrison Phillips

THE CONFESSION

It was a miserable day - grim and dark, the sky filled with thick, weighty clouds, which blackened the earth as far as the eye could see. A heavy rain was falling once again, as it had been, on-and-off, for the past four weeks. Occasionally, violent flashes of lightning illuminated the countryside (it was early afternoon, but one could be forgiven for thinking it was midnight). Thunder rumbled and echoed through the open countryside, like the footsteps of giants rambling over the hills.

The trailing road, which cut through the countryside like some black snake winding its way through deep grass, was practically empty. George hadn't seen any other cars for the past half-hour or so. A few lorries had lumbered along the road, undeterred by the persistent storm. But the road was devoid of cars. *Perhaps he was the only one crazy enough to drive in such unforgiving conditions.*

Sure - most people didn't like driving in the rain. Most people considered bad weather - especially weather as unrelenting as this - to be too much of a hazard. But George didn't really mind.

The radio was on, volume turned up as high as it could go (without causing too much undesirable distortion, of course). But the noise of the rain, as it hammered the flimsy sheet steel of the car's roof, perforated the sound of the latest chart toppers with ease.

The wipers beat back and forth at full pelt, swiping the rain away from the glass, only for it to be replaced microseconds later by further floods of cascading rainwater.

Through the sheet of rain that ran down the windscreen, refracting George's vision, twisting it into some blurry, nightmarish world, he saw a sign. 'H.M.P. TUDOR HOUSE – 10 MILES' it read.

He was getting close.

George reached over to the passenger seat, glancing for only a second at a time, before returning his eyes to the treacherous road ahead. His hand fumbled past the flimsy, rain-soaked cardboard files, paper hanging out of them, the edges roughly creased where they'd been stuffed in unceremoniously, over to where his jacket had been slung earlier. He groped his way into the pocket and removed a packet of cigarettes. He took one, inserted it into his mouth and then spent the next few minutes trying to find the lighter which he knew he had hidden in some other, secret pocket on the inside of the jacket. When he failed to find it, he decided to resort to the car's built-in cigarette lighter. He pushed it in and waited the required duration, before it popped out, confirming it was ready to go.

He lit his cigarette and inhaled the smoke, a long, drawn out drag. He savoured the taste. So many times, people had told him he'd ought to quit. He told them he would, knowing full well that it would never happen. He just enjoyed it too damn much.

As George took the last puff of his cigarette, he saw he was approaching another sign. This one informed him that he was now only five miles away.

He wound down the window, just a crack. A rush of air poured in, the thunderous rattle of the road booming into the car. Rain flickered off the frame of the door, splattering over George's shoulder. He flipped the cigarette butt out of the car and quickly wound the window back up.

Sooner than he'd expected, George reached the outer perimeter of the prison. A high fence - at least twelve feet tall, he guessed - stretched up towards the grey sky, the top line laced with bales of razor wire, like the metallic teeth of some terrible creature, threatening to tear at the clouds above - or at the flesh of any man who dared to cross its path. This fence stretched on as far as George could see, which, with the weather as vile as it was, was not very far at all.

He continued along the road, the entire stretch of which was lined on both sides with the steel mesh. George felt like some wild animal, locked inside its cage, ready to be presented to an adoring audience of adults and children alike. *Actually,* he thought, *more like I'm the prisoner.* Beyond the fence, as far as George could tell, was nothing - just open fields.

A sign offered directions towards the visitor's car park. George followed them.

A few minutes more and he had arrived. He pulled up in the visitor's car park, lining himself up perfectly within the confines of his space, his OCD daring him to leave it askew and see what would happen. He ignored it, of course. There were hardly any other cars there. Few cars meant few visitors. It was probably the weather keeping them away. *Good.* George had managed to secure a space close to the door, perhaps less than ten feet away.

George flipped up his jacket, retrieving a tie from underneath. It was red - *a little too confrontational*, George thought - but it'd have to do. He tied it around the collar of his shirt and straightened it up. He looked at himself in the rear-view mirror. His black hair, saturated with rain, was a mess. He slicked it back with his hands, running his fingers front to back. Better.

Struggling, he contorted himself in the car until his jacket found its way onto his shoulders.

He took a deep breath. He grabbed his files. He was ready.

Quickly, George opened the door, exited the vehicle, and sprinted for the prison doors, locking the car with the remote as he went.

***

The halls of the prison were bare and white, although you'd be hard-pressed to argue with anyway who tried to say they were actually yellow, what with the dirty light the aging fluorescent tubes cast upon them. The walls were practically featureless, save for the occasional poster, which either urged inmates to give up the drugs or to rat on the people they knew were dealing the drugs. Neither scenario struck George as being likely - not in this environment. A few plastic chairs - their bright green bodies faded on the seat due to the numerous behinds that had planted themselves there at one time or another - sat on either side of the occasional door. George had no idea what lay beyond those doors, nor did he care to find out.

The floor had been rendered with a sleek grey resin. It was slippery underfoot. There had been a mat just inside the entrance, but it had done an inadequate job of soaking up the rainwater which George had dragged in with him. A guy, who looked to be in his seventies - lanky, scrawny, his grey hair thinning on top - mopped the floor ahead. George would almost certainly leave dirty footprints on the freshly cleaned floor. That wasn't his problem - it was a thankless job that this old man had been tasked with. Besides, this old man probably enjoyed his work, after all, he was beyond retirement age and was clearly only here to top up his pension.

"Have you been here before?" George's escort asked him. She had introduced herself as Kathy, although she had since told him that Kath was perfectly fine. She was as tall as he was, but broader. Her hair was cut short, brown, but bleached blonde on top. She's wore it spiked. She had an oddly square chin for a woman. If it weren't for her cartoonishly large breasts, she could easily have been mistaken for a man.

She was dyke, no question.

"Erm... No," replied George, the question catching him off guard. It was a feeling he wasn't a quite used to. *Surely she'd have known if he had been?* This made him feel a little nervous, but he was used to dealing with his nerves by now. *Piece of cake.* His voice was soft, almost delicate in comparison to Kath's gruff tone. "I've been to plenty of other prisons, of course. But never here."

"Well," said Kath "I expect our rules are the same as any other."

"I'm sure they are."

They reached the end of the corridor, where they passed through a set of double doors. Beyond these doors was another corridor, the same as the last - a long, boring, off-white tunnel, devoid of anything that may spark even a little interest.

"But just to be on the safe side," Kath continued, skipping over whatever it was that George had just said. "We'd best go through them again."

George could sense that Kath didn't quite trust him. He looked too young to be a 'real' journalist. The ID he had presented stated that he was twenty-eight, but, had she have been asked, Kath would've placed him at no older than twenty-four. But then, that didn't really mean much. Perhaps he was enthusiastic. It was by no means an impossibility that an enthusiastic graduate with a talent for writing could get a job at a national paper. Almost certainly at a tabloid.

"Please do," replied George, not really wanting her to, but knowing she would regardless.

"Do not give him anything that he may use as a weapon," Kath told him, stating the obvious. "No sharp objects. No pens. No pencils. Nothing with staples, or paperclips on or in. Paper only."

George nodded his understanding.

"Do not hand anything directly to him. Anything you do wish to give him, place it flat on the table and allow him to take it from there."

They turned a corner and continued along the corridor. There were windows here, looking out over the fields. The rain outside continued in its persistent onslaught. Soon enough, George found himself standing before another set of doors. These were barred on both sides. A sign confirmed to him that he was about to enter maximum security and that only authorised visitors were permitted entrance. This amused George no end - *surely all visitors had to be authorised, regardless of where they were headed?* There were two guards - both tall, heavy-set men - waiting here, one on each side of the door. The man on this side of the door was stood to attention, his feet shoulder width apart, hands behind his back. He was staring at George, his face a blank canvas. The man on the other side of the door was sat behind a desk, flicking through CCTV images on a small black and white monitor. It wasn't something that George had considered, but now that he thought about it, it seemed obvious - there were CCTV cameras covering every inch of the building.

As they neared, the guard on this side of the door stepped forward. His face cracked into a smile and, all of a sudden, he looked a lot less threatening. "Hi Kath," he said, taking her ID card and swiping it through a device on the wall. "How's it going today?"

"Same shit, different day," said Kath.

The guard smiled and snorted half a laugh. He then took another step towards George. "Hello sir," he said. "How's your day been so far?"

"Oh, not too bad," said George.

"Glad to hear it. Can I see your ID please?"

George's ID card hung loosely around his neck, on the end of a scrappy blue lanyard. He removed it and handed it to the guard. The guard looked it over closely. George tried to remain as neutral looking as possible, as the guard's eyes scanned over his face and compared it to that in the photo.

"Thank you, sir," said the guard, handing George his ID. "Okay, so I hope you don't mind, but

I've got to give you quick once over before we can let you through."

"No, not at all." George didn't mind - it wasn't as if he was carrying anything he shouldn't be. Besides, at this point it was all just a formality. He lifted his arms as instructed and remained still as the guard ran his hands across every inch of his body. Once he was finished, the guard stepped aside and ushered George and Kath along. "You're good to go," he said, smiling once again.

George nodded his thanks. Kath swiped her ID card through the reader at the side of the door and the lock clunked open. The guard pushed the door open, and she and George continued. As far as George had noticed, the security guard sat at the desk hadn't once taken his eyes from the screen. Come to think of it, he might not have even blinked.

"I'll be close by, keeping an eye on things," Kath continued, snatching George's attention. "He'll be chained to the bench, so he can't stand."

"Why? Do you consider him dangerous?" George asked.

"Personally? No. Not exactly. But he is a maximum-security prisoner. It's just standard procedure. *You know what he did.* But since he's been in here, he's never been a problem."

"That's good to know."

"If he gives you any trouble - any trouble *at all* - just stand up and walk away. Somebody will come over and deal with you immediately."

They arrived at another set of doors. These ones were wooden, with a small glass panel in each. Behind these doors was the sports hall. Through the

Idle Hands

window, George could see him, sat at a small desk in the middle of the room.

Kath stopped him before they entered, placing her palm on his chest. "Can I ask you something?"

"Please do," George said, intrigued, but fairly certain that he knew what she was about to ask.

"Do you really think he's innocent?" she said. Indeed, that *was* the question George had expected she'd ask. In fact, he was surprised nobody had asked him sooner. Rumours would, more than likely than not, have run wild as to why George was here. He had some funny ideas, or at least most people seemed to think. But maybe, Kath would've said if anybody had bothered to ask, just maybe he was on to something.

"I don't know," George replied. "Maybe. Maybe not."

"Well, it wouldn't surprise me to find out that he didn't do it. He doesn't seem capable."

"You'd be surprised at what some people are capable of."

"I don't think I would. I've worked here long enough."

George smiled. It was only then that he thought about all the other prisoners that had served - or indeed, were *still serving* - their time here. Kath would've met all manner of psychopath. "Well, regardless - hopefully I'll find out."

"I wouldn't count on it," Kath huffed, as she pushed the door open. "He really hasn't said anything worthwhile to anyone in a long, long time."

With that, Kath and George entered the room.

Oftentimes, when private interviews were granted with the maximum-security prisoners, they would be set up in the sports hall. That way, with the room being as large as it was, the guards could remain present, inside the room at all times, while still granting them the privacy that seemed to still be a human right afforded to even the most deranged of psychopaths. The sports hall that George now found himself standing in was bigger than he had expected. The waxed wooden floor was littered with a multitude of intertwining coloured lines, unintelligible to the untrained eye, which seemed to map out the zones for a number of sports. It was enough to make anybody dizzy, should they look at it for too long.

At the side of the room, another guard - a black male, overweight, yet still fearsome looking - was stood, motionless, hands behind his back. He was watching George. Just like the other guard, he didn't appear to blink.

As they crossed the hall, Kath whispered a *good luck* to George. Before he could thank her, she was gone. She peeled away from him and joined the other guard at the side of the room. George couldn't hear what they were saying, but he could see their lips moving. The male guard chuckled at something and then they were both still, both staring.

George approached the man sitting in the middle of the room. His name was Alan Morrissey. He was 47. He was overweight and his hair, shaved close to the scalp, was thin and grey, but still held on to faded hints of the ginger it used to be. His eyes were a deep brown, wide and inviting. But something about them was off. They were blank. He too was staring. It was as if he was looking *through* George. And he was smiling. It was a dry and slimy smile - the kind that liars and cheats used when they believed themselves to be untouchable. It was a smile that George had seen many times before, even, on occasion, when he looked in the mirror.

George arrived at the desk and pulled out the chair. He dropped his files on the table and offered his hand. "George Parsons," he said. "Pleased to meet you."

Alan lifted his hands, palms facing upward. He raised them as far as they would go before the chain of the cuffs that bound them together bottomed out on the steel loop fixed to the table. "Sorry," said Alan. "As much as it would be a pleasure to shake your hand, that's pretty much an impossibility at present. Still - I'm very pleased to make your acquaintance, also. I'm Alan.

George smiled and nodded. He took off his jacket and hung it over the back of his chair. He then took the seat opposite to Alan and straightened out his files.

Alan continued to stare. He no longer seemed to be looking *through* George - now it seemed more like he was looking *into* him. His eyes probed George's, examining his posture, attempting to work him out, as if he were a predator trying to predict the next move of his prey.

George reached into his jacket pocket and took out a Dictaphone. It was an old-fashioned model, one that still required a tape to record to. George preferred the old ones over the newer digital models - he didn't trust them to work properly. At least with the old ones, you could see the tape winding and you knew it was recording. He placed it on the desk, stood up on its end. "You mind?" he asked Alan.

"Please do," Alan replied, shaking his head.

George pressed the record switch, and, with a buzz, the tape began to turn.

"Okay. So - do you know why I'm here?" George asked, already fully aware that he did. Even if he hadn't been told explicitly, it wouldn't have been too difficult for Alan to have worked out.

"Of course," Alan replied, a smug laugh hidden somewhere beneath his words. "You're a journalist. You're here to ask me some questions. Then you'll go home and write an article, most likely full of lies and mis-quotes."

"I'm not that kind of journalist," George said, defensively.

"Oh really? I thought *all* journalists were *that kind* of journalist?"

"Not me. I like the truth."

Alan's smile had widened. "Well - that's good," he chuckled. "So - where do you want to start? I can't think of anything I could tell you that I haven't already told the dozens of others that have come before you."

Alan spoke with some intelligence, but it struck George as being forced, as if he were somehow pretending to be smarter than he truly was. But then, that was another gift that all liars and cheats were in possession of - that's what made them so good at what they did.

"Well..." George thought for a second, composing his words in his head, trying to decide on how best to put it. "The first thing I wanted to ask you was, I guess, a pretty straight-forward question."

"Go ahead."

"Did you kill Melissa Saunders?"

Idle Hands

Alan cocked his head slightly, like a puzzled dog. He was still smiling, although now it seemed more confused - and certainly a lot less smug - than it had before.

Melissa Saunders had been just two days shy of her ninth birthday when she was taken. She was a skinny little girl, tall for her age. She was as pretty as a picture. She had long blonde hair, which hung halfway down to her backside. Her eyes were sea green. She was last seen playing with her friends on a local park. At approximately 17:35, she'd said her goodbyes, before leaving to head home - her parents had expected her home by 18:00, you see. When she hadn't arrived home by 19:00, her father had gone to look for her. Finding no trace, he had returned home and phoned the police. Two days later, she had turned nine and her presents had remained wrapped. The following day, her parents had held a press conference in which they pleaded with the kidnapper to let their beautiful, intelligent young daughter go. Her naked body was found by a fisherman six days later, floating face down in the River Arrow. She'd been sexually abused, before her kidnapper had strangled her to death with what seemed to be a length of electrical cable. Her skin was blue, and decomposition had already begun, indicating that she had been killed, and her body had been disposed of, within hours of her being reported as missing.

"Why did you say you were here?" Alan asked, his smile fading, the early signs of a frown beginning to show on his face.

"I told you, I like the truth," George replied. "Did you kill her? It's a simple question - yes or no."

"I think you know I did."

George shook his head. "I'm not so sure."

Alan's smile was now completely gone. He'd not met anybody who seemed to question the validity of his claims before.

"And what about Suzie Connors?" George continued.

Suzie Connors was twelve when she was taken. Like Melissa Saunders, she was tall and skinny, although the onset of puberty had caused her to fill out somewhat. She was a very pretty girl. She had a smile which most would describe as infectious. Her brunette hair was cut into a short bob, which she almost always wore in a ponytail. The night she had been taken, she'd been to the cinema with a group of friends. Her parents had told the police of how they had been concerned, of how they had known something bad was going to happen. It was the first time they'd let her go out alone like this. Apparently, the group (which consisted entirely of girls, with Suzie being the youngest) had taken the bus to and from the cinema. It was only a short walk home from the bus stop. The film finished at 20:45 - Suzie's parents had insisted on knowing before allowing her to go. They had expected her home by ten. When she was still missing by midnight, they had phoned the police. Much like Melissa Saunders, her body had been found floating in the River Arrow. That was three weeks after she had gone missing. Much like Melissa Saunders, she was found naked and partially decomposed. She too had been sexually abused, before being strangled. As before, the killer's weapon of choice appeared to be a length of cable.

"I killed her too," Alan replied, shrugging his shoulders as if it were obvious. It seemed now that he was much less confident in his power to shock. George thought that this was probably a peculiar feeling for Alan - most people were repulsed by his actions, but the young man sitting opposite him didn't appear to be.

"I'm not so sure about that one either," said George.

"What's not to be sure about?" Alan asked. "The jury was sure. *I* killed all those children."

There had been nine victims in total. Over a period of two years, nine children, all young girls whose ages ranged from seven to thirteen, had been abducted from the streets of Brookhaven. Melissa Saunders was the first; Suzie Connors was taken six weeks later. Then, with months separating each murder, they continued to disappear. Melissa Saunders. Suzie Connors. Ellie Carter. Emma Maud. Scarlett Evans. Jess Cooper. Sally Thompson. Harriet Scott. Jennifer Hobbs. None of them were related. One or two of them attended the same school, but that was as far as their relationships extended. In all cases, the victims were sexually abused and then strangled with an electrical cable. In all cases the bodies were found floating in the River Arrow, sometime days - more often, it was weeks - after the girls' initial disappearance. The location in which the victims had been found had led to the killer being dubbed the 'Riverside Ripper', a name that always struck George as being somewhat odd, what with the killer's MO being strangulation and all.

Regardless of how ill-befitting the name was, the media's branding of the killer had made him into a kind-of macabre celebrity. This branding, many were sure, had pushed him into killing more frequently than perhaps he would have, had he not been thrust into some morbid, tabloid-inflicted limelight. In the final months, letters had been sent to the local police, goading them, daring them to catch him.

Then, one morning, the very day after the ninth body had been found (that of eleven-year-old Jennifer Hobbs - a pretty girl whose school photo had been used on the front of the papers, a photo showing her wide, happy smile, her braces making her none-the-less beautiful), Alan Morrissey walked into Brookhaven police station and confessed to the murders.

His trial lasted all of four weeks. He was, of course, found guilty of the murders. He was given nine life sentences, one for each of his victims.

That was five months ago.

Now George was sat opposite Alan, the man convicted of killing those children, claiming that Alan's confession may have been false.

"I've read your statements," George told Alan, his demeanour cool, surprisingly relaxed. He didn't fear the alleged psychopath sat before him at all. "Very impressive. There's a lot of detail in them." He was fairly sure there was a somewhat patronising tone to his voice now, but he didn't really care.

"Why wouldn't there be?" Alan questioned.

"Those details... They're mainly repetitions of what the police had already confirmed to the media. They mostly consist of details published in the daily newspapers."

"There are details in my statements that only I could've known."

"I don't think so." George shook his head, as if he were admonishing a young child.

"Then you know nothing." Alan was growing angry now. George felt as though he could read his mind. He was thinking - *How dare this cocky little shit accuse me of lying?* His cheeks were growing red, no doubt a result of the increased heart rate he was experiencing. George sat opposite him, his expressionless face giving nothing away.

"A lot of those details seem to be false," George went on, sucking the air over his teeth, a whistle that accuse Alan of straight-up lying. "I think the police ignored a lot of those inaccurate details, just to gain a conviction."

"So, you're accusing the police of being incompetent."

"Not incompetent, as such. I'm pretty sure they knew what they were doing." George sat forward a little. "I imagine they were desperate."

Alan didn't respond. He just stared at George, his eyes flicking side to side. His vision seemed clearer now; he no longer looked *through* George, or even *into* him. He now *saw* him completely. George was a threat.

George opened one of his files, retrieved the papers from inside and spread them out before Alan. Each one was a crude, child-like drawing, vivid colours, smeared across the page in wax crayon. The first depicted a man, knife in hand, standing over the dismembered corpses of children. The second was very similar to the first, only, in this one, the man held an axe instead of a knife. Another of the pictures showed the man holding a decapitated head, streams of blood (actually frantic scribbles of wax) cascading from the detached neck. One of the pictures showed the man tearing the innards from one of his victims. In the picture, the man was smiling.

George tapped on the pictures, motioning for Alan - whose eyes had remained fixed on his - to take a look. "Did you draw these?" he asked.

Alan nodded.

"Why?" said George.

Alan shrugged his shoulders. "They asked me to draw what I saw in my mind," Alan waved his hands over the drawings, claiming ownership. "That's what I did."

"But they strike me as a little odd," George said, sitting back in his chair. For sure, Alan didn't like the fact he was making himself comfortable. "If this is you, why draw yourself cutting children into pieces? That's not how you killed your victims."

"So?"

"So why draw them that way?" Perhaps this was the way a man befitting the title 'Ripper' might draw his victims. But not a man who strangled them.

"Maybe that's what I would've liked to have done. Maybe I just didn't have the guts to go through with it. Maybe I decided that they didn't deserve that."

"But they *did* deserve to be raped and strangled to death?" That was a rhetorical question, which George answered himself with a shake of his head. "No. I think you drew these just to be shocking." George raised his hands, his fingers spread wide, and waved them in front of his face, as if to emphasise the word *shocking*. "You thought that if a psychoanalyst saw these, their verdict would be almost guaranteed - *you're insane, buddy!*" George laughed. He was almost giddy with excitement now, so much so he could barely contain it.

Alan just stared.

Idle Hands

"And I've got to give it to you," George scoffed a laugh. "You were right."

Alan said nothing. By this point it would've been futile; George knew the truth and there was nothing he could've done about it.

George opened the second file and pulled out a series of newspaper cuttings. They each showed the same story. Another young girl, Sarah White, had disappeared six weeks ago. No body had been found yet, but the authorities were searching the river. They expected they'd find it soon. Somehow, for some reason, the press hadn't connected this kidnapping to those committed (or so they seemed to believe) by Alan Morrissey. It was as if they didn't want to - there was a man locked up, convicted of the murders, and there was no way they were about to profess his innocence, admitting to their own negligence at the same time.

"This wasn't you," George said, holding up one of the clippings. "It *couldn't* have been."

Alan looked the article over. He'd seen this on the news. "They haven't found the body yet, have they?" he whispered, as if he wanted to cling on to his lie just a few seconds longer.

"No, no. But I understand your concern. If they find her body, they'll know she's a victim of the 'Riverside Ripper', won't they?" George made mock quotation marks with his fingers as he quoted the name. "And they'll know that you - my friend - you aren't the real killer. Your little game will be over."

Alan didn't respond. He stared, wide eyed, like a rabbit caught in the headlights of an oncoming car.

George leaned over the desk, in close to Alan. "So, if *this* was the real 'Riverside Ripper'," he paused for a moment. He looked Alan over. "Who are you?"

Alan continued to stare, lost for words. His neatly spun web of deceit was unwinding before him. "*I'm* the real 'Riverside Ripper'," he pleaded, unconvincingly.

George smiled and shook his head. He collected his Dictaphone from the table and hit the stop button. He slipped it back into his jacket pocket. He then stood and stuffed his papers back into his files.

Alan watched him closely. George could see that he was trying desperately to figure out just what his next move might be, having no idea what he might say next. If George had been in his position, he imagined that would be the most frightening part - the total and utter loss of control.

George leaned in over the table. "Don't worry," he whispered. "I'll keep your secret, if you keep mine."

Alan looked deep into George's eyes.

George smiled. "They haven't found the body of Sarah White yet, because she's *still alive*. I have her in my cellar." His psychotic mind was whirring away, delighted in its own ability to deceive whoever it chose to. Even those who should've been able to see through his masquerade had been fooled so easily. Nobody knew who he really was. Nobody ever would - not until *he* wanted them to.

With that, George turned. Without looking back, he picked up his jacket, draped it over his arm and walked away from the table.

Idle Hands

George could feel Alan's eyes probing him, staring, watching him as he went. But he thought little of him - his mind had shifted and was now transfixed on little Sarah White and how her delicate skin would feel against his own.

Kath met George at the sports hall door and escorted him out of the room. "Did you get everything you needed?"

"Yes, I do believe I did," George nodded in thanks.

"And - do you still believe he's innocent?"

"You know what?" George said, looking back through the glass pane, into the sports hall beyond. Alan was still sat at the desk, hands still chained. He was still staring. "I'm not so sure anymore."

***

Outside, it had stopped raining. The clouds had cleared, and the sun was beating down fiercely. The pools of rainwater that had collected on the tarmac of the car park were slowly evaporating away, thick clouds of vapour rising up and dispersing into the warm surrounding air.

It'd probably rain again soon.

George waved back to Kath, who had remained at the door, in thanks for her assistance. No sooner had he done so, she'd turned her back and walked away, on to the next task. It would probably only be a few moments before she forgot he was ever even there.

George was happy about that. The sooner she forgot, the better. The authorities would be finding Sarah White's corpse sooner rather than later.

George opened the boot of the car and flung in his jacket. He pulled his tie loose, lifted it over his head and tossed it in too. He then took his ID off and looked it over in his hand.

"Thanks for this, George," he said, as he looked at the photo on the ID. It was remarkable really, that anybody could've mistaken him for the man in the photo. Sure, they were both white, both had short brown hair, both had a moderate amount of stubble. But realistically, if anybody took more than just a few seconds to look, they'd have seen that he and the man in the photo looked barely alike. The *real* George even had a large mole on his left cheek - that should've given the game away immediately. "You've been very helpful today."

He tossed the ID into the boot. It landed on the chest of George Parsons, who lay in the boot of his car, his mouth sealed tight with silver duct tape, his wrists and ankles bound with thick lengths of electrical cable.

He tried to sit up, tried to scream for help, knowing full well that he too would soon be dead. But the stranger outside slammed the boot shut.

George Parsons was entombed in darkness.

THE END

ALSO AVAILABLE

The Whores Of Satan
Bloodhounds
Superfan
Idle Hands
In The Valley Of The Cannibals
Nazi Gut Munchers
The House Of Rotting Flesh
In The Name Of The Devil
Shotgun Nun
Return To The Valley Of The Cannibals
The House Of Rotting Flesh: Episode 2
Teddy Bears Picnic
Night Of The Freaks
Shotgun Nun Vol.2: The Wrath Of God
Feces Of Death

ALSO AVAILBLE FROM D&T PUBLISHING

Field Trip

Printed in Great Britain
by Amazon